PEARLS

OF

SECRETS

Teresa A Swift

FUNTEXT BOOKS
"Enlightening readers in a fun way"
Upper Marlboro, MD

Funtext Publishing
Upper Marlboro, Maryland

Cover Design: Chris Beaver

Library of Congress Control Number 2012936861

ISBN-978-0615612751

Printed in the United States of America

Christine thanks for being the best listener.
I know you're still listening.
Jewell and Christa thanks for seeing the vision.

PEARLS
OF
SECRETS

Chapter 1

Ann sat fearfully on the floor, naked, her hands trembling. Desperately trying to control their movement, her hands wobbled like a runaway train on an old rusty track. For a moment, she knew her soul had briefly left her body. Slowly scanning the room one last time, she tried to remember every item in detail.

This is it, she thought as the gun's barrel was pressed against her temple.

For months, she had thoroughly considered this final step, and wondered if the plan could be carried out. Pondering and rehearsing it over and over in her mind. She lit a cigarette and began to puff frantically. When the time drew near, she began to weep. Although she knew that love surrounded her most precious gem, she couldn't help wonder what he would think about his mother. For the moment that was her only fear. As she stared into darkness with empty eyes a tear rolled down her face. The trigger was pulled. Bang! Her body fell lifelessly and slumped over to one side.

It was a sunny and breezy October day. The rustling leaves in the treetops softly whispered as they sparkled like the bright colors of a rainbow. The weather was brisk enough to wear a sweater. No more shorts, tank tops, bikinis, and flip-flops. It wasn't time for coats, gloves, and scarves just yet—but in a short few months that would change. When Old Man Winter arrives, people would be bundled up from head-to-toe trying to conceal every inch of their body from the brutal cold. The broken end of a broom's handle propped opened the kitchen window as a gentle wind wafted through the crack, tossing the lace curtain into the air, swinging it softly, while releasing a fresh aroma of fall. Precisely at that moment, a strange twinge of concern raked through Janet's mind. She instantly knew something was wrong. As she stood in the kitchen, an eerie feeling engulfed her body. She grabbed the telephone and dialed Ann's number. After several rings, the answering machine came on. Janet patiently waited for the voice of Ann's recording to finish. She left a brief message and continued cooking dinner.

It was about 3:00, time for Trevor to come home from school. He rushed into the house, slamming the door behind him. He threw his backpack in the corner of the floor and yelled, "Mom, I'm home."

There was dead silence in the house. Trevor headed towards the backyard to retrieve his bike. He pedaled past Shelly and Sabrina playing hopscotch and picked up speed as he scurried around the corner. Up the hill, he zipped passed the Collins' house and down the block toward the park. Several boys were playing tag, while two little girls tossed a Frisbee back and forth. Trevor parked his bike and stood at the chain link fence watching as giggly kids squealed with excitement as they twirled on the merry-go-round. Trevor hopped on his bike and cantered back down the hill passed the Collins' house and turned into his driveway. Thirsty from the long ride he leaned his bike against the garage door and rushed into the house to get something to drink. After entering the house he yelled for his mother. No response. Once he reached the kitchen he looked on the table in their usual spot for a note that would probably read: Trevor—Gone to the store. Do your homework. See you soon. Love, Mom. However, on this cool October day there was no note.

Check the garage, he thought.

Trevor rushed downstairs to the garage, yanked opened the door and he noticed both cars were parked inside. Racing back outside to his bike, he mounted it like a cowboy hopping onto a horse. He gripped the handlebars and pedaled effortlessly along. Trevor loved to show off his custom made Mongoose Spinn Freestyle Bike. The shimmering frame's hue resembled a red delicious apple and the saddle was black as licorice. The spokes spun around giving off a whistling sound. The other kids were amazed when he cruise the streets demonstrating jaw dropping tricks. Much to the amusement and delight of Trevor's bike, every boy

2

on the block wanted to ride it, but he didn't allow them, because the bike meant so much to him.

As darkness fell, the first street light flickered to life. The neighborhood kids began trickling inside their homes for dinner. Trevor decided to go in as well. As he rode his bike up the narrow driveway, he had no idea that from this moment on, his young life was about to change forever.

Chapter 2

The sky had darkened quickly as the moonlight illuminated on the rooftops below. Trevor stepped in the house and he felt a compelling urge to walk down the long hall that led to his mother's bedroom. The thickly covered carpet cushioned each step as he approached the room. The door was closed. He attempted to turn the doorknob but it was locked. That's when fear overcame him. Trevor nervously paced the hallway. He didn't know what to do and suddenly he decided to call Janet.

"Hello Aunt Janet, this is Trevor," he said slowly.

"Hello, Baby. How was school today?"

"School was fine," he paused. "Aunt Janet did you talk to my mother today?"

"No, Baby, I did call her earlier and left a message, but she has not returned my call yet. Isn't your mother at home?" Janet asked sounding irritated.

"No, ma'am, and her bedroom door is locked and there wasn't a note today. She always left a note for me. It's dark and I'm scared."

"Maybe she went to the store?"

"No, ma'am, her cars are in the garage."

"Maybe she walked?" Janet said, cheerfully as she could.

Giggling slightly, Trevor mumbled, "My mother walking to the store. No way!"

"Give her an hour and hopefully she'll show up. Call me as soon as you hear something,"

"Yes ma'am, I will."

They expressed their love and Trevor hung up the phone. He dashed into his bedroom and popped in his favorite CD by the Back Street Boys. He sat in complete darkness and was suddenly

4

overwhelmed with sorrow. Trevor began to sob. The telephone rang blaring like a school bell, which halted his tears.

"Hello," he said with happiness in his voice.

"Hello. May I speak to Ann?"

"I'm sorry, but Ann isn't home."

"Yes she is," the female voice said. "She needs your help as soon as possible before it's too late," she stressed.

"Excuse me, who is this?" Trevor asked, with fear in his voice.

"Hurry, Son before it's too late! Your mother is in her bedroom and she needs you. Go now," she shouted.

Then the telephone went dead. Trevor lay across the bed speechless, recalling the words of this strange voice. He leaped to his feet and hastened to his mother's room. After several attempts of kicking and thrusting his shoulder against the heavy wooden door, it did not bulge. Trevor rushed into the kitchen to look for a something to pry it open when he noticed the black knife stand on the counter. He carefully removed a stainless steel knife and returned to the door. With all his might he applied leverage to the locked door but failed miserably. The words of the caller ignited unparalleled fear in his heart. Trevor waddled back to his bedroom and phoned Janet.

"Hello Aunt Janet."

"Is your mother home now?"

"No ma'am and I'm scared. I just received an anonymous phone call. A woman told me to go to my mother's bedroom, that my mother needed me as soon as possible before it was too late."

"Do you think someone is playing a joke on you, Trevor?" Janet asked, hoping her voice was not breaking apart.

"No ma'am. Right before the phone call I started crying."
With gentleness in her voice, Janet tried to reassure him.

"Stay put, do not leave the house or answer the phone. I'm on my way."

Trevor placed the phone on the receiver and turned up the volume on the CD player, pacing the floor. His slim body was drenching in sweat as he marched fearfully up and down the hall. Forty-five minutes later Trevor heard the doorbell ring, he glanced through the peephole and quickly unlocked the door. Janet and her brother William walked in. Trevor collapsed in her arms with relief.

"Aunt Janet, I'm so happy to see you. Thank you for coming."

He placed a kiss on her cheek.

"Are you okay?" Janet asked while staring down the hall, looking for anything unusual.

Trevor nodded and the three of them proceeded down the hall toward Ann's bedroom. Janet could feel the chill in the air. That same creepy feeling she had felt earlier overcame her once again. Before they reached Ann's door, Janet redirected Trevor with her eyes.

"Why don't we go in your room while Uncle William tries to get your mother's door open?"

They turned toward Trevor's room. Then she nodded at William to continue on to Ann's bedroom. William stopped at the door, took a deep breath and tried to turn the doorknob. He noticed the knife on the floor. Without hesitation, William picked it up and jimmied the door like Trevor had done earlier. After several attempts, the door opened. A sick feeling gripped William's stomach as he walked in the room, yet he walked in unwillingly. *There's no turning back now*, he thought.

William clicked the light switch, his body flinched at the unimaginable horror he saw. It was the bloodiest mess he had ever seen. Although he was raised on a farm and witnessed pigs slaughtered, nothing had prepared him for this. He quietly embraced himself and closed the door behind him, not wanting Janet or Trevor to see the gruesome scene.

"Oh my Lord!" he exclaimed. "Ann what have you done?"

He inched over to her body, trying not to step in the blood. William's body began to shake with fear. His voice became like wind. For his words were not in him.

"Please, Lord, do not let her be dead," he prayed as he crept silently closer.

Her small, bare frame had slumped over to her side in a large pool of blood. An area of the wall was saturated with blood spatters. A tiny hole to the right side of her temple was steadily leaking blood. It ran down her head, neck, and covered her perky breasts. An ashtray was on the right side of her body, along with a note and a picture of Trevor on her left side. And finally, he saw the small gun, which lay beside her right thigh. William wanted to feel her pulse to see if she was still alive, but he couldn't find the nerve to touch her. Trevor left his room and approached his mother's door.

"Uncle William, Is everything all right?"

William shivered as he tried to compose himself viewing the bloody mess that was before him.

"I'll be out in a minute."

William's body instinctively settled on the edge of the bed. The devastation was too much for him and he began to weep.

"Why Ann?" he muttered, gasping for air. "Why did you do this? How can I explain this to Trevor?"

William rose from the bed and shuffled across the room. He had no idea how slowly he was moving. It was as though his body was struck in a time warp. William dried his tears, with a big sigh. He somehow found strength to leave the bedroom. Trevor eagerly approached William, hoping he had good news. He looked directly in William's big brown eyes and asked with a look of dismay.

"My mother—is my mother in there, asleep?"

"No, Trevor, your mom is not in there."

William hated lying, but he knew the truth would have shattered him. William stood in front of the door unable to move. The casualty was too much for him to bear, but he had to remain calm for Trevor's sake.

"Where's Janet?" He asked pensively.

"Oh, she's in my room."

"Will you tell her I'd like to speak to her?"

William staggered into the kitchen. A pot of old coffee was on the stove. He didn't mind that the coffee was cold and stale. He just needed the caffeine to calm the fiery ache that burned his soul. William's mind was stuck on what he had just seen. He wanted to scream, but his mouth had gone dry. He then quickly grabbed a coffee mug and poured a cup. The more William realized that he had to face the awful truth, the sadder he became. He took the pack of cigarettes out of his shirt pocket and tossed them on the kitchen table and sat down. He sat there for a while, and then lit one. Janet could tell by William's expressionless face that something was wrong.

"Baby, do me a favor. Go back to your room while I talk to Uncle William." Janet said with a grateful look.

Trevor disappeared into his room, William sadly stared at Janet. He pulled a chair out from under the table, directing her to sit down. The shock of the tragedy was on his face.

"What's wrong? Something is wrong, isn't it?" she insisted.

William looked at Janet and said without blinking, "Yes, there is something very wrong."

"What is it?"

He paused for a moment and the stern look on his face was harder than rocks. William fretfully said, "Ann shot herself."

Janet sat there for a long time in disbelief. Her happiness was instantly zapped away like a deflated balloon. The only sounds that filled the house were the thumps from the CD in Trevor's room. Janet finally broke the silence.

"What do you mean, she shot herself? William what are you talking about? This can't be true?"

"Ann shot herself," William glumly repeated.

"Where at?" Janet asked looking worried, leaping to her feet, and nervously pacing the kitchen floor.

"She shot herself in the head."

"No, William. This must be a joke," Janet whispered as her head wagged.

"Janet, listen to me."

William gently pulled Janet's arm and led her back to the chair.

"This is no joke. Ann is lying nude on her bedroom floor with blood covering her body. There is an ashtray on the right side, a note and a picture of Trevor on the left, and a small gun beside her thigh. Other than the blood, the room is spotless, the bed is made and there's no evidence the room was ransacked."

Janet kept her jaws clenched tight so that he couldn't see the effect his words had on her. After a long pause, she said, "I'm going in. I must help her."

Janet tried to get up, but the heaviness in her heart kept her in the chair. The scope of their problem was far worse than she could imagine.

"No Janet," William said weakly, gently rubbing her hand.

"You shouldn't go in there. You must take Trevor to your house so I can call the police. We *cannot* let Trevor see his mother like this."

Sitting frozen in the chair, Janet stared down the hall toward Ann's room.

"William," trying to avoid the inevitable question, "Is Ann dead?"

"Janet, I don't know. I wanted to take her pulse, but I was afraid to touch her—her body is too bloody."

"Oh my God, William, this is terrible." Janet let out a loud scream. "Why? Why did she do this?"

Janet sat crying quiet, silent sobs. She tucked her head between her hands; tears rolled down her face and her body shook uncontrollably.

What a horrid thing for Ann to do, Janet thought.

William gently hugged her. He took her shoulders in his hands and looked deeply into her eyes.

"Janet, you must get yourself together right away and take Trevor to your house so I can call the ambulance. Time is wasting and Ann may need medical attention if that's necessary."

William slowly stood up and handed her a wad of tissues.

"William. I can't do this. I'm too nervous. I know I won't be able to drive," saying as she wiped tears away and blew her nose.

William gripped Janet's hand and held it tightly.

"You must, Janet. You must do this for Trevor."

Now Janet's facial expression was a mixture of concern and fear, hoping that the news William had just revealed to her was all a dream. Janet and William realized, as they sat at the kitchen table how intense the sadness was that now burdened them. The more Janet realized that she had to face the painful truth the more forceful her tears flowed.

"Okay, William," she said as she tried to compose herself, still wiping tears away.

"I will call you as soon as I hear something."

He embraced her with a long hug, ensuring her that everything was going to be okay. Janet faked a smile and left the kitchen. As she walked in Trevor's room, her head was still reeling from the news that William had just delivered. Janet plopped down onto Trevor's bed and gazed at him speaking in a mild tone.

"Guess what, Baby? Since your mother isn't home, I'm going to take you home with me. Is that okay with you?" she asked with a smile. "Uncle William is going to wait here for your mother," she continued.

He loved his Aunt Janet. She was like a second mother to him and going over her house was like going on vacation. Trevor turned off the CD player and grabbed his backpack from the corner on the floor where it had been laying since he got home from school. He removed each book one-by-one.

"Do I need any clothes," he asked, tossing the books on his desk.

Janet nodded, almost imperceptibly. She smiled, trying not to show any sad emotions. He stuffed a few clothes into the backpack. Janet looked up and noticed William standing in the doorway. Tears began to flow down her face, but William glanced at her and whispered.

"Be strong for Trevor."

Janet wiped away the tears before Trevor saw them. Her frown became pronounced as she left the room. As Janet forced her body to walk back into the kitchen, she simply looked up toward heaven, hoping that she would control her feelings for the boy's sake. She then turned her full attention down the hallway toward Ann's room and recited a prayer. By that time Trevor had finished packing. He walked out of his bedroom in the direction of the kitchen and yelled with excitement.

"Hey, Auntie, I'm ready. Race you to the car. Last one there is a rotten egg."

They entered the car without words. Slowly and cautiously Janet drove with a blank stare. She looked at Trevor and back to the house that contained the secret as the car turned the corner.

Chapter 3

William picked up the phone immediately and dialed 911.

"911, what's your emergency?"

"I need an ambulance as soon as possible," William said with a quavering voice.

"Sir, what seems to be the problem?"

"My niece was shot."

"Is she breathing?"

"Ma'am, I don't know. Please send help now."

"Help is on the way—stay with me sir. What's your name?"

"William Jones. Please—please help me. I can't breathe. "

Sudden fright and imminent fear squeezed the air out of him like a bora constrictor and he had begun wheezing.

"Mr. Jones I need you to calm down. Can you do that for me?" she asked with compassion.

In those few breathless seconds it felt like hours for William. Then there was a loud thunderous knock at the door.

"Help is here," William said keenly.

He dropped the phone, rushed to the door, greeted by two very tall firemen standing on the steps.

"Sir you reported a shooting?"

"Yes," he answered as his voice trembled.

"Where's the victim?"

"She's in the bedroom."

"Is there anyone else here with you?"

William shook his head.

"Can you take us to her?"

William led them down the hall to the bedroom. When they entered, the blonde haired fireman rushed to Ann's aid. William walked back into the living room where he noticed a small black Bible on the bookshelf. He instinctively picked it up, turned to Psalm 23 and began reading aloud.

"Tom, check her pulse," the other fireman said.

They rushed over to her body trying to avoid stepping in the large puddle of bloody soaked stained carpet. Tom wiped blood off of her wrist with an alcoholic swab while the other fireman paged the dispatcher at the station from his walkie-talkie.

"Mary, this is Matt, we have a possible suicide shooting, send help now."

Mary quickly responded. "Help should be there in a few minutes."

"Thank you, Mary." He placed the walkie-talkie into its holder.

"Matt!" Tom shouted, "I feel a slight pulse."

Matt rushed to her side and proceeded to administer CPR.

"Matt, do you think she will make it?"

"I don't know," Matt replied while blowing fresh air into her mouth. "It would truly be a waste if she didn't," he continued as he came up for air and pressed her chest. "Never figured out why a person would want to kill themselves anyway. Life can't be that bad," Matt said as he continued administering CPR.

Meanwhile, Tom tried controlling the bleeding by placing a patch around her head. William was pacing the living room floor and puffing on a cigarette when he noticed the fireman approach. He stopped cold—dead in his tracks and waited to hear the worst.

"Sir, we found a slight pulse, she's alive."

William lifted his head and threw both of his arms up toward the ceiling and shouted, "Thank you, Lord!"

Suddenly, he dropped to his knees and began to say another prayer. More paramedics and the police had arrived. They rushed passed William, who was still on his knees and followed Matt into the bedroom. They crammed themselves in the bedroom each one geared up for their assigned duties. William rose from his knees and entered the kitchen, listening to the confusion that filled the air. The only voice he recognized was Matt's.

"Hurry man, I think she can make it but it's all up to her now," Matt said steadily.

The house was swamped with medical personnel and police officers. They were back and forth like barnyard chickens in a coop. The louder the sounds, the more nervous William's fears grew. He couldn't help but listen to the hustle and bustle in the bedroom; machines beeping and paper being ripped opened. That didn't stop him from praying and thanking God that Ann was alive. William so desperately wanted to call Janet to give her the good news, but he knew that she hadn't made it home yet. Moments later, a tall, thin policeman wearing a well-trimmed beard approached William.

"Good evening. My name is Detective David Brown," extending his hand. "I'm with the Criminal Investigation Department."

William stood and extended his hand in a firm handshake.

"It's nice to meet you Detective Brown. My name is William Jones. I'm the victim's uncle."

"I need to take a police report, mind if I ask you some questions?"

He took out a note pad and began to scribble. William sat in the chair and lit another cigarette.

"What's the victim's name?"

"Her name is Ann Sanford."

"Are you the person who called for help?"

William nodded yes as he took a sip of the cold coffee.

"How long did you wait before you called for help?"

"About ten minutes," he said as he gently placed the cup on the table.

"Why did it take you so long to call the authorities?"

William's voice began to decline. "Well sir, her son was here and I didn't want him to see his mother like this, so I asked my sister to take him to her house. Once they were out the house, I phoned you."

"Is that where her son is now?"

14

"Yes."

"So he doesn't know that his mother has been shot?"

"No, sir, he's only a little boy and he loves his mother very much so I couldn't allow him to see her like that." William offered.

"How old is her son?"

"He's eleven."

"You did the right thing," Detective Brown stated as he continued to write on his note pad.

"What can you tell me about this?"

"Well around 5:00 today, my sister Janet called me and told me that Trevor, that's Ann's son, called her to tell her that his mother was not at home. It was dark outside and he was getting scared. So I told Janet to let me know if she needed me to drive her over here. My sister informed me that Trevor was going to call back in an hour if his mother didn't come home within that time. About ten minutes later Janet called me back and said that Trevor received a terrifying telephone call."

"What kind of phone call?" the detective asked while scratching his head.

"Trevor stated that someone called and told him that his mother was in her bedroom and she needed his help immediately."

"Did Trevor say who it was?"

"Trevor said it was a woman's voice. A voice he didn't recognize."

"Do you know if they have caller ID?"

"Yes, I believe they do," William answered looking somewhat confused.

William briefly paused and simultaneously removed another cigarette from the package on the table.

"When Janet and I got here, I quickly proceeded to her bedroom, but the door was locked."

The detective noticed William's nervousness because he smoked one cigarette after another, not to mention, the kitchen was filled with a mist of thick, gray smoke. He watched William as he took several very long puffs on his cigarette.

"Sir, did you say the door was locked?"

William continued speaking as the smoke spurted through his mouth and nose forming circles.

"Yes it was."

"How did you get in?"

"There was a knife on the carpet. I'm guessing Trevor tried to get in but couldn't, so I picked up the knife and jimmied the door open and that's when I found her," he said almost breaking up again.

"Did you touch her?"

"No, I didn't. I was too afraid."

"Did you move anything?"

William shook his head no.

"I immediately went to the kitchen to let my sister know what I saw. Then I convinced her to take Trevor to her house so I could call for help. Once they left, I called you guys and that's all I know."

"Is that it Mr. Jones, can you remember anything else?"

"That's it, sir, that's all I know."

William took another long drag on his cigarette and held out his hand to catch the fallen ashes.

"Thank you for your time, Mr. Jones. I will let you know if I have any more questions."

The detective went down the hall as William followed him with his eyes until he disappeared into the bedroom. The detective checked the caller ID. He noticed a call from Janet around 2:30 and a call earlier, but there was no call after 2:30. In the meantime, he phoned the telephone company to have a trace placed on all incoming calls to the house that day. The detective went back into the kitchen. William was holding the Bible when the detective approached.

"Mr. Jones what is your sister's last name?"

"Her last name is Price, Janet Price."

"What's her phone number?"

"Her number is 555-3022."

"Thanks," he said as he swiftly turned to exit the kitchen.

"Is everything okay?" William asked, looking puzzled.

"No need to worry Mr. Jones, everything is fine, thanks again for your help," he responded.

William clutched the Bible close to his heart. The detective joined the others in the bedroom carrying his note pad in his hand. Moments later, the telephone company called. Detective Brown answered on the first ring.

"Detective Brown this is Kathy from the phone company. I've checked those records for you. Here's the information," she began.

The detective removed his note pad from his back pocket and began to take notes on a clean sheet of paper.

"There was in incoming call at 9:00 from Sears Department Store and another call from the residence of Janet Price at 2:30." The phone went quiet.

"Do your records show any other incoming calls?"

"No," Kathy said.

"Are you sure?"

"That's it, detective."

He cleared his throat and asked, "How many outgoing calls do your records reflect?" Now his voice had a discouraging tone.

"Detective, I'm showing two outgoing calls, one at 4:30 and another outgoing call at 4:50 to the residence of Janet Price."

"Kathy are you sure there are only two incoming calls?"

"Yes, I'm sure, I checked the records twice," she answered sounding a little frustrated.

They said their good-byes and with a click she was gone. Detective Brown began to write quickly on the note pad, looking somewhat deranged.

"Mr. Jones," he yelled.

William responded quickly and followed the detective's voice.

"What time did Trevor say this lady called?"

"Well, I didn't ask Janet what time she called, but it had to have been a little before 5:00 because my sister called me around 5:00.

"Mr. Jones we have a slight problem. I checked the caller ID and I didn't see any call after 2:30. The telephone company checked their records and they don't show a record of any incoming calls after 2:30."

"Detective Brown, I don't understand. Trevor distinctly said that there was an incoming call and I don't think he would lie about it."

"I'm not saying he's lying, I just need clarity. What's your sister's address I need to speak to Trevor?"

"Sir, Trevor doesn't know that his mother has been shot. Why do you need to speak to him?"

"Well, Mr. Jones," the detective said as he peered at his notes. "I'm going to be quite honest with you. Before we can rule out an attempted suicide, I must first prove it wasn't attempted murder." William was stunned that the detective was having such thoughts. "Who would want to murder Ann?" He quickly blurted out.

"I don't know, but it's my job to find out."

"Detective Brown are you saying Trevor may have something to do with this?" He asked looking appalled.

"No, Mr. Jones, I'm not saying that, but I really need to speak to him to help me tie up the loose ends. Maybe he saw something or heard something that can help with the case. For right now he's the last person to see his mother."

"I assure you that Trevor had nothing to do with this," William said as he stared at the detective with waving eyes. His voice began to crack as he angrily grumbled, "Trevor loves his mother very much. They are best friends and she had always been there for him. Unfortunately, his father never had been around to help. Ann would do anything for him," William pleaded. "They need each other. It's always been that way."

"Mr. Jones I understand what you are saying, but I must do my job."

"I understand, just give me some time to make arrangements for you to speak to him."

"Okay Mr. Jones. I'm really sorry about all of this. And I hope everything works out for your niece."

"Thank you, Detective, I'll be in touch with you," William continued. "But you're wrong about Trevor and I hope you don't put him through any unnecessary dilemmas. I have a terrible feeling he's going to go through enough when he finds out that his mother has been shot," he said, trying to sound convincing.

The detective lowered his head and walked away. William continued to read the bible desperately trying to forget the conversation he just had with the detective. For now he needed to focus on his strength. Somehow he wanted to know what happened in the house that he had spent so much time with the family. In the very house he was standing was a mysterious secret that he wished he knew. Why would his niece attempt such a horrible action? What was the guarded secret that the house held and why didn't he see signs before now? William closed the bible and wept silently as the drama in the bedroom continued to unfold.

Chapter 4

The paramedics carefully placed Ann's bloody body on the stretcher and covered her with a white sheet. When they rolled Ann past William, he looked down at her and whispered.

"Stay strong, we love you."

Within seconds, she was rushed to the Emergency Room. The majority of the emergency unit had left. However, Detective Brown was still in the bedroom reviewing the crime scene as William approached him with a sarcastic gesture.

"Excuse me Detective Brown; sorry to interrupt you, but when I was in here earlier I noticed a note on the left side of Ann's body. Have you read it yet?"

"Yes, Mr. Jones I have."

"May I read it?" William asked as he scanned the room.

"Not at this time. We will let the family read it after I take it to the station for review and tagged for evidence. I'll be in contact with you as soon as possible."

"Thank you, sir; I'm going to the hospital to be with Ann. If you need me here's my phone number."

William handed the detective a scrap of paper.

"Thanks for all your help and cooperation today. Good-bye Mr. Jones."

They shook hands and William called a cab company and soon left the house. Detective Brown remained in the house and continued examining the room. The Forensics Department took photos of the crime scene and placed the knife, the picture, the gun, the ashtray and the suicide note in plastic bags. They also dusted for fingerprints, gathered all the evidence and exited the house.

When William arrived at the hospital, he immediately went to the front desk. The receptionist was busy assisting another person. William approached her and waited patiently until she was able to help him.

"Good evening, may I help you?" she asked while typing on the computer's keyboard.

"Yes, I'm looking for my niece. The ambulance brought her here about forty minutes ago."

"What is her name?"

"Her name is Ann Sanford."

As she keyed the information into the computer her eyes brightened with concern. "Sir, are you talking about the gunshot victim?"

William nodded yes.

"She's in the shock trauma center."

"Where is that?"

The receptionist stood, pointing her finger and said, "Go to the end of this hall and make a right. At the second corridor make another right and the trauma center is on your left."

William quickly proceeded down the hall. It was a long walk down the corridor but the words of the detective continued to echo in his head. The closer he came to the trauma center the more scared he became. He didn't want to be there, but he had no choice. He noticed a phone booth in the lobby and decided to stop and phone Janet. As William inserted the coins into the slot, he noticed that his hands were extremely heavy from exhaustion. William knew in his heart this would be the hardest phone call he would have to make in his life. After several rings, the tiny voice on the other end answered.

What can I say to him, William thought.

"Is this you, Trevor?" William asked trying to camouflage the concern in his voice.

"Yes."

"Where's Janet?"

"She's in the bathroom."

"May I speak to her please?"

21

Then the one question came that he dreaded hearing.

"Uncle William did my Mom come home yet?"

"No Trevor not yet."

"Where can she be?" he whispered. "I miss her and I want her to come home so I can talk to her. Is anything wrong?" Trevor asked softly.

"No son, there's nothing wrong." He lied.

"If you say so, Unc, here's Aunt Janet."

Janet's hands began to shake when she took the phone. She was afraid of the words she might hear.

"Hello William."

"Hello Janet," he began slowly. "Can you talk?"

She laid the phone on the nightstand and asked Trevor to go downstairs to play with his friend Charles for a while. Trevor grabbed a game from the den, and hurried over to Janet to let her know he was leaving as he bent down to kiss her on her cheek. After hearing the door slam behind him, Janet picked up the phone.

"William, I can talk now. Where are you?"

"I'm at the hospital."

"Which hospital?"

"Riverside County," William said, heaved a sigh of relief and continued, "Ann is alive."

Janet's voice froze for a moment. She wanted to ask a question, but her tight lips wouldn't open.

"The paramedics found a slight pulse," William added.

"Do you think she'll make it?" She asked without hesitation.

"I don't know, Janet, I just got here and I haven't had a chance to speak to the doctor yet. Oh by the way Janet, a detective by the name of David Brown may be calling you."

"Calling me for what?"

"He wants to talk to Trevor."

"Talk to Trevor, What in the world for?" Her breathing was hard and fast.

"To ask him some questions."

"William what kind of questions does he need to ask an eleven-year-old boy?"

"Well Janet," William said, trying to remain calm. "The detective needs to talk to Trevor because the phone records indicate there were no incoming calls to the house after your last call to Ann around 2:30. Trevor was the last person, he think, to see his mother."

"What are you trying to tell me, William?"

"The detective told me that before he could rule out the possibility of an attempted suicide he has to determine whether or not it was not attempted murder."

"Murder are they kidding," she said rudely.

"Janet this is no joke. They feel some of the information that was given is not verifiable and they must investigate it."

"What information are they talking about?"

"The telephone call—Janet."

"What telephone call?"

Dead silence. Janet was irate now and William could hear the frustrated tone of her voice.

"The anonymous phone call that Trevor said he received from the strange woman. The detective told me that the telephone company's records don't show such a call to Ann's residence during the time Trevor indicated."

"No way, William. Trevor told me that there was a phone call and I believe him."

"I do too, Janet, but still the detective said he had to do his job."

"What do I tell Trevor?"

There was a brief silence before William continued.

"Janet, wait until the morning to talk to him. I'll come over to help you."

"Tell him what?"

"The truth." He calmed some and said again, "the truth."

Janet realized that she had to tell Trevor what has happened to his mother. She agreed to tell him in the morning.

23

The sooner the better, she thought, *but not for her sake. It's for the little boy that she loves so much.*

"Okay, William we'll tell him in the morning, keep me posted on Ann's condition. We'll talk later."

"Yeah, talk to you later."

With a click he was gone. Janet's heart felt like it had stopped beating for a moment. How would Trevor react from the news? Will he be strong or will he fall apart. The answer to that question haunted her because she had no clue how he would respond. Janet placed her hand over her heart and could feel that it was beating a mile a minute. She desperately needed to calm down so she went into the bathroom and ran some water in the tub to take a bath. A long hot soak always helped her to relax. As the tub began to fill with water she poured some of her favorite bubble bath under the faucet and watched the tub fill with floating bubbles. Janet sat on the edge of the tub and began to feel pains in her chest.

"Lord," she whispered, "please give me the strength. I need Your help. Please don't leave me now."

Janet went into the kitchen to get a glass. She filled the glass with ice. Afterwards she went into her bedroom to retrieve the secret bottle of Gin she kept hidden behind her dresser. Janet always kept a drink for guests. It's been a while since she had a drink. Janet knew that drinking wasn't going to make it easier for her. She just wanted to calm herself. Janet poured the liquor, swirling the glass and sniffing and then she took a big, long swig. After emptying the glass, Janet refilled the glass and took another big swallow. She placed the glass filled with ice cubes on the nightstand and returned to the bathroom to take the soak that her body was yearning. While Janet was in the bathtub she slowly began to relax.

Her mind began to ease as her heartbeat slowed to normal. While she lay in the tub glancing at the ceiling, she began to weep.

Ann, why did you do this? What could have been so bad that you couldn't talk to me? I thought we were friends. I thought you loved me?

Through her broken sobs, Janet continued, *why couldn't you just talk to me? I have always been there for you and I never left your side and now you're trying to leave me. What will your baby think of this? Will he blame himself for what you've done?*

Janet continued to speak to Ann as though Ann could hear her.

Why are you putting us through this? We don't deserve this because we love you deeply.

A tear dripped off Janet's cheek and splashed into a layer of bubbles. The horrifying image of Ann's bloody body raced through her mind and her body quivered with fear. The sound of the front door slamming quieted Janet's thoughts and tears.

"Aunt Janet, I'm home."

"I'm in the bathroom, Baby, be out in a minute."

Janet continued to soak, thinking, and speaking to herself. Although Trevor had settled down in the den and turned on the TV, his mind was restless. He tossed and turned on the sofa fighting until he finally fell off to sleep. Janet came out the bathroom, calling Trevor's name. There was no answer. She slowly walked into the den where she found him asleep on the sofa. She took the multi-color blanket that she had crocheted and gently laid it across his shoulders. While rubbing his innocent face with great passion, she placed a soft moist kiss on his forehead. Janet thought within but then said aloud.

"Sleep tight," Janet whispered, "Your life will never be the same after tonight."

Even after the long bath, her body was still drained. Yet she found enough strength to drag herself to her bedroom. The house was quiet now. As Janet turned on the TV, she lay across the bed, and restless thoughts of Ann's bloodstained body began to race through her mind again. Although she didn't see her that way, the description that William gruesomely painted was extremely vivid. Every time Janet tried to close her eyes, she saw every word William described. A picture of Ann's body covered in blood made her muscles quiver and ignited her anxiety. She tried hard to think of other things but she couldn't concentrate and her thoughts always returned back to Ann.

25

At 3:00 in the morning, Janet lay wide-awake watching the moonlight shine through her window. The house was lonely and silent, so much so that she didn't want to be in the room alone. Janet got up and sat on the edge of the bed. She instinctively took another sip of the watered-down drink sitting on her nightstand. No matter what she did, her thoughts would not ease up. They were coming fast and strong now. She could not erase the grisly scene of Ann's gory body lying on the floor with a bullet hole in her head covered in her own pool of blood. Nor could she erase the thought of her not surviving. Struggling with her own grief, she grabbed her pillow and blanket and turned the TV off. Janet walked into the den to be near Trevor. His innocent boyish face was perfect as he rolled over on his side. She placed the blanket on the floor and lay quietly beside him. She wanted to get up off of the cold hard floor but her heart wouldn't let her.

I must be near Trevor, she thought. She couldn't force herself to move even if she wanted to.

"I will never leave you, Baby," she murmured under her breath.

She watched Trevor snoring in his peaceful sleep, knowing his dreams were probably about his mother and eventually she fell asleep, too.

Chapter 5

Awakened by the warm morning sunlight beaming on her face, Janet's head was throbbing. She didn't know if it was from the bad news or the alcohol she drank the night before. She rubbed her eyes from the bright morning glare and suddenly remembered William's horrible words. The memory of yesterday's chaos came back so strongly, she began to shake with fright. Janet was in pretty sad shape. Her body was still tired from the restless sleep, and not to mention the soreness from lying on the cold hard floor. She picked up the blanket and pillow and tipped out the room trying not to disturb Trevor.

It was 7:00 *"I must cook Trevor's favorite breakfast,"* Janet thought. Shaky from the lack of sleep, still pursuing a logical explanation for the shocking event that occurred last night, she hurried into the kitchen and turned on the light. There were a few dishes left in the sink from the day before. The coffee pot had just started brewing and the fresh smell of Maxell House filled the air. Around 7:30, the telephone rang. She quickly answered it hoping that it didn't awaken Trevor.

"Good morning, Sis," William said from the other end of the line.

"What's so good about it," Janet said grouchily.

"How's Trevor?"

"He's still asleep."

"What time will you be over?"

"I'm on my way now, but I have to make a stop first. I should be there by 8:00."

"Okay, William, breakfast will be ready when you get here."

Janet went into the bathroom and washed her face and hands and brushed her teeth. She could barely brush her teeth and her legs ached. She wanted to awaken Trevor, but she needed him to sleep as long as possible, knowing that this will be the last good sleep he will have in a long time. Janet walked back to the kitchen on her aching legs and began to prepare pancakes. She knew pancakes were Trevor's favorite breakfast food. As she mixed the batter, she began to weep.

"Lord, I know this will be the hardest day of my life and I know this will be the hardest day of Trevor's life but grant us the serenity to accept the things we cannot change, the courage to change the things we can and wisdom to know the difference."

Janet opened the refrigerator, searching for some sausages through her tears. Her heart began to panic when she couldn't find the kind of sausages that Trevor liked.

"I must have some link sausages in this house somewhere," she mumbled under her breath.

Janet opened the freezer and began to toss everything on the table.

"Trevor doesn't like anything but link sausages, she thought. *"I must find some."*

The freezer was almost empty when she noticed a package wrapped in aluminum foil tucked away in the corner. She removed the package and slowly opened it.

"Link sausages, thank you God. I found some," she said with a smile.

Janet placed everything back into the freezer, not caring that it was sloppily done. She leaned her aching body against the door until it closed. She removed the frying pan from the cabinet and placed it on the stovetop. She grabbed the griddle pan from under the sink and made giant-sized pancakes just the way Trevor liked them. After making four huge pancakes, she placed them in the preheated oven to keep them warm. Janet then reached for some eggs and cheese and began to scramble them in a bowl. Afterwards a beautiful cream color tablecloth was draped across the table before she went into the hall closet and retrieved her favorite napkins—the ones that her mother had willed to her. These napkins had been in their family for over one hundred years and she only used them on very special occasions. In her mind, today was a special occasion.

Janet was not a young woman. She was in her late seventies, but aging was her friend. Her complexion was what people considered as fair skinned. She was too dark to pass for white and too light to be black. At times she felt like a miss-matched shoe. Although, she was walking in the same direction, they had different soles. Her shoulder-length hair was naturally curly. She was a tall full-figured woman, growing up the kids teased her and called her dirty red—tall enough to make you scared. The lovely warm-hearted woman lived in a dangerous part of town. The two-bedroom apartment in the inner city was filled with gangs, thugs, and frequent sounds of gunshots.

Her living conditions were not desirable, but she made do with the little she had. The only comfort was Sunday mornings when the ringing of a nearby church bell would chime every hour. When she heard those bells she knew she'd made it through another week. She has lived in the same apartment for thirty years. Janet was neighborly and the people loved her and kids adored her. From time to time, she baked cupcakes for the neighborhood kids. Janet loved life and life loved her. Her spiritual stimulation resonated through everything she touched. She gave birth to a son, who however over the years had forgotten about his mother. He didn't visit often. He was always getting in and out of trouble. After her son moved out she turned the extra bedroom into a den. He relocated out of state years ago and didn't write and barely called. When she did get a phone call, he always needed money. Everyone could see the good in her except him. Trevor and Ann were her life. She loved Trevor's company and she wanted to spend as much time with him as possible. Sometimes Trevor slipped and called her grandmother and she loved that. The two of them were inseparable.

Janet's restlessness was apparent on this nippy and dreary morning. Her hair was matted and the dark circles under her eyes were very noticeable. This was the first day in seventy-plus years that she felt old. As she glanced at the clock, it was 8:00. Janet finished cooking breakfast and returned to the bedroom to fix her-self up. She didn't want

Trevor to see her looking haggard. In her mind she wanted to look nice for him. Janet brushed her hair and pinned it up in a bun. She wore little or no makeup, but today she painted her lips with lipstick. As she rooted through her closet to find a shirt, Janet picked up several blouses; she wasn't impressed and quickly tossed them back in the closet on the floor. She finally found a blue shirt with the words "THE WORLD'S GREATEST GRANDMOTER" embossed on the front. Trevor had given her that shirt as a gift several years ago.

"*This is the one,*" she thought.

"I'll get it, Aunt Janet." Trevor yelled as he dashed to the door.

She was surprised to hear Trevor's voice.

"Trevor you're up?"

"Yes ma'am can't sleep with those sweet smells coming from the kitchen. Who wants to sleep when they can be eating," he said giggling.

Trevor opened the door after recognizing his uncle through the peephole.

"Good morning, Trevor," William said as he entered the room.

"Good morning, Unc."

"Where's Sis?"

"She's in the bedroom getting dressed."

William could tell Trevor was in a good mood, but he also knew it would be temporary. Once they tell him the truth about his mother, his laughter would turn into tears.

"Are we going anywhere?" Trevor asked surprisingly.

"No. Why did you ask that?"

"Because you're over here early."

"Yeah, I know—I must talk to Sis."

"Must be important to get you over here so early huh?"

"Yeah, it's important," he said as he turned his head trying not to look him in his eyes.

When Trevor walked past the dining room, he noticed the beautifully decorated table with the tablecloth, china, and napkins.

"Hey Unc, must be very important because Aunt Janet dressed the table," he said thrilled.

William pretended to be busy trying to avoid answering the question. Trevor knocked on Janet's bedroom door and she responded softly and instructed him to wash his face and hands and brush his teeth.

"Only have to tell me once," Trevor said, chuckling. "It smells good in the kitchen Auntie. Must be a special occasion?"

He hurried into the bathroom to brush his teeth and wash his face and hands. Meanwhile, Janet went into the living room where William was sitting and gracefully sat on the sofa beside him in complete silence. Then Trevor strolled out of the bathroom and joined them.

"Hey, Auntie what's for breakfast?" he asked while taking a big sniff.

"Your favorite—pancakes, link sausages, and scrambled eggs with cheese," she answered with a smile.

"Wow—all this for me? I'm ready to eat," Trevor hungrily said as he pulled the chair from the table and plopped down on it. He licked his lips in anticipation of the tasty meal before him.

Janet and William followed suite and sat down beside him. Then instantaneously Trevor leaped to his feet.

"Oh before we get started I must phone my mother. I don't think she knows I'm over here. I didn't leave a note."

"Wait, Trevor," Janet said as she grabbed his arm. "Don't call her yet, she's probably still asleep." She sounded a bit agitated. "Uncle William left a note for you."

"You did, Unc. Thank you," Trevor said with a grin.

William turned his head toward the window because he knew it was a lie. Trevor smiled toward Janet. He placed his napkin under his chin. Relieved, Janet settled back against her chair, turning her attention to Trevor, while the words of William's findings raced through her mind.

"Aunt Janet, why is the table set so pretty this morning? Are we expecting company? You only use the good china for special occasions and I can't remember the last time we used the napkins."

"No company, Baby, just felt like setting the table today."

Janet interrupted him because both she and William knew why the table was set so beautifully and why she put on that special shirt and lipstick. And after breakfast Trevor would know as well.

"Trevor, you say the grace," Janet said trying to change the subject. As they gathered hands, Trevor began slowly speaking.

"Father, thank You for the food we are about to receive for the nutrients of our body...and Father bless my mother, Amen."

It took everything within Janet not to break down and cry. As she sat there watching Trevor stuffed his mouth with the pancakes, sausages, and eggs, Janet wished she didn't have to do what she had to do next.

"Auntie are you okay?" Trevor asked as he sipped his orange juice?"

"Sure, Baby, why do you ask?"

"You look a little tired this morning. Did you sleep well?"

"Yeah, I just have a lot on my mind."

Janet knew this was another lie and like her brother she hated lying. The three hours of uncomfortable restless sleep on the cold hard floor made every muscle in her body ache. She thought she fooled Trevor by putting on lipstick and pinning her hair up, but he could see right through it.

"Me too, Auntie," saying as he slurped the sticky syrup off his fingers.

"Trevor, what's on your mind?" she asked as her heart throbbed.

"My mother, this is the first time she has ever done this and I surely miss her."

Janet could tell that Trevor was concerned about his mother by the tone of his voice and needless to say, so was she. Janet and William both watched as Trevor grubbed out. The only thing either one of them could digest was the coffee, and it took all their strength to do that. Trevor wiped his plate clean. After breakfast, Janet cleared the table and turned off the coffeepot. Trevor offered his assistance by taking the trash out. Grabbing his shoes and jacket, he headed outside for the trash dumpster. Upon hearing the door slam, Janet looked at William. Her body began to tingle when he said, "It's time Janet. We must tell him."

Janet nodded solemnly. Trevor rushed up the stairs and entered the apartment, slamming the door behind him. Janet was standing at the sink when he came in to ask if he could go out to play. Janet stopped cold.

"No, I really need to talk to you first."

"Talk to me about what?" he asked as he washed his hands.

"Yesterday."

"What about yesterday?"

Janet ushered him back to the table and joined William. When Trevor sat beside his uncle, Janet took a seat across from him. Once they were comfortably seated, both pairs of eyes were on Trevor. Janet paused, took a sip of coffee and then started with the questions.

"Trevor, tell me about yesterday?"

"What do you want to know, Aunt Janet?"

"Did you see your mother?"

"Yes. She woke me up for school. Then she went back in her bedroom. About five minutes later she came back into my room and asked me if I wanted breakfast. I was surprised because we never eat breakfast during the weekdays together. I told her all I wanted was a bowl of cereal. So, she fixed the cereal and we sat at the table and ate cereal together."

"Did she act strange to you?" Janet asked, eyeing him closely.

"Strange, no ma'am, we joked for a while and I had to leave. She told me not to stay after school today because she wanted to take me to the mall to get some new sneakers. I said okay, and then she kissed me—told me she loved me and I left."

"Trevor, what happened when you got out of school?"

"I ran home, because I knew my mother was waiting for me. When I arrived, I yelled for her, but she didn't answer, so I went outside to ride my bike. About an hour later, I went back in the house to get something to drink and to see if my mother was home yet. I went to the kitchen to get some punch and looked on the table for a note, but the table was empty. I went back outside—but first I went to the garage to see if her cars were there. There I saw both cars and assumed she was visiting a neighbor."

Trevor sighed and continued.

"Around 4:45, I decided to go in because it was getting dark outside and all my friends were going in for dinner. Back inside the house I called for my mother again and still no answer. So I went to my room to listen to a CD. I was lying across the bed and then I started to cry."

"Crying," Janet interrupted. "Why were you crying?"

"I felt a sadness come over me," Trevor continued with a weary expression. "I can't tell you what it was but I was just sad. About ten minutes later the telephone rang, and it was a woman on the other end."

"Who did she sound like?" asked Janet.

"Her voice was nice, soft; it reminded me of what an angel might sound like."

"What did she say to you?" William asked as his eyes were fixed on Trevor's lips.

"She asked for my mother. I told her my mother was not home. Then she told me that my mother was home—that she was in her bedroom and she needed me as soon as possible. She told me to hurry before it was too late. So I rushed into the kitchen to get a knife and tried to pry open the door. When I couldn't get the door open, I got scared and that's when I phoned you. I stayed in my room and waited for you there." Trevor paused and then said, "Auntie, what's up with the questions?"

"Trevor are you telling me the truth?" she asked glaring straight in his eyes.

"Yes." Trevor said honestly. "I have no reason to lie, besides you and mom always told me that lying only makes life harder."

"Trevor, I believe you," Janet said remorsefully.

"Aunt Janet, why are you asking so many questions? Is there anything wrong with my mother?"

Janet stood and walked around the table and grabbed Trevor, holding him tightly.

"Baby, I have something to tell you and what I'm about to say is the hardest thing I ever had to do in my life."

"What is it?"

"It is your mother."

"What about my mother?" His voice was hostile.

Janet stopped for a few seconds and look directly in Trevor's face.

"She's in the hospital."

"The hospital! Why is she in the hospital?" he declared.

"Your mother has been shot."

"Shot! No! Not my mother," he said violently shaking his head. "My mother is not in the hospital! She's home, and I'm going to call her right now."

Janet risked a glance at Trevor who was biting down on his lip, his hands clenched into a puny fist on the table. Then he leaped from the chair and headed toward the telephone.

"No Trevor," Janet yelled as she grabbed him by the arm.

"Your mother was found in her bedroom shot in the head yesterday."

"No!" he shouted at the top of his lungs. "No, not my mother," he kept repeating. "Aunt Janet, stop playing games with me."

During their conversation, Janet had become aware that several times his voice had risen in a high pitch tone.

"Trevor I'm not playing. Look at me," she said as she gently grabbed his face. "Your mother is seriously injured."

Trevor stepped back, not wanting her to touch him, fell to his knees and began a strident cry.

"Lord," he pleaded in anguish, "please say it's not so. My heart can't take this. I want my mother."

He sat on the floor, rocking back and forth. His eyes were shut tight but the tears found a way to escape. William looked at Janet and then at Trevor with penetrating sadness. Janet rushed over to hold Trevor but he jerked away from her and darted out the door.

"Trevor, come back," she shouted.

Janet ran as fast as her old body could carry her but Trevor disappeared out of her sight once he hit the stairs. William followed Janet outside the apartment door. He took Janet's hand and led her back into the house.

"Sis let him be—he needs some time alone. He'll be back."

Janet paused and breathed heavily. "I pray that you're right William," she replied looking at him through watery eyes.

Chapter 6

The hours passed quickly. William and Janet waited for Trevor to return. Janet kept herself busy, trying not to think about Ann, and yet worrying about Trevor's disappearance at the same time. William finally forced her to sit down and at least try to relax. She did to appease him, but it only lasted for a moment when she was up again, constantly pacing the floor and peeping out the window. After three hours had passed and still no sign of Trevor, William announced he was going to the hospital to be with Ann and told Janet to page him if she needed anything. She stood in the hallway and watched William walk down three flights of stairs until his body faded out of sight.

As the sun began to set, and still there was no sign of Trevor. Fearing the darkness for Trevor's sake, Janet grabbed her sweater, purse, and keys and bolted out the door. Janet's head and heart were competing as she wandered aimlessly through the streets, guided by her own grief searching for Trevor. She stopped at the corner store and peeped in the window. Mr. Chan spotted her through the glass and waved her in.

"Ms. Canet, no need today?" he asked.

Janet answered, "No Mr. Chan, not shopping today."

"What can do for you?" His smile was enormous.

"Have you seen Trevor today?"

"No, did you send here to shop?"

"No, I'm just checking."

"Sure you don't need?" he asked while pointing to a bunch of bananas.

Janet shook her head no, smiled and left.

Mr. Chan was the owner of the 4th Street Deli. He knew Janet and Trevor well. Janet always brought the daily newspaper from him, a loyal customer. Days that Mr. Chan didn't see her or Trevor in the store, he would send his son to deliver the paper to her apartment.

The cool autumn breeze caressed Janet's face; she didn't mind that the temperature had dropped ten degrees but she had to find Trevor. Janet tired and aching joints wanted to give up but her heart would not allow her. She kept stepping as if she was marching in a band. Janet continued to browse the neighborhood, looking at every young face that crossed her path. A few blocks away from the 4th Street Deli, she noticed a boy standing on the corner who resembled Trevor.

"Trevor," she yelled taking huge steps toward him.

As the boy slowly turned, she realized that it was not him. She was disappointed, not to mention exhausted. She had been walking for over an hour and her legs began to swell and ache. Refusing to give up she decided to walk to the neighborhood park. It wasn't really a park, just a run-down tennis court with no net and the kids played tag football on the blacktop. It was there that Janet came upon a group of boys playing football when she spotted Charles amongst the crowd.

Charles was Trevor's best friend. They had been friends since the age of four. He was a cute little boy, kinda on the chubby side with short black hair. Janet noticed him from a distance and yelled out his name. He recognized her immediately as she stood under the streetlight. When he reached her, he was breathing heavily.

"Have you seen Trevor?"

"I saw him early this morning," Charles said trying to catch his breath. "He was running like the wind. I tried to catch up but he wouldn't stop."

"Do you have any idea where he could have gone?"

"No, ma'am."

"Can you ask the other boys if they have seen him?"

Charles trotted over to the other boys and almost instantly returned with no good news. He looked up at Janet and noticed that she was crying.

"What's wrong, Ms. Janet? Why are you crying?" he asked with passion as he grabbed her weak, frail hand.

"Charles, I have a heavy load on my heart. I've been walking for hours looking for Trevor and I can't find him."

"Can I help?" he asked sincerely.

"You mean you will help me look for Trevor?" she said with sagging eyes.

"Sure, I'll get my friends and we will look all over the neighborhood for you."

"I really appreciate this Charles."

"Any time Ms. Janet, and try not to worry—if he's around, we'll find him."

He smiled at her as he ran to join his friends. It was very late in the evening when Janet returned home. Once at her apartment she slowly walked up the flight of stairs, stopping on each floor to take a break. She licked her lips and noticed they were dry and chapped. The lipstick she painted on them early that morning was long gone. She landed on her floor, hoping Trevor would be in the house. When she turned the knob and pushed the door opened, the house was cold, damp, and silent. Janet walked into the kitchen, flung her purse and keys on the counter and reached up to a cabinet, took out a glass. She dropped several ice cubes inside and then she headed down the hall to her bedroom to find her bottle. As she poured her drink, the phone rang. She answered it on the first ring.

"Hello, Janet this is Mae. What's going on girl? How have you been?" The Southern voice asked.

"I'm okay."

"I thought I would call you girl, you've been heavy on my mind lately."

With that Janet couldn't hold it any longer, she broke down and began sobbing.

"Janet, what's wrong?" Mae asked with concern.

She tried to talk but the words would not leave her chapped lips.

"Wait girl, I'm on my way."

The phone went dead. Janet sat on the bed and a sharp pain shot through her heart like a knife. The first sting was bad enough, but the second was excruciating. She grabbed her chest and began to weep louder.

"Lord, please remove this load from my heart and bring my baby home safe."

Then there was a soft knock at the door. Janet jumped to her feet and hurried to answer it. She unlocked the door wishing for good news. Charles's face was gloomy and instantly she knew that wasn't what she wanted or needed to hear.

"Ms. Janet, sorry but can't find Trevor," he said. "We looked everywhere. We checked all our favorite places and even our secret hiding place and he's nowhere to be found."

"Thank you, Charles for looking. Should you see him tell him to come home immediately?"

"Will do. See you later."

Just before closing the door Janet heard a familiar voice in the hallway.

"Janet," Mae said loudly from the bottom of the stairs. "Wait, it's me."

Janet peeped down the stairs and she could see Mae gradually climbing up the stairs breathing hard with every step she took. When Mae entered the apartment she said while huffing, "Girl, those steps can kill an old woman."

Before Janet could reply she fell into Mae's arms.

"Girl, sit down and tell me what's wrong," Mae directed Janet to a chair.

"Mae, my life is falling apart. I wish I could go back and erase yesterday."

"Girl what are you talking about?"

"I have lots of problems," Janet proclaimed while shaking her head.

"It can't be that bad. I'm here now, let me help you."

Janet looked on, her eyes wet. She put her hand up to her face. It started with a sniffle and then her aging face crumbled.

"I don't know where to begin."

"Let's start from the beginning."

Janet relayed the whole story leaving out nothing. The room became quiet as Mae stared into Janet's eyes. She felt her pain and her eyes began to water, too.

"Mae, I told Trevor what happened to his mother this morning and he ran off. Now I don't know where he is. His friends and I searched the neighborhood and we couldn't find him. I'm so afraid," she said outwardly displaying her fear.

"Ann is lying in the hospital fighting for her life and I can't find her baby. Mae, what am I going to do?"

Janet laid her head on Mae's shoulder, sobbing uncontrollably. Mae's heart reached out to Janet. She held Janet in her arms and gently stroked her hair. Then words finally broke her lips.

"First of all Janet, you must calm down."

Mae took her handkerchief from her handbag and wiped Janet's tears away.

"You know your heart can't take this. Are you taking your heart medicine?"

"Yes," Janet whispered.

"When was the last time you've been to the doctor?"

"Last week," she answered with a grunt. "Mae, the sad part of this, Ann nor Trevor doesn't know I have heart problems. I never shared that, because I didn't want to scare them."

Janet glanced at the clock and sighed woefully. Then she continued.

"After the death of her husband and losing the baby, and Tyler, I didn't want to add more stress to her life."

"So in other words, Janet, you have been hiding this from them for months," Mae stated, looking somewhat surprised.

"Yes, I know and now everything is backfiring on me."

Mae rose from the sofa and went toward the phone.

"Well girl the first thing we must do is call the police and file a missing person report."

Janet leaped to her feet, wringing her hands with worry and responded, "Mae, we can't call the police."

"Why not?" Mae asked puzzled. "The boy is missing and we must find him before he gets into some trouble."

"Mae, believe me when I say you can't phone the police, so please hang up the phone," she said with conviction.

"What are you saying, girl? Your baby is missing."

"Mae, there's something I didn't tell you." Janet took a breath, hard swallow and continued. "A detective wants to question Trevor."

"Question Trevor for what?" she asked quickly placing the phone back on its receiver.

"Well, according to the police, Trevor was the last person to see his mother and they are investigating an alleged phone call that Trevor received."

"What phone call are you talking about?"

This information unnerved Mae and she instantly thought of Janet's poor heart condition. But Mae struggled not to react.

"Mae, I don't want to talk about this anymore." She shrugged and crossed her arms. "I just want to rest—couldn't sleep last night. I slept on the cold, hard floor all night just so I could be close to Trevor. I just didn't want him to be alone. Help me please?" Janet cried!

"Girl, first you need to get some rest. I'm here now so I want you to lie down and try to get some sleep and I will stay here until Trevor shows up."

"Are you sure, Mae, I really need to rest? I'm tired," she said simply.

"Oh girl, I'm sure. You've been like a sister to me and there is nothing I wouldn't do for you."

"Can you call William to find out about Ann's condition? Dealing with Trevor's situation I didn't have time to call him."

"Okay. I'll fix some tea to relax you and then you must get some rest. You must stay strong for that little boy. He's going to need you more than ever."

"Yeah, Mae, I know." They hugged and Janet went to her bedroom.

Mae found the phone number on the board and she paged William as Janet requested. About five minutes later he called back.

"Janet," the strong gentle voice said.

"No, this is Mae. Janet is resting."

"Hello Mae."

"Hi William. How's Ann?"

"Everything is okay. Her vital signs are getting stronger. The doctor will try to operate tomorrow to remove the bullet. The bullet is still lodged in her head. They were afraid to operate today because they felt she wasn't strong enough, but they must remove the bullet before it causes an infection."

"Oh no William." Mae heard her own whisper.

"Did Trevor come home yet?"

"No, not yet. We're hoping he will come in soon."

"Tell Janet to call me once she gets up. I'll probably stay at the hospital all night. Let me know as soon as you hear from Trevor. I'll take to you later Mae, and thank you for coming to see about Janet. She really needs you."

They exchanged their good-byes and hung up. Mae fixed Janet a cup of tea but by the time she took it to her she had fallen asleep. She turned quickly not to awaken her and scampered into the den and turned on the TV. She plopped down on the sofa and cuddled up watching the news while her best friend was snoring in the next room.

Mae was a very attractive woman. Her flawless skin was as smooth as a milk chocolate M&M. You would never find her hair out of place. It was always well groomed, so perfect people thought she wore a wig. She spoke with an accentuated southern tone, making sure she pronounced all her words correctly. She had a sophisticated style—the way she dressed the way she walked and the way she talked. She oozed out class and elegance at the same time. Her four grown kids; all married with kids of their own. Mae and Janet had been friends for over forty years. They worked at the post office before retiring. And if you didn't know them you would think they were sisters. There was nothing she wouldn't do for Janet and vice versa.

A car backfiring in the parking lot startled Mae. She roused to her feet and peeped out of the window, making sure it was not gunfire. Janet was still sleeping when Mae crept into her room. She was grateful that Janet was finally getting the much-needed rest. She looked so relaxed and peaceful. Making sure not to awaken her; Mae covered Janet with the blanket that was lying on the edge of the bed. She gently squeezed her hand and stroked her face passionately.

"My friend, I'm here for you. Don't worry everything will be all right," she whispered.

Chapter 7

As Mae stood watching Janet, she was once again startled. This time it was a loud bang at the door. She raced to the door fearing that the noise would awaken Janet. When the door swung opened, there he stood. His clothes were covered with filth. His face and hands looked like they had not been washed in weeks.

"Get in here, boy," Mae said as she grabbed his shirt and yanked him through the door. "Had your Auntie worried all day? Go in the bathroom and take a bath right now," she said with authority.

He did just what she ordered him to do. Mae went into the kitchen to page William again to report Trevor's return.

I'll cook dinner. I'm sure they're probably hungry, she thought.

When she opened the refrigerator, she noticed cut-up chicken in a bowl that had been washed and seasoned. Janet had apparently placed there earlier. On top of the stove was a clean black cast iron skillet. Mae located the shortening and poured it in the pan, lit the pilot, and turned up the fire to get the pan nice and hot. While drenching the chicken with flour, Mae started humming *Amazing Grace*. She had a pleasant voice, been singing in the church choir for years. Fresh from his bath, Trevor quietly slipped into the kitchen and was listening to her for a moment as she placed the coated chicken into the hot bubbling oil. His bright, Ivory soap scented body glowed like a ripe orange.

"Aunt Mae, I'm sorry that I made everyone worry about me today," he said solemnly interrupting her humming.

"But when Auntie told me about my mother my mind snapped. I wanted to run away forever. I just wanted to get lost and never come back. I thought about my mother and Auntie. I didn't have the nerve to abandon them. We need each other now more than ever and I gotta support them and show them the love that they always show me."

45

His bright face began to show signs of distress. He started to grieve audibly. Mae waited for him to regain his composure.

"Aunt Janet and my mother are all I have now."

He looked up at the matronly woman standing before him and asked sadly, "Aunt Mae how is my mother?"

"Son, I spoke to your uncle earlier and he said that your mother will have to undergo an operation tomorrow. We're praying that the operation will be a success and the two of you can go home to be a family again."

She forced a smiled while turning the chicken over in the skillet.

"I really hope so. Aunt Mae, was my mother really shot in the head?" His voice began to tremble as he waited for the answer.

She took a deep breath and replied, "Yes."

"The head!" he exclaimed. "Can people live after that?"

"Sure, Honey, if it's not your time to go, God will not allow you to be taken," Mae said with a weak smile.

"Well I surely hope it's not time for my mother to go," he muttered. "We still have a lot of living to do together."

"Trevor, listen to me." Mae stopped in her tracks and stared at him as though he was her own grandchild.

"You are a very smart young man, but you must be strong for your mother and Janet."

She wanted to tell him badly about Janet's heart problem but that was a secret only Janet could tell.

"Remember, son everything happens for a reason. You don't know the reason yet but one day it will be revealed to you. I know your mother loves you and everything will be just fine. So, Trevor, what did you do all day?" she asked shifting the conversation.

"I walked for miles, talking to my mother and praying to God. I ended up in a park on the north side. While I was sitting on a bench, I saw a woman and a little boy. The boy was probably around four or five-years-old. I watched his mother toss a ball to him and he giggled. He looked so peaceful and content. His laughter reminded me of myself

46

when I was his age. I could tell that they were special together just like me and Mom. I became jealous and sad."

Trevor dropped his head and a tear rolled down off his chin.

"Aunt Mae, why did she do it? Doesn't she love me?"

By now, Trevor was trying to hold back the tears.

"Son, I don't know why she did it—only God and time can answer that question."

"I do know I prayed to God over a thousand times today. He's probably tired of me by now, repeating the same thing over and over. Telling him how much I love my mother and how badly I wanted her to live. You know Aunt Mae; our lives have not been the same since Ed died. After losing Ed, Tyler, and the baby, she always seems so sad. She pretended to be happy for me, but I could see through that fake smile and I know she hurts. I miss Ed and Tyler, too. I wished we were still a family."

A tear rolled down his face and he quickly wiped it away. His focus tried to roll back to joyful times, but living with so much pain for the past year had begun to wear the boy down.

"Well, son, we can't bring Ed back, but you, Tyler, and your mother can still be a family," she said as she patted his shoulder.

"I know, I will keep praying and I know one day my prayers will be answered."

The pain became intolerable and he couldn't hold them in any longer and tears started pouring down his cheeks.

"Come here, son." She held him close to her bosom. "No need to be wary any more. We will get through this together, I promise," she said with a smile as she wiped the fallen teardrops with the back of her palm.

"You promise?" Trevor asked as he choked on his words.

"Yes I promise. Now try to unwind until dinner is finished. It should be ready in fifteen minutes once the biscuits are done."

Trevor disappeared from the kitchen. Instead of going to the den he walked towards Janet's room, stopping at the threshold. He stood there staring at her in complete silence. The glare from the streetlight reflected on her face, and for the first time in his life she looked old to him. The gray in her hair was noticeable and her skin didn't have that glow that it always had. As Janet turned over, she noticed his presence. She quickly sat up on the bed and her eyes lit up like lights on a neon sign.

"Come here," she announced with outstretched hands.

He rushed to her and collapsed in her arms. They chatted for a few minutes holding each other tightly.

"Auntie, I'm sorry about today."

"Shhh," she said, placing her finger over his lips. "No need to say a word."

The room became stone quiet as they held each other.

Chapter 8

The thunderstorm that had awakened him earlier had subsided and the sun finally made its appearance. Trevor lay on the sofa staring vacantly out the window at the big blue sky now filled with huge white clouds. He noticed that the leaves on the trees were almost gone. He loved the fall; it was his favorite time of the year. Trevor lay there thinking about the time they went hiking in the mountains when he was six-years-old. They packed a picnic lunch and off they went—disappearing all day. They hiked through caves and on the trails, talking and picking up various colored leaves. They had a contest to see who could collect the most colorful leaves. Trevor smiled to himself because he always won, but deep in his heart he knew his mother let him win. Trevor reassured those moments. As he looked at the clock, he jumped to his feet because it was almost time for church. He heard the chiming of the nearby church bell and broke into a big grin. The house was extremely quiet. He didn't hear Janet at all so he peeped into her room but she was not there. He trotted down the hall toward the dining room and there she was, sitting at the table drinking a cup of coffee. She was pre-occupied and full of yesterday's stress, fears of tomorrow, and unanswered questions of today.

"Good morning, Auntie," he said as he leaned over and planted a kiss on her cheek. "Why didn't you wake me?"

"Wanted you to sleep."

"Going to church today?" he asked in a joyous tone.

"No, don't feel like it this morning," Janet answered taking a sip of coffee.

Trevor sat down next to her and placed his arm around her shoulder. He stared deeply into her eyes and faintly said, "Aunt Janet, we need God *now*. We can't afford to turn our back on Him. We must go to church. We must pray for my mother."

Janet looked at him with amazement.

"Trevor you are so right. What in the world was I thinking about? Church will start in forty-five minutes. Think you can be ready?"

"For God—anytime," he grinningly said as he rushed into the den to change his clothes.

Trevor was so skinny; his mother told him smilingly that he didn't weigh more than a bag full of quarters. But he had speed like lightning. Being the fastest boy in school, every day someone challenged him. However, he never lost a race. He was smart for his age and got along well with others. Ann never had a problem with him. He was polite and well mannered. A little on the shy side and didn't talk much in public, but he loved to play jokes on people. Janet always said he would make Ann proud of him one day. Although, he was an only child, he was very giving. He loved to share his toys with his friends. Material things were never a factor for him, it was the gift of giving that he adored. He was not the typical kid who wanted name brand clothes; he was satisfied with what Ann purchased. Being an only child most people thought he might become a spoiled brat, until they met him.

When Trevor finished dressing he went back into the living room and Janet was waiting for him.

"My, my, my, don't you look handsome," Janet complimented as she tucked his shirt into his slacks.

He had on black slacks, a gray shirt and black loafers. Trevor took a bow. They both chuckled and proceeded to leave. Just as Janet locked the door, Trevor mentioned that he had forgotten something. She quickly unlocked the door to let him in. Trevor rushed into the den and then he ran back to join her.

"Now I'm ready," he said as he stuffed a piece of paper in his pocket.

"Are you sure?" Janet asked with a big smile on her face as she locked the door.

The sky was hazy and the temperature was in the low fifties. They proceeded up the sidewalk in the direction of the church. Janet lived only two blocks away. Trevor had been going to this church with Janet ever since he was a baby. He knew everyone there and they knew him. Because Trevor had a very soulful voice, the choir director had been trying to get him to sing in the choir for years but he was too shy. As they continued to stroll along the sidewalk, Trevor head was tilted downward. Janet took her hand and lifted his face toward the sky.

"Hold your head up, Baby. Remember what I told you. Always walk tall and proud."

"Yes, ma'am," Trevor said as he straightened up and grabbed Janet's hand. "Auntie, can we go see my mother today? Last night Aunt Mae told me that my mother will be having an operation and I want to be there with her."

"Sure, we'll call Uncle William after church."

"Thank you," he said as he kissed her hand.

"I see someone is in the kissing mood this morning," Janet said giggling.

"Today is a happy day, because today my mother is going to live."

Janet was quiet. She didn't want to say anything wrong to destroy his hope and joy. When they arrived at the steps of the church, several people greeted them. Deacon Green welcomed Trevor.

"Good morning, Deacon Green"

"Haven't seen you in a while."

"I know, haven't been to visit my Auntie in a while."

"Pleased to see you, son." He tapped him on his shoulder with his bulletin.

Once inside the church, Trevor took Janet's hand and led her to the front.

"Where are you taking me?" Janet whispered.

"To the front," he said, "must be close this morning."

They sat down on the front pew. Trevor glanced over his shoulder and then he looked in the of direction the Pastor's Pulpit.

"Trevor, keep still," Janet quietly reprimanded.

But within moments he started fidgeting and looking around again.

"Aunt Janet, have you see Deacon Rogers?"

"Yeah, he's standing in the back talking to that lady in the yellow dress."

"Do you mind if I go talk to him?"

"Hurry before service begins," she said smiling at him as he proceeded to the back of the church.

Janet followed him with her eyes and watched carefully as Trevor spoke to the Deacon. Within seconds he reached into his pocket and handed the Deacon a piece of paper. The Deacon nodded his head pleasantly and Trevor returned to his seat.

I wonder what that was all about, Janet thought.

She wanted to ask him, but when he returned the organist started playing. When Pastor Getrite stood up to speak, he looked directly at Trevor. He couldn't take his eyes off of him.

"Good morning, church," he stated in a blissful tone.

"Good morning," the congregation responded in unison.

"Before we get started on the message this morning, I have a special request from a very special young man. Trevor come to the front please."

He motioned him forward with his hand. Trevor rose from the chair, walked up to the altar and stood tall and proud next to him. His slim body was as straight as an arrow.

"Son, you have the floor."

Janet was looking with astonishment because she didn't have a clue as to what was going on. He stood perfectly still, cleared his throat and finally spoke.

"Good morning Pastor, members, and friends. First I would like to give honor to God. I come to you this morning in need of prayer. You see, my mother is very ill and she's having a life threatening operation today. I need you to pray for my mother and my family. I'm scared and my Aunt Janet is doing all she can to help me through this difficult time and I love her for that."

The congregation said, "Awe" and Janet couldn't hold back the tears any longer. She removed her handkerchief from her purse and wiped the tears that were flowing freely down her face. She was amazed at what he was doing. Janet stared at Trevor, recalling his shy personality. *This can't be Trevor*, she thought, *couldn't get him to talk in front of an audience if you paid him.*

The longer he spoke, the stronger his voice resonated with power.

"This thing that has crippled my family is sad, but there is nothing that God can't handle."

"Amen," hollered the Deacons.

Then Deacon Rogers rose to his feet and shouted with great enthusiasm. Every pair of eyes in the church was glued on Trevor as he continued to talk.

"Will you please bow your heads and pray with me?"

Within seconds, every head bowed and waited for Trevor's prayer. He began.

"Our Father which art in heaven, bless my family oh Lord and keep us safe from harm. Bless my aunt for her strength for we know this comes from You alone. And finally Lord, bless my mother because she's Your child and she's in need of Your healing power. Bring her out of surgery safe and secure. Bless her all the days to follow. Guard her heart and her mind. Amen."

After Trevor's prayer, there was not a dry eye in the church. Even the children were weeping as they clung to their mothers and fathers.

"Before I go, I would like to dedicate a song to my mother. This is her favorite song. *His eye is on the Sparrow*. Maybe if I sing it loud enough she'll hear me."

Trevor cleared his throat and then said, "This is for you, Mom."

The organist began to play; he joined in singing like he never sang before. By the time Trevor finished singing, the whole congregation was standing on their feet. They clapped and shouted loudly; you could

53

hear the roars blocks away. Janet knew Trevor could sing, but until today she had no idea he could sing as well as he did. She was very proud of him and when he returned to his seat, she grabbed him and gave him a great big hug and a kiss then she told him how much she loved him.

"Hurry up, Baby," Janet said, pulling his arm as she swiftly walked down the street. "We must hurry home so we can go the hospital to see your mother."

Once they were in the house, she marched over to the phone and called the local taxi company. Janet noticed that the light on the answering machine was flashing. The news about Ann's tragedy was out and everyone was calling to share their concerns.

"Do you want me to play the messages?" Trevor eagerly asked.

"No we don't have time. We'll check them once we get back. Change your clothes so we can leave for the hospital."

"Auntie, do you mind if I keep my church clothes on? I would like to look nice for my mother."

His voice was mixed with happiness and sadness at the same time.

"Sure, but I must get out of these panty hose and girdle. The girdle is killing me." Janet chuckled as she left the room.

She darted into her bedroom and exchanged her Sunday's best for a pair of black slacks, a gray sweater, and pair of low-heeled black shoes. Satisfied with her selection she returned to the living room to join Trevor. His eyes were filled with delight when he saw her.

"Wow! Auntie, you look nice. We look like twins," Trevor said, almost giggling.

Just before they walked out the house, the phone started ringing.

"Want me to answer that?" Trevor said as he turned in the direction of the ringing telephone?

"No, Baby, I'll get it. Now run downstairs and see if the cab is here."

Janet rushed over to the phone and answered.

"Hello."

"Hello, Mom."

"Hi, son."

"How have you been?"

"Just fine."

"I heard about Ann. Is she ok?"

"She's hanging on. I'm on my way to the hospital to see her now."

"Where's Trevor?"

"He's waiting for me downstairs."

"How is he handling it?"

"Little rough last night but we got through it."

"I would like to come home to see you, Ann, and Trevor, but I don't have any money."

There was silence. Normally she would have said *I'll send you some*. But today she didn't offer.

"Don't worry; she wouldn't know you're here anyway. Just sent her a card and some flowers,"

Janet's voice became impatient and she began to rush him off the phone—today she didn't have time for his foolishness.

"I'll call the hospital tomorrow and get the address. I'll try to come home for Christmas."

Their conversation was interrupted from the shouting of Trevor's voice from the bottom of the stairs.

"Must go now, the cab is here. I'll talk to you later and take care."

"Yeah, talk to you later."

With a click he was gone.

"Coming, Baby," Janet said as she locked the door and rushed down the stairs.

When they reached section B12 of the hospital, Trevor noticed William sloped in a chair.

"Hello, Unc."

"Hey, Trevor," William said as he tried to sit up straight. He limply waved his hand at Janet. At her guess, he was too tired to speak.

"Man you look a mess," Janet murmured. "Go home and get some rest. Trevor and I are here now."

"Ann is still in the operating room Janet. I will leave once I hear something."

Janet could tell he had a rough night because his eyes were red and full of sleep. His clothes were wrinkled and reeked of tobacco smoke.

"How does it look?" Janet asked.

"Don't know. Everyone is too busy to talk."

Trevor was staring at a nearby vending machine when Janet noticed him.

"Trevor would you like a snack?" She reached in her purse and handed him fifty cents.

Trevor rushed over to the machine and inserted his money. He stood there for a moment, contemplating what he wanted. Janet looked at William's exhausted face and whispered under her breath.

"William, Trevor did an amazing thing in church today."

"What's that Janet?" William said barely opening his mouth—too drained to talk.

"He prayed for Ann and dedicated a song to her. Made me so proud," she said with a big smile.

"Wow," William sighed. "That boy always amazes me."

"He's truly a blessing, William," Janet said with a proud grin.

"Yeah, sis I know."

"Michael called me today," she continued.

"Did he ask you for any money?"

"No," Janet sighed in a low voice. But William could see the lie on her face.

"He said he'd try to come home for Christmas."

"Yeah, Yeah, Yeah," William said as he rolled his eyes.

"Are you okay, William?"

"I'm tired sis, that's all."

Janet could see the tension on his face.

"Why don't you lie down and take a nap. I will wake you as soon as I hear something," she quickly offered.

He took off his jacket and balled in up to make a pillow, placing it on a chair and laid down across three chairs and quickly fell to sleep.

After being in the hospital for several hours, Trevor was becoming restless. His empty potato chip bag lay on a chair next to him.

"Auntie may I go to the maternity ward to check out the babes, I mean babies?"

"You don't know where the maternity ward is?"

"I'll find it. Gotta learn my way around the hospital—it seems I'll be spending a lot of time here," he said staring down at William who was snoring.

"I guess you're right, but don't get lost and remember where we are."

"Got it Auntie, section B12."

"Hurry back and don't get into any trouble."

He kissed her on her cheek and skipped down the hall and disappeared out of her sight.

William slept peacefully as Janet watched him, remembering when he was born. The midwife that delivered him said he was the prettiest black baby she had seen. His head was coated with big curly locks and his skin was dark and rich like an espresso coffee bean. William was Janet only sibling and they were very close. He was much younger than her and sometimes she had to catch herself from not treating him like her own son. William was a handsome man. His hair was jet black because of the frequent application of Just for Men. A thin mustache outlined his face. He was in good shape and very muscular. Outside the scent of cigarettes he always smelled good. He was quiet—only talked if you asked a question, never married and didn't have any kids.

As Janet quietly sat watching her baby brother sleep, she mumbled, "Thank you. I couldn't have endured this without your love and support."

Trevor skipped down the hall; he stopped briefly to find out where the maternity ward was located. After getting directions from a nurse he continued walking. At the maternity ward he stopped and took a long look at the babies through the glass window. He couldn't help but notice a tiny one in the back. It had several tubes connected to a machine that were attached to his diminutive body.

"Must be sick," Trevor mumbled. "Sure hope the little guy makes it."

A nurse who was working in the back noticed Trevor gazing through the window and motioned him in with her hand. Trevor hurried in to meet her.

"Wanna help me with the babies?"

"May I?" he asked as his eyes lit up with excitement.

"Go over to the sink and wash your hands, then put on this robe."

The nurse handed him a blue robe. His exhilaration filled the air. *Wow, this is neat*, Trevor thought.

"What's your name?"

"My name is Trevor."

"Hi Trevor. My name is Sue."

"I know."

"How did you know that?" she asked with a raised eyebrow.

"I read your badge."

"Smart huh," she snickered.

"No, not really, I can read that's all."

"Why are you visiting? Do you have a new brother or sister here?"

"No ma'am. I'm waiting for my mother to come out of surgery."

"Where is she?" Sue asked with sincere sentiment.

"Oh she's on another floor." He began blinking his eyes, fighting back the tears. "She's in the Trauma Center," he said in a gloomy voice.

"Must be serious huh?" Sue said sighing.

"Yeah, gunshot to the head," Trevor answered as he put his hands over his face to hide the tears.

"Who shot her?"

"Don't know. I was at school when it happened."

"Did you come home and find her?"

"No ma'am. My uncle found her. He's downstairs with her now. I was bored so I decided to come up here and check out the babies."

"Trevor it's certainly nice to meet you and I hope everything will be okay with your mother."

"Thank you, Sue," he said as he tried to break into a cheerful smile.

Hours had passed and Trevor was having so much fun with Sue and the babies, he forgot about the time. Almost three hours had slipped away and he knew he needed to get back before his Aunt sent the bloodhounds after him.

"I have to go now, Sue. Can I come back and help you again?"

"Anytime, Trevor. I work Sunday through Thursday."

"Then I'll see you tomorrow."

He handed her the robe. She smiled at him while rubbing his hair back in place.

When Trevor returned to section B12, he found Janet and William in the same position.

"I guess no word yet?" Trevor stated as he stood close to the chair next to Janet.

"No, not yet, but what took you so long. I started to worry."

"I was having so much fun with Sue and the babies I forgot about the time."

"Sue! Who's that?" Janet asked while staring at William as he shifted positions.

"Sue is my new friend. She's a nurse in the Maternity Ward and I helped her with the babies. She told me to come back anytime."

"Well you're going to stay right here with me for now."

Janet took his hand and plopped him down onto the chair next to her.

"Gotta hear something soon," she said gesturing impatiently.

"We'd been waiting a long time."

About an hour later a tall distinguished looking man wearing a white robe approached Janet.

"Excuse me; are you here for Ann Sanford?"

"Yes," she answered quickly and roused to her feet.

"May I talk to you," he said as he motioned her to follow him out the waiting room.

Janet went over to William and tapped him on his shoulder. They followed him out of the waiting room into an office. He offered them a seat and then he settled into a big black chair behind the desk. Trevor stood beside Janet.

"Is this young man her son?" the doctor asked eyeing Trevor.

The only thing Janet could do was nod, yes. He took Trevor to an adjoining room full of toys and closed the door. Janet watched the perfect posture of the doctor when he returned.

"My name is Doctor Garfield."

"It's nice to meet you doctor. My name is Janet Price and this is my brother William Jones."

"I am the neurosurgeon who operated on Ms. Sanford."

He paused briefly and continued, "Well, I have some good news and some bad news. The good news is the operation was successful. The bullet has been removed. We had a difficult time removing it, trying not to cause any serious damage in the process."

He rose from his chair and went to an x-ray board that showed a picture of Ann's brain and began to explain the procedure to them. He spoke for ten minutes—his words sounded like a foreign language to them. They sat solemnly still—nodding as though they understood.

"Excuse me, Doctor Garfield," Janet finally interrupted him. "I don't understand a word you are saying and I'm sure William is clueless too."

William shook his head in agreement.

"Can you tell us in layman's terms what you are talking about?"

"I'm sorry, get carried away sometimes," he said, paused, and sat on the edge of his desk.

"It gets a little complicated," he said compassionately. "There are some damages due to bleeding and swelling causing inadequate oxygen that affected the cerebral hemispheres and cerebellum."

Janet heard that word before, but she couldn't recall what it meant.

"Cerebellum," she repeated.

"Ann is unconscious," Dr. Garfield responded as he stared at the board.

"Oh my Lord!" Janet shouted. "A coma, will she come out of it?"

The doctor's voice rose slightly as he continued.

"Ann is an extraordinary person and very strong. She has been fighting for her life and refuses to give up. It's all up to her now. Brain injury victims usually come around in their own time. There's nothing more we can do for her medically. There are several factors that have saved Ann's life. The small caliber bullet—bullets are funny things no two ever act exactly alike. Then there's the angle of the impact and finally luck," he said.

"What will happen if she doesn't come out of it?" Janet asked as she choked on her words.

"Well, someone in your family would have to make the decision whether or not to continue to let her live in a comatose state or end it," the doctor said as he cleared his throat.

Janet thought about it briefly and then she responded.

"We couldn't make such a decision," she said, shaking her head rapidly.

"Well Ms. Price, I know this is hard for you and your emotional state isn't clear right now, but this is very serious and you will have to weigh all of your options."

"So then what you're telling us is that she will just lie there like a vegetable?" William finally asked.

"In layman's terms yes."

William squeezed Janet's hand, he could feel them sweating like ice rolling off a hot mountain.

"It's going to be okay, Janet," William whispered, as he rubbed the sweat off her palms.

"At least she's still alive and we know Ann's will power. She's come out of this on top."

"William I hope you're right," Janet said with a sigh.

The room suddenly became very quiet. So Dr. Garfield finally broke the silence.

"There's no need for you to stay here tonight." His smile slowly faded.

"We need to get her settled in her room and it's going to take a while. She'll be okay, so why don't you go on home and get some rest and come back in the morning."

"Trevor." Janet yelled, as she rose from the chair. "We're leaving."

Janet shook the doctor's hand, and forced out thank you Lord. Then she hung her head and mumbled, "Thank you doctor for helping our Ann."

"You're welcome," he said with a smile, escorting them to the door.

Chapter 9

The ride back to Janet's house was long, gloomy, and quiet. William normally played his oldies but goodies CD, but today he wasn't in the mood to listen to music at all. His thoughts were on Ann. Trevor broke the dreary silence.

"Auntie, will my mother be all right?" he asked in a soft humbling tone.

"Baby," she said as she swung her body around to look him directly in his eyes. "Your mother is very ill and it may take her a long, long time to recover." She let out a big sigh.

"What do you mean a long time?" he asked as he leaned toward her.

"Maybe months."

"Months, why months?" he asked trying to hold back his tears.

"Well Trevor," Janet continued gently, not wanting to upset him. "Your mother has brain damage, and the healing of the brain is something you can never put a time limit on. She may be up in a day or it may take months."

"Can she talk?"

"No, not right now."

"Can she walk?"

After a brief moment of silence Janet answered, "No, Baby."

"Can she see?"

"Nope," she responded trying to remain calm after the hard questions but her voice began to tremble.

"Well if my mother can't talk, walk or see what can she do?"

The car went silent again. Janet tried to find the right words to say but her mind went blank.

"Well Trevor," she said as she winced, "Right now the only thing she can do is hear."

Trevor paused for a moment and then spoke.

"Well, I'm going to talk to her all the time and I will also read to her."

"She'll like that," Janet said as she faked a small grin.

"And when she can walk again, I'm going to take her to the mountain for a day. We haven't been to the mountain in a long time."

"That's the idea, Trevor," Janet said grateful for his optimism. "We must help your mother through this so we can be a family again."

"Aunt Janet," Trevor sighed, "I have faith that my mother is going to be okay. God answered my prayer today and if everyone we know prays for my mother, do you think God will hear one of us?"

Janet studied him slightly and answered, "Trevor I'm not sure if God hears all prayers, but I believe He will hear yours."

"Well I'm going to pray for my mother right now."

Trevor sighed and leaned back in his seat, closed his eyes and bowed his head. Janet and William became quiet as they listened to Trevor's conversation with God.

When they reached Janet's house, the coldness hit Janet and Trevor in the face once she opened the door. She rushed to the thermostat to turn up the heat. Janet took off her clothes and replaced them with a house gown. After settling herself, she went to her room to return some of the phone calls from earlier. Even though Trevor was sitting in the den watching TV; he could hear his aunt on the phone discussing his mother's circumstance. He walked in the room and asked if he could sleep with her because he was scared.

"Bring your pillow with you," Janet said while still engaged in her telephone conversation.

Trevor hurried to Janet's room with a pillow in his hand and dropped down on the bed beside her. He laid his head on her chest as she continued to chitchat. When she finished returning all the calls Trevor commented about school.

"Oh Lord I forgot all about school tomorrow. Do you want to go?" she asked staring at him as he lay on her chest.

"Can I stay home with you tomorrow?"

Janet couldn't refuse his request, and quickly replied, "I'll call the school in the morning and let them know what happened and maybe William can go to the school to get your books and assignments. You still have to get a good education," she said with a smile.

"I know, Auntie; my mother always told me that getting an education is not a choice, it's something you gotta do."

"She's right, can't be a doctor without education."

"Aunt Janet can I call Tyler and tell him about my mother."

At first Janet hesitated and then said, "I don't see why not. Do you know the telephone number?"

Trevor nodded yes, as she scooped up the receiver, feigning a smile. Trevor recited the numbers and Janet dialed. Trevor's conversation with Tyler was brief. When he hung up, he covered his eyes with his hands and began to sob. He cried so hard and loud that big teardrops rolled down his cheeks and his body shook out of control.

"Made me sad to tell Tyler about Mother, he took it kinda hard."

She smiled at him sympathetically, knowing that it wasn't his fault.

"It'll be okay," she whispered in his ear while continuing to comfort him. She held him tight in her arms. Trevor expelled a sigh of relief. He knew her love for him was very strong. Her tight grip was squeezing the air out of him.

Trevor squealed, "Aunt Janet, you're suffocating me. I can't breathe."

They both burst out with laughter.

The house was serene as Janet and Trevor both slept until 8:00 in the morning. The loud ringing of the phone had awakened Janet. Trevor was lying on his back with one arm thrown around her chest. She slowly removed his arm and eased out the bed without disturbing him and answered the phone in the kitchen.

"Hello." Janet said in a sleepy voice.

"Good morning, Aunt Janet, this is Bernita. Did I wake you?"

"No, sweetie, I need to get up anyway." There was squeakiness in her voice and Bernita could hear it.

"I just heard about Ann. How is she?"

"Bernita, she fine. The operation was successful yesterday and now she's recovering in God's hands."

"How bad is it?"

"Well, sweetie," Janet said as she pulled up a chair and began to whisper.

"Ann is in a coma."

"A coma!" Bernita shrieked.

The news was overwhelming for her. It was not what she had expected.

"Oh my Lord, I had no clue it was this bad. I need to get there as soon as possible, Ann needs me," she said faintly. "I will book my reservation right away. Are there any nice hotels near the hospital?"

"A hotel, you don't need a hotel. You can stay right here with Trevor and me."

"Don't wanna put you out,"

"No, sweetie, you're not putting me out. Trevor and I need some company."

"Are you sure?" Bernita asked.

"I'm positive. You're Ann's best friend and I just wouldn't feel right if you stayed in a hotel."

Bernita could hear the loneliness in Janet's voice and agreed to stay there. The call ended.

Janet went into the bathroom to take her bath. While waiting for the tub to fill, Trevor woke up. He could hear the water running and he knew exactly where she was. He hurried into the kitchen washed his hands in the sink and put on a fresh pot of coffee. *If I hurry*, he thought, *I could fix breakfast for Auntie*. Trevor took the bacon out and began to fry it. He placed a slice of bread in the toaster and then fried an egg. When Janet came out the bathroom she noticed that Trevor was no longer in bed she called out his name.

"I'm in the kitchen." He answered persistently.

Trevor placed the burnt bacon, the over-fried egg and dry toast on a plate. Then he poured a cup of coffee in her favorite mug and sat them on the dining room table. Janet smiled when she looked up and noticed him standing in the kitchen.

"I don't believe my eyes, Trevor you cooked?" she asked nodding towards him.

"Yeah," he said with a grin. "Hope it tastes all right?"

Janet sat down and began to eat. The food wasn't tasty, but she didn't have the nerve to tell him. His effects were good enough for her.

"Wow, this is good," she lied as she took a sip of coffee that was worse than the food.

"You like it?" he asked as he munched on a piece of crispy bacon.

"Yes, it's delicious. I didn't know you knew how to cook?"

"My mother taught me how," he said grinning.

"But you're only eleven-years-old."

"Yep, I know. My mother told me she wanted me to learn so I wouldn't have to depend on a woman to cook for me. She also told me that women are impressed with a man in the kitchen," he said as he giggled.

"What else has your mother taught you?"

Janet stared at him from the rim of her coffee mug.

"Well she taught me a lot of things. Like how to do laundry and iron my clothes, wash dishes, and oh yeah how to vacuum."

"Wow that's terrific, Trevor. I didn't know you were so knowledgeable around the house. You can be a stay-at-home-dad," she said beaming from ear to ear.

"No ma'am, I'm going to be a doctor," he said as he stuck his chest out.

Janet giggled.

"Oh I forgot, Auntie; Mom taught me how to shoot my BB gun."

"Shoot a BB gun," Janet said, puzzled. "How long have you been shooting a BB gun?"

"About three months now," he said as he stuffed the final piece of bacon in his mouth.

"Aren't you scared to shoot a gun?" There was a look of concern in Janet's eyes.

"At first I was, but not now."

Hmmm, Janet thought, *Ann never told me that*. She sat frozen in her fears, hoping that the detective wouldn't find this out.

"What time are we going to the hospital?" Trevor asked trying to change the subject once he noticed the concerned look on Janet's face.

"Visiting hours are from 10:00 until 7:00. We'll take the first shift and Uncle William will take the second."

Trevor removed the dishes from the table and placed them in the sink.

"So what time will we be leaving?" he yelled from the kitchen.

"Around 9:30."

"Oh did you call my school this morning?"

"Yep, I spoke to your guidance counselor Ms. Day. She will get all your assignments together for the week and William will pick them up at the office. She told me to tell you that she's sorry to hear about your mother and for you to take care of yourself. She said that her prayers are with you and the family." Janet rose from the table and continued. "If you need her for anything just give her a call. And she also said if you have any problems, or questions about any of your assignments you can call her at home."

Trevor smiled as he turned to dress leaving Janet standing at the table lost in her own world.

Trevor and Janet arrived at the hospital at 10 exactly. They stopped at the front desk to ask which room Ann was bedded in. When they entered the room, she lay with her eyes closed, her body as motionless as a corpse. She looked so fragile lying there, as if she was in a deep sleep. Her head was wrapped in a big white bandage. The only parts of her face revealed were her eyes, nose, and mouth. There were IV's attached to different parts of her body and a tube was inserted in her mouth that was attached to a large machine that pumped up and down. Janet had never seen anything like this in her life and it frightened her.

Her worn-out body instantaneously took a step backward as she placed her hand over her heart.

"Oh Lord, give me strength," she mumbled.

She took hold of Trevor's hand and they walked slowly over to the bed. As Janet and Trevor approached Ann's motionless body, they began to shudder with fear. For a brief moment, they stood there in amazement. The room was completely silent. No one said a word.

"Good morning," the voice said from behind.

As they turned around, a nurse came into the room pushing a cart.

"Good morning," they chorused at the same time.

"Have a seat; she's not going to bite you."

The nurse leaned over Ann's body to observe her bandages. Janet and Trevor walked slowly over to the chair and forced themselves to sit down. Trevor's eyes began to water.

He whispered, "Aunt Janet, can she hear me?"

Janet's lips were dry and tight so she moistened them with her tongue. Then speaking in a crackling voice, she said, "Sure, Baby, talk to her."

Janet took her hand and nudged Trevor on his side, forcing him to stand up. He stood quietly beside her, and then he bent down and kissed her on her eyes, nose, and mouth. Afterwards he placed his right hand on her chest.

"Mom," he said humbly, trying not to cry. "I can feel your heart beat." After a long pause he let out a big sigh. "And one day soon, I want you to be able to feel mine? You can do this, Mom. I know you can. I miss you so much. Can't sleep at night because all I do is think about you. Aunt Janet is here with me. I'm living with her now. She's taking great care of me and we both miss you so much and we want you to hurry up and get well so we can go home and be a family again."

Trevor turned to Janet who now placed her hands over her eyes.

"Tomorrow I'll bring a book to read to you. Would you like that?" he asked, shaking his head yes as through she answered for him.

Trevor stared at Janet with tears in her eyes.

"Auntie, do you want to say something?" He whispered.

Janet didn't realize that she had sat down. She struggled to stand up and then she began to weep.

"No, Baby, not right now." She gloomily answered.

Janet quickly returned to her seat holding her heart saying, "I'll talk to her later."

Trevor began to talk to Ann again as through she was listening. He talked all afternoon, asking her questions and then quickly answering as if they were carrying on a two-way conversation. The hours passed quickly for Trevor but felt like eternity for Janet. As they sat there together, mother and son, Trevor spoke to Ann, as a child speaks to their best friend. Pausing from time to time, holding back tears that threatened his speech.

It was around 3:00 and Janet thought *William will be coming soon.* Trevor asked if he could go to the Maternity Ward to see his friend Sue and the babies. Janet winked at him and off he went skipping down the hall greeting each guest, the patients, and the staff as he passed by.

Around 3:45 William strolled in the room. He noticed Janet sitting in an oversized chair by the window looking pitiful. He bent down and kissed her on her cheek.

"Hi, sis, it takes you back a little when you see for the first time."

"Yeah William I know, almost didn't make it in the room. If it weren't for Trevor being here with me, I don't think I would have had the nerve to come in."

Then it had occurred to William about Trevor. "Why is Trevor in the hall talking to that detective?"

"Detective," Janet shrieked.

"What detective are you talking about?"

"The one that was at the house taking the police report the night of the incident."

"The one who wanted to question Trevor—I didn't know he was out there?"

Her protective instincts rose, as did her fear. She jumped to her feet and stuck her head out the door and looked down the hall. *I'm going to get my baby*, she thought.

She walked down the long corridor until she noticed Trevor talking to a man in a pair of blue slacks and blue blazer. She walked up to them angrily and said, "It's time to go Trevor."

She grabbed him by the hand and yanked him along.

"How many times have I told you not to talk to strangers?" Janet asked irritably.

She pulled him even hard, making it almost impossible for him to keep up.

"But, Auntie, he called me by my name so I asked him how did he know me? I didn't recognize him."

"Well, you're going to stay with me from now on."

"Oh, Auntie," Trevor whined, "I didn't do anything wrong."

In her heart she knew he didn't, but she knew the detective was up to no good.

"I know, just a little scared that's all, I don't want to lose you," she said as she quickly rushed back to Ann's room never letting go of his hand.

"Auntie," he said with a chuckle, "you're never going to lose me. I'm here for life."

It's been one week since the incident occurred and Janet and Trevor have gone to the hospital daily like clockwork. But still there was no improvement in Ann's condition. Trevor was experiencing difficulty sleeping ever since the night of the horrible shooting and it was getting worse. His insomnia had nothing to do with the sympathy that he so desperately needed after the incident or living with his Aunt Janet. The nightmares are what disturbed Trevor's sleep—the ever-recurring thought of his mother lying in the hospital room with a small chance of her surviving the ordeal. He continued to sleep with Janet and some nights the nightmares would be so terrifying he would wake up in a cold sweat, blubbering as though the incident had just happened. He started losing weight and barely went outside to play. Janet would talk to him and ask if he wanted to visit his friend, Charles. But whenever she offered, he would kindly refuse. Trevor was satisfied spending evenings alone, eating ice-cream right out the box, watching Flintstones re-runs on TV, reading a good book, listening to music, or just daydreaming about his mother.

Later that evening Charles came to visit. "Hello Ms. Janet." he said as he trotted past her in the kitchen.

"Hi, Charles," Janet said and smiled.

"What's in your hand?"

The brown bag that Charles was holding was swinging back and forth.

"It's something for Trevor. I thought I would try to cheer him up."

Charles lifted the bag in the air, opened it to show Janet what he brought.

"He never comes out to play anymore and every time I see him he looks so sad," Charles said while sealing the bag.

"Thank you, Charles," Janet gave him the okay sign. "Trevor should like that. He's relaxing in the den."

He nodded and proceeded to the den. Charles stopped in the hallway and tapped on the door. Trevor acknowledged the knock but never looked up.

"Hello Trevor," Charles said as he plopped down on the sofa beside him. "I thought I would bring you something."

"You didn't have to do that."

Charles handed Trevor the bag and he eagerly opened it, his eyes lit up with excitement. There was a card and a game cartridge for his play station. He read the card aloud and then he placed it on the table and gave Charles a massive smile.

"Hope you don't already have this one?" Charles murmured.

He reads the title and said, "This is cool, man—and no I don't, but now I do," Trevor said with a laugh. "Thanks, I really appreciate this. Wanna play?"

They played for hours. Janet could hear the boys in the room giggling, talking, and playing. Sounds of great pleasure filled the air that had not been there for quite some time. *Trevor really needed that*, she thought. In her mind he was sounding like a typical little boy again.

"Going trick or treating with me and the guys tomorrow night?" Charles asked as he pressed the control panel trying to block Trevor's move.

"Nope, not in the mood for candy and Halloween is silly anyway."

"Come on and go with us," he begged. "We're going to have a lot of fun."

"No thanks, Charles. I'm going to stay here with Auntie—don't want her to be alone on such a spooky night."

"Man, I am really sorry to hear about your mother and I hope she will be all right. I truly miss playing with you and I miss our friendship."

Trevor placed the control panel on the floor and then he looked at Charles.

"Charles, you haven't lost me as a friend. I've had a lot on my mind lately that's all," Trevor sighed.

"I know, but you haven't been the same since this whole thing happened but I understand. I'd be the same way if it had happened to my mother."

At that moment it dawned on Charles that Trevor's heart was damaged.

"Guess I should go home now, it's getting late. I'll see you tomorrow."

"Yeah, see you tomorrow. And man thanks for the present," Trevor said cheerfully.

"Anytime," he said as he walked out of the den. Charles waved good-bye at Janet and left the house.

Chapter 10

Janet was standing in the bathroom combing her hair when she heard a knock at the door. The door swung opened and all she could see was a big bouquet of flowers.

"Hello Aunt Janet," the timid voice said from behind the flowers.

Bernita rushed into the house and placed the flowers on the table.

"It's nice to see you, sweetie," Janet said as they embraced.

"How was your flight?"

Janet grabbed her bag and suitcase from the hall and placed them inside the apartment.

"Oh the flight was fine. The food was awful," Bernita said, laughing.

"Yeah, never knew why they wanted to serve food on an airplane anyway. You can't get a good meal in the air."

"I know," Bernita said still laughing, "Just come to Aunt Janet's house for some good soul food."

Janet joined her laughter.

"Where's Trevor?"

Janet pointed to her bedroom. Bernita tipped toed into Janet's room. She stared at him for a while as he slept. She noticed his long brownish eyelashes and a mole on the side of his forehead that she hadn't recognized before. He was frowning and tossing in his sleep, apparently not enjoying the dream he was having. She kissed him, closed the door and went back in the living room in search of Janet.

"How long can you stay?" Janet asked while placing her suitcase in the closet and shutting the closet door.

"I have to leave Monday evening. I have a very important meeting on Tuesday. I tried to reschedule it but unfortunately I couldn't."

74

"I understand. We're just glad you could come," Janet said as she embraced her again.

Bernita was a small-framed woman. She had long black hair that bounced as she walked and dressed nicely, mostly in skirts. She kept her house so neat and clean; people teased her and said you could eat off her floor. A lover of joking she always kept you laughing. Bernita was forty-years-old, two years older than Ann. They have been friends for over thirty years. As long as Janet can remember, they have spent a week together every July. They called it 'the girl's week.' No husbands, no kids, just the two of them. Bernita was married to a minister, a very charming man. He pastored a small church that has less than one hundred members. They lived in an elegant house in a rural town in Jersey. They were a blessed couple—she had to sift through a lot of trash to find him. After Ann lost Ed, they spent a lot of quality time together, mostly chatting on the phone. Many times, they didn't know how long they had been speaking. Some days they would talk for hours. Bernita listened attentively and never rushed her off. Bernita was Ann's support and Ann was hers. She counseled Ann as much she could and tried to keep her spirits up after her tragic loss.

"Bernita, let's go in the living room and relax. We have much to discuss. Would you like something to drink?"

Bernita nodded yes and Janet poured her a cup of coffee. They sat on the sofa, staring at each other first. Neither one was ready to break the silence but Bernita finally spoke.

"Aunt Janet, do you really think Ann shot herself?"

"Bernita, I was thinking the same thing. I'm so bewildered by this. It's been on my conscious every day."

"Why do you think she did it?"

"Couldn't answer that, sweetie—I didn't see any signs."

"The last time I spoke to Ann, she was doing well. She was ecstatic that she joined that support group. It did a lot for her self-esteem and for Trevor. Her heart was getting stronger. I made sure of that. For her to attempt such a thing is a shock to me." Bernita said, holding her coffee cup to her mouth. She started to take a drink but didn't. "We must figure out why she felt this was the last straw. She had so much to live for."

"When was the last time you talked to her?" Janet asked while she sipped her coffee.

"About two weeks before the incident. She was planning to visit in January for our women's retreat at the church. We were looking forward to it."

"Did she say anything that would have yielded some clues regarding her mental state?"

"No ma'am not at all. She talked about the business and how well Trevor was doing and that they were going to visit Tyler in a couple of weeks."

"Sweetie, this just doesn't make any sense. I know how badly they wanted to see Tyler. Why in the world would she try to kill herself?" Janet said as she shook her head in shock.

The thought of Ann trying to kill herself finally turned Janet's dream into reality. At that point it finally registered to her that Ann didn't want to live.

"Aunt Janet, do you think there is some foul play?"

"Well since you said that let me tell you about the phone call."

"What phone call?" Bernita asked as she forced a small sip of coffee.

"The phone call Trevor received."

"When?" Bernita's eyes became bright. Janet's words struck a nerve.

"Right before he called me the last time."

"Who was it?"

"Don't know. The detective is investigating it now."

"A detective? Did you speak to him?"

"Nope, he spoke to William."

"What did he say?"

As Janet took another sip of coffee, her hands shook with dismay. "The detective wants to speak to Trevor."

"Why?" Bernita asked as she stood up putting her hands on her hips.

"According to the detective Trevor was the last person to see or speak to Ann."

"How do they know that? And what can Trevor tell the detective?"

Bernita paced the floor nervously. She was uncomfortable and it showed.

"They want to ask him questions about the alleged phone call?"

"What phone call?" Bernita asked as she plopped down on the sofa.

"Bernita, I don't know, but I'm so afraid. My heart is weak and it's getting weaker by the day. My doctor wants to operate on me soon. He told me that my heart is so weak that if I don't have the surgery in the near future, I may not live to see another year."

Janet finally told her secret to someone besides William, Mae, and Michael. She sighed and closed her eyes.

"You must have the operation, it is very important that you do."

Bernita passionately stroked her hand and Janet opened her eyes.

"I lost my brother about a year ago from congenital heart failure. We can't afford to lose you too."

"Bernita, I can't have the surgery until I know Ann will be all right." She began to cry, "Gotta to be here for Trevor."

Bernita held Janet tight. They rocked and cried together.

"Aunt Janet, everything will be all right. First I must help you find an attorney for Trevor."

"Why? Trevor doesn't need any attorney. He didn't do anything wrong."

"I know—but before he speaks to the detective, I would like to get legal advice. I want to make sure everything is going to be fine."

Janet dropped her head for a moment. When she finally looked up she then said, "I don't know any attorneys."

Bernita was ready and responded, "I have a friend with a successful law firm downtown. I will call him tomorrow and see if he can see us before I leave."

"How will that make Trevor feel, he's just a baby?"

"We must explain it to him—it's for his own good."

"Sweetie you make it seem like he may have something to do with it?" Janet said with suspicion.

"No that's not what I'm saying. We must protect him for Ann.

"I know. I don't know what Ann would do if anything happened to her baby?" Janet said with a frown.

They sat there nonchalantly and didn't utter another word. Both of their minds were on Ann, Trevor, and now the detective.

Ann was very pleasing to look at. She was strong, sensitive, and a giving person—one who would give you the shirt off her back. Ann didn't have many friends. She stayed to herself a lot. Her sexy legs and walk was the envy of every woman. Men stared at her when she entered a room. She was tall and petite and sported a short sassy haircut. Ann was very professional and well organized. She left Trevor's father when he was only nine months old. Ann didn't remember much about her own father, he died when she was only five. Her mother raised both she and her brother alone. After many years of suffering, her mother died. During her mother's days of sickness, Ann never left her side. After her mother's death, Janet became like a second mother to her. Janet was her mother's aunt.

About three years ago, Ann met Ed, a single father. His son Tyler was only three at the time. When they meet they instantly fell in love. Trevor and Tyler shared everything and they were elated to have each other. Ed owned a landscaping business. Shortly after they started dating, Ann quit her job at an advertising firm to help Ed grow his business. After one year she was able to turn the business into a million dollar empire. Their affection for each other churned deeply after six months of dating. Ed proposed. Their wedding was in Hawaii. Only a few close friends and family attended. It was the most beautiful romantic sunset wedding one could imagine. With the good fortune of the booming business, they purchased a huge house in the country about thirty miles west of the city. The ten acres lot was surrounded by woods and a large natural stream edged the property. Ed planted a large vegetable garden and flowerbed behind a maple tree. Ann loved flowers and every morning she would cut fresh flowers from her flower bed, placing them in her favorite vase and set them on the kitchen table. Ed always dreamed of owning a large piece of land; he so desperately wanted to raise horses one day. They had a blissful life together. Everyone said they were truly meant to be together.

While Ed was out of town for a business trip Ann became ill. She decided to have a check-up. To her amazement, Ann found out she was pregnant. After being gone for a two weeks Ed was returning from his trip, so she packed-up the boys and sent them to Janet's house. She couldn't wait to share the good news with Ed. She prepared a nice candlelit dinner with wine and soft music while waiting purposefully. Ed called from his cellular phone when his plane landed. He told her he was just leaving the airport and he would see her in a half an hour. He told her how much he missed and loved her and he couldn't wait to hold her in his arms again. Ann felt the same way, but she had a surprise for him. A secret she had been holding for three days. No one knew her secret. Not Janet, Trevor or Bernita, she wanted Ed to be the first to hear the words leave her lips. She waited and waited. An hour passed and she was getting restless. Every time a headlight shined through the window she would peep out to see if it was Ed. Impatient, she called him on his cellular phone. No answer. She left a loving message and hung up. Another hour had passed, she called him again and still no answer. She decided to relax on the sofa and wait for her love to come through the door. She fell asleep with a big smile on her face.

A thunderous knock awakened her; she rushed to the door thinking it was Ed. To her surprise there was a short stocky cop with bland features standing on the porch. He flashed his badge and she invited him in. He asked her if she was Mrs. Sanford. She nodded yes. For a second there were no sounds, just pristine stillness.

"Mr. Cop why are you here?" she finally asked with concern.

What came out of his mouth next stunned her to a point of no return. He informed her that Ed was in a terrible car accident three miles from the house and he was MEDEVACed to Riverside County Hospital. The cop continued to speak, but she couldn't hear a word. His lips were moving but her mind went blank. Ann grabbed her purse and keys and jumped in her car and rushed to the hospital not knowing the seriousness of his injury.

Ann drove like a bat out of hell and praying all the way. She was hopeful that Ed was not severely injured. By the time she pulled into the parking lot at the hospital she had broken several traffic violations—speeding, running red lights, when possible and not coming to a complete stop at stop signs. It was no time for her to obey the law, she had one thing on her mind—her concerns were compounded on Ed's condition.

When she arrived in the Emergency Room, she was ushered quickly to a small area. There she saw his lifeless body laid on the table. The doctor tried to console her but her grief had swallowed her up. She yelled from the top of her lungs with a rumbling roar and then collapsed to the floor. His death took her by surprise. She never had a chance to tell him about the baby or how much she loved him. Her heart was broken and she sank deep into depression.

From the description in the police report Ann knew exactly the location where Ed's car skidded off the road and struck the tree. That street became a no-drive zone. She couldn't muster up the nerve to drive or ride down that street again. She took another route home—it took a little longer, but in her mind that was okay. One of her employees wrapped a large yellow ribbon around the tree as a memorial for Ed.

Shortly after Ed's funeral, Ann went to the hospital for observation, due to fatigue and emotional stress. She started experiencing problems holding down food and she only slept for thirty minutes at a time. Bitterly disappointed, her health began to deteriorate and consequently she lost weight. After several days in the hospital, she had a miscarriage. Bernita and Janet supported her through it all. They felt sorry for her and her predicament. Less than one month, she lost the love of her life and the baby she so desperately wanted.

It wasn't long after Ed's death, the fight between Ann and his ex-wife, Barbara had begun. Barbara wanted Tyler to move back with her. Ann and Barbara were in a custody battle for months. Even after hiring the best attorney, the judge awarded Tyler back to his biological mother. Ann spent a lot of the money Ed left fighting to keep Tyler. She didn't want to lose him, and he didn't want to go. Ann loved him—like her own child. She fought until the very end trying to hang on to anything that reminded her of Ed.

Ann and Trevor joined a support group to help them get through their trauma. The group met every Tuesday night. Ann never missed a session because attending the meetings was helping her get her life back in order. Her beauty had resurfaced and she started looking like herself again. Gradually her smile and weight came back and she was able to enjoy life. Ann took Trevor on his first cruise for a week. The cruise helped them and their bond grow stronger as they tried hard to adjust to their new life.

"Aunt Be, I didn't know you were in town, "Trevor said, giving her a tender hug.

"Arrived this morning, Snook," she said while hugging him back. Snook was a nickname that she had given to him when he was a baby.

"How long are you going to be here?"

"I can only stay a couple of days—leaving Monday."

"How's Uncle Terry?" Trevor asked while admiring her hairstyle.

"He sends his love and prayers and he will try to come soon."

"Good morning Auntie." Janet acknowledged him with a smile.

"Aunt Be," Trevor said as he sat down between her and Janet. "I miss my mother and I dream every night that she was here. I'm trying to think positive but it's getting hard. You and Uncle Terry always told me to keep the faith, but to be honest with you, I'm about to lose it."

"Snook, you must always pray and never lose faith," Bernita said softly as she tried to compose him. "Your mother will be all right. She wants to live—if she didn't, she would have given up already. She loves you and we love you and when you find yourself getting sad or about to lose your faith, pick up your Bible and read it. And don't forget you know you can always call me?"

He agreed with her and then said, "I would love to read my Bible, but it's at the house."

"I'll call the police department to arrange for us to get some of your things. Would you like that?" she asked with a smile.

"Yeah, that'll be cool. I need some clothes and I would like to get my bike."

"Well consider it done; now get ready so we can go see your mother. I can't wait to see her."

Bernita smiled at Trevor and allowed her focus to remain on him.

"I feel the same," Trevor said as he stood to exit the room.

"Aunt Be," Trevor said as he swung around, "thanks for coming. Mom will like that."

Bernita nodded as she suppressed a smile. The two women continued to sit and chat as they waited for Trevor. He dressed quickly and soon after, they left for the hospital.

Chapter 11

As Bernita drove her rental car to the hospital, they couldn't believe how quickly their lives had changed. Less than two weeks ago, everything seemed normal. Nonetheless, they all realized that Trevor's life had somewhat fallen apart. The ride was fun for once. Anticipated joy filtered from Trevor and Bernita as Bernita told her corny jokes, while stiff fortitude of sadness filled Janet's head. Each one was eager to obtain their goal of finding peace—but their individual techniques would be quite different. Once Bernita turned the car into the parking lot of the hospital everyone's laugh dried-up and they became strangely solemn. Bernita pulled up to the entrance of the hospital; put the car in park, and opened the door for Janet and Trevor. Before pulling off, Bernita handed Trevor that big bouquet of flowers while they waited for her to park the car.

When they arrived in section B12, there was a mob of people gathered in the brightly lit waiting area. A few men were standing in a huddle chatting by the door. There were two ladies from Janet's church standing by the window staring out to the vacant lot next to the hospital. Some were sitting in black chairs with their arms folded, trying to watch TV and others were reading magazines. As Trevor walked past each group, they acknowledged his presence. Trevor knew most of the people, but there were some strangers amongst the crowd. Only three people were allowed in at one time to visit Ann. As three went in, the others waited for their turn. There was not a happy face among them. Janet knew Ann was loved but she had no idea so many people cared. When Bernita, Janet, and Trevor entered Ann's room, everyone's eyes lit up and the room was flooded with flowers, balloons, and cards. They could barely make it through the door. The floral aroma filled the atmosphere. Everyone, who knew Ann, knew she loved flowers. Trevor tried to find a place to put the flowers he had in his hand. With help from Bernita, he found a spot close to Ann's bed.

"Good morning, Mom," he said as he kissed her on the eyes, nose, and mouth. "I brought someone special to see you."

Ann was lying there. Nothing had changed from the day before. As Bernita stood staring down at her best friend, her body began to tingle.

"Hello Ann," she said in a low tone. She slowly reached out to touch Ann but her hands began shivering so she quickly pulled back and placed them in a crisscross position.

"Ann, my beloved friend, how are you dear? I know you can hear me. I miss you so much. Please fight. Fight for those who love you. It's not time for you to go and I can't live without you, so fight, dear fight."

Her voice was soft but yet hostile at the same time.

"Remember today is a gift—that's why they call it the present and now you must live for tomorrow."

She bent down on her knees and started praying. As she prayed the room became respectfully silent and the prayer vibrated down the hall to the waiting area. All the visitors choked as Bernita prayed. After the prayer she placed a gold cross above her bed, and kissed Ann on the bandage of her forehead and slowly walked out the room. Janet quickly followed and called out her name.

She gradually turned around and said, "Aunt Janet, I can't do this. I thought I could handle it, but now I realize that I can't. It's too much for me. I don't want Snook to see me like this. I must be strong and right now, I'm too weak and my heart is in so much pain. Seeing Ann like this is killing me. I just don't understand why she would do such a thing?" Bernita placed her hands on her cheeks and continued walking down the hall, never once looking back.

After their visit to the hospital they returned to Janet's house. Trevor retired to Janet's room to watch TV. When she peeped in on him, she noticed that he had peacefully fallen asleep in the middle of her bed. So she tucked him in, gently kissing him, closed the door, and then left the room. Bernita made Janet feel so comfortable that for a moment she had forgotten about the tragedy that had surrounded them. They laughed and talked all evening as the kids knocked on the door to receive their Halloween candy, while yelling trick or treat.

William arrived later with a large pepperoni pizza. They sat around the table, eating, laughing, passing out treats and talking about Ann and Trevor. For a brief moment things almost felt normal as they relived the special times they've shared throughout the years. When William left several hours later and the knocks stopped, they took their tired aching bodies to bed.

Trevor had awakened late the next morning. Janet and Bernita were reading the Sunday paper in the dining room when Trevor walked in.

"Good morning ladies," he said as he reached for a glass to pour some orange juice.

"Good morning, Baby," Janet stated as she peeped from behind the paper.

"Hello, Snook. Come here and give me some sugar."

Trevor went to Bernita and kissed her on the cheek.

"Oh Auntie, I haven't forgot about you," he said as he swung around and kissed Janet too.

"What are you lovely ladies up to this morning?"

"Not much, just relaxing and checking out the news."

"Going to church this morning?" he asked as he took a sip of orange juice.

"No Snook, not today. We have to meet the officer at your house at 10:00 to get some of your things," Bernita offered.

"Yeah, I forgot about that. Aunt Janet are you going with us?" Trevor asked as he looked at her gleaming.

"No, I'm going to stay here and cook dinner. Can't send Bernita home without some of my home cooking," Janet said with a grin.

"What time will we be leaving Aunt Be?"

"As soon as William arrives, we can go."

"Well I'm going to take my shower and get dressed. See you lovely ladies later." He smiled and left the room.

Chapter 12

William arrived about an hour later and they marched to the car in a line. The ride was fun with Bernita's wacky jokes keeping things lively. After they turned into the driveway on the north side, the empty garden and deserted flowerbed was noticeable. Many of the flowers had died due to the cool weather and neglect. A police car was parked on the street in front of the house. They exited the car and headed up the flagstone sidewalk; the officer approached them.

"Hello. My name is Officer Moore. I need you to wait here until I signal you to come in."

They stood patiently on the flagstones and watched the officer stroll over to the front door. He removed the yellow caution tape that outlined the door, opened it and disappeared inside. A bright light coming from the shade in the living room flickered on when the officer turned the switch. Officer Moore came to the door and motion for them to come in. When they hit the entrance of the door, the stench of dried blood engulfed them and by the time they entered the foyer, the smell of death slapped them in the face.

"Must have the carpet cleaned," William stated as he pinched his nose.

Bernita was aware of the appalling odor but she chose to ignore it. Trevor walked slowly behind William holding on to the back of his shirt.

"Unc, I don't feel good. My stomach is upset," Trevor said as he held his hand over his mouth. "This house is spooky, creepy, and I'm scared," he said, as he peeked around the corner with fearful eyes.

"I know, I feel sick too," William whispered.

"Can't we leave now—I don't want to go any further?" Trevor stopped dead in his tracks.

"Trevor, don't you want your bike?" he asked.

86

"Yes, but I can't stay in here." His feet were still plastered to the floor.

"Nothing is going to hurt you. I'm here. Aunt Bernita and that big strong cop over there are here," he said pointing in the policeman's direction. "We will never let anything harm you. Follow me, and I'll make sure nothing happens."

Trevor reluctantly grabbed William's hand and they walked slowly toward his bedroom. The big house carried an unwavering moment of fear. Trevor followed them through the house to his room. Once in his room he saw familiar things and began to relax. He looked at some of his sports trophies, toys, and books. The closet door was slightly open. He went to the closet and removed some of his clothes. Bernita removed several items from the dressers. They were placed in two large plastic bags. William sat quietly on the bed and watched as they pranced around the room gathering his articles.

"How are you doing?" Bernita whispered to William.

"I'm nervous," William whispered back. "Feel my hands?"

William held out his hands and Bernita gently touched them. His hands were cold as ice. This was all so unreal to William. Less than two weeks ago, this was a happy home—now it was unnerving.

They packed the car with the plastic bags and Trevor's bike.

"Need anything else, Son?" William asked as he closed the trunk.

"Oh snap, I forgot my Bible and some school books."

"Wait here and I will get them for you."

"I'll go with you Unc, don't think you can find them."

Trevor followed William back into the house. They rushed past the officer, while Bernita waited in the car. Once in the house, Trevor grabbed his Bible and some books from his desk. There was a brown chest sitting on the dresser. After searching through it, Trevor removed an item.

"What's that?" William asked with curiosity.

"Oh, just a key."

"A key to what?" he asked suspiciously.

"A key to lock my bike."

"Oh yeah, you will need that. Any kid would love to get their hands on that bike."

"I know, Unc, Ed brought this for me as a Christmas gift and I know he spent a lot of money for it."

"Yeah, trick bikes are expensive," said William as they returned to the car to join Bernita.

The officer clicked off the light and re-taped the door. Officer Moore waved to them as they drove away.

Bernita had a few errands to run that afternoon which included telephoning her attorney friend, Paul. After briefly explaining the situation to him, Paul advised her to bring Trevor to his office in the morning. As Janet set the table for dinner, Trevor rushed to the closet to get the napkins. When he opened the box he looked jolly and for once he seemed happy.

"Using the napkins today?" he asked Janet as he took them out the box.

"No, Baby, the next time we use the napkins your mother will be eating with us," she said as she carefully placed the napkins back in the box.

Trevor stared intently at the napkins and then spoke. "Auntie what do the initials A.L. means?"

This was the first time he noticed the lovely embroidery in the corner of each one. With a wide grin Janet said, "A.L. stands for Auntie's Love."

Trevor giggled. He didn't understand why she would have napkins with the initials A.L., but if she said they stood for Auntie's love then he had no reason to doubt her. She winked at him and he quickly placed the box back in the closet on the top shelf. They ate quietly. No one uttered a word. Trevor played with his food for a while.

"Stop playing, Baby and eat up," Janet finally said as she passed him another piece of chicken.

Trevor loved Janet's fried chicken—it was his favorite. To him, no one in the world could fry chicken better than Janet, not even his mother. Trevor took a drumstick and began to nibble on it. Bernita cleaned her plate and sat there gazing at Trevor as she sipped her lemon-flavored tea.

"Snook, I would like you to speak to my friend?" Bernita said in a happy tone.

"Who?" asking as he banged his drumstick on the plate.

"His name is Paul Domingues."

"Who is that?" he asked surprisingly.

"He's an attorney," Bernita answered trying not to look directly at him.

"An attorney! Why do I need to speak to an attorney?"

Bernita rose from her chair and stood behind Trevor massaging his shoulders.

"Snook, a detective would like to ask you some questions and before we let you speak to him we would prefer you talk to an attorney first."

"Aunt Be why do I need to speak to a detective?" he asked as his eyes widened with fear.

"Well Snook," she said trying to keep her voice calm. "He would like to speak to you for several reasons."

"What reasons?"

"Well," she said as she continued rubbing his shoulders, "Because they think you were the last person to see or speak to your mother, and the phone call. According to the detective, they can't find a record of that mysterious telephone call to the house."

"I promise there was a phone call," Trevor said as his voice shrilled. He pushed his plate away from him as if he just lost his appetite. Then he crossed his arms and sat back forcefully against the chair.

"Snook, settle down," she clamored instantly. "These are only police procedures. There's nothing to worry about."

"Why can't they just leave me alone? I don't know anything?" Trevor added angrily.

"Snook," Bernita said as she continued trying to calm him down. "We understand, but maybe you can tell him something to help solve this case?"

"What case—this is no case. My mother didn't want to live so she tried to kill herself. She doesn't love me and she doesn't love herself. She probably thought this was the best way to end it."

He pushed the chair from underneath him.

"Snook, listen to me. Have I ever told you anything wrong?"

Trevor nodded as the tears sparkled in his eyes.

"Well I'm not going to start now. I promise you, we will protect you," Bernita continued speaking and tried to console him.

"But first you must speak to the detective and tell him everything you know."

"Like what Aunt Be?" He looked up at her somewhat surprised. "I don't know anything."

"Think Snook, think. Any little thing can help."

Trevor pleaded, "Aunt Janet, why can't people just leave us alone? I just want to be left alone."

The conversation ended abruptly. He rose; walked into the den, and shut the door. Janet was weeping, trying to conceal her tears.

"Bernita, why can't they leave us alone? Why does Trevor have to go through this? It just isn't fair," Janet managed to say.

"I know Aunt Janet, but it's something we can't avoid."

"It's just breaking my heart," she murmured as she withdrew herself from the room.

The house was cast in gloom. Gradually the sun began to set overtaking the bright sunlight that once beamed in the house. As they rode to the hospital, no one uttered a word. Their minds were still focused on what happened during dinner. Bernita did not tell one joke. There was no laughter or music coming from the car. Trevor didn't speak and Janet read her Bible and hummed to herself.

When they approached the hospital waiting room, they noticed a small crowd waiting to see Ann and they rushed past with greetings. Trevor went to Ann and kissed her as he always did. He talked to her for a while and read a couple of verses from his Bible. Janet and Bernita watched with pleasant smiles on their faces. Neither one forgot what happened earlier that day but somehow they were able to let it go once they saw Trevor's contact with his mother. Several incidents of tragedies happened to them this year, and now they don't know which one was worst.

Trevor finished reading the verses and asked Janet if he could go to see Sue and the babies. She hesitantly agreed. As Trevor marched down the busy hallway he noticed a little boy in a room alone.

"Hello," Trevor said as he peeked in his room. "Mind if I come in?"

It was apparent the little boy was very ill. Trevor felt sorry for him and wanted to be his friend. Being in the hospital was frightening, boring, and lonely. After scanning the room, he noticed that no one was visiting him.

"Sure," the boy said delicately.

"What's your name?" Trevor asked when he reached his bed.

"My name is Alonza, and yours?"

"I'm Trevor. Nice to meet you, Alonza. Why are you here alone?" he asked as he sat down beside him.

"I don't have parents, brothers or sisters."

"Where are you parents?" Trevor asked with compassion.

"My parents are deceased."

"Then, who takes care of you?"

This made Trevor aware that this could be him. It never dawned on him before, but if he lost his mother, then he would not have parents either.

"My grandmother, but she couldn't make it to the hospital today," he said with sad eyes.

"How old are you?" Trevor asked.

"I'm six."

Trevor stared at him because he was so tiny for six and his bald head made him look older.

"Why are you here, what's wrong with you?"

"I have leukemia," he said gasping for air.

Trevor couldn't stop staring at him. He looked so frail and weak.

"I'm sure you will be all right. Would you like to play a game?"

"Okay," Alonza said as he sat up in the bed.

"Do you have any cards?" Trevor asked as he glimpsed around the bare room.

"No, I don't think so."

"Do you have any board games?"

Alonza shook his head no. "I never had anyone to play with," Alonza said as he gasped for air again.

"Well, that's okay, we can think of something to play."

Trevor looked in the drawer and found some paper and pencils.

"Hey look what I found, we can play hang man," he said with excitement.

"Do you know how to play?"

Alonza shook his head no.

"I'll teach you."

Trevor was eager to play with the little sick boy. He placed the paper and pencil on the tray and taught him. Alonza quickly learned and Trevor and Alonza played for an hour. The nurse came in and asked him to leave so that Alonza could get some rest. Trevor said good-bye and told him that he would be back tomorrow.

The halls in the hospital seemed to be getting shorter. Trevor had learned different short cuts to maneuver to and from the maternity ward. After being in the maternity ward for several minutes, he realized he couldn't find Sue. He walked up and down the halls searching for her. Finally he noticed her in a break room eating a sandwich.

"Hello, Sue," Trevor said waving at her when he noticed her blonde hair.

"Hi Trevor."

Her face broke into a happy smile.

"How long have you been here?"

"About ten minutes," he said with a grin.

"Taking a lunch break, would you like to join me?"

Trevor sat next to her at the table. Sue took out several chocolate chips cookies and offered him some. As he crunched on his cookie Trevor started with the questions.

"Sue, what's leukemia?"

Sue looked up at him and asked, "Who has leukemia?"

"I met a boy name Alonza in room 517 and he told me that he has leukemia. I didn't ask him what it was because I felt sorry for him. He's so small for six and he had not one visitor. His parents are decreased and his grandmother was unable to make it to the hospital today. I played with him for hours. Since he had no toys or games, so we ended up playing hang man."

"Trevor," Sue said trying to digest her sandwich. "Leukemia is a malignant disease affecting tissues of the bone marrow. A rapid increase in the number of immature blood cells makes the marrow unable to produce healthy blood cells."

Trevor looked at her as he bit into his cookie.

"It's like cancer huh?"

She nodded yes.

"Will he be all right?" Trevor asked she took another bite of his cookie.

"It can be fatal if it's not properly treated."

Trevor sat there quietly. Finally responding in a humble voice he added, "Well, I will have to add Alonza to my prayers."

Trevor looked at Sue with sad glassy eyes.

"He'll like that, Trevor," Sue commented as she cleaned the table and tossed her trash in the nearby waste basket.

Back in section B12, Trevor noticed that the crowd had thinned out. Bernita, Janet, and William were having small talk.

"Hello Snook," Bernita said as he entered the room.
He spoke as he plopped down on the arm of her chair.

"How are the babies today?"

"I didn't get a chance to see the babies. I met a new friend named Alonza in room 517. I played with him for a while and then I had lunch with Sue."

"What's wrong Snook?"

It was obvious that he was sad. She squeezed his hand and exchanged a warm smile.

"My friend, Alonza has leukemia and he looks so sick and sad. There was no one visiting him and he has no toys or games to play with." Trevor said as he leaned his head against her chair. "Aunt Be can we buy Alonza some toys and games to play with? I can go play with him every day. The little guy looks so lonely."

Bernita could see the disappointment on Trevor's face. Buying the sick little boy games were the honorable thing to do and she quickly agreed. Trevor planted a kiss on her cheek and thanked her for her kindness. As time drew near for their departure, they gathered around Ann's bed and held hands. Bernita said a heart-rending prayer. Trevor interrupted by adding Alonza's name at the end of the prayer.

Chapter 13

The next morning, Janet, Bernita, and Trevor left early to meet the attorney. The drive through the city was delightful for Trevor. The air was crisp and chilly. He preferred the excitement and variety of the tall buildings instead of the quaint country lifestyle. Trevor loved Washington DC, and he could never understand why they moved to the country. He watched the people as they hurried to catch their buses. Business people bustled along the sidewalk toting their briefcases. Taxicabs rushed down the street and horns honking at pedestrians jaywalking through the crosswalks. When they pulled up to the office building, Trevor admired the architectural design. The building was tall, strangely shaped with tinted windows. People were dashing in and out of a revolving door. They sported their fancy coats, scarves, and hats. Bernita looked back at Trevor and announced.

"We're here."

She smiled as she drove to the parking lot, stopping long enough for the attendant to hand her a ticket. Bernita placed the ticket on the dashboard and found a parking space. Before long, Janet, Bernita, and Trevor walked up a long ramp and entered through the same revolving door that led to an elevator.

"What floor?" Trevor asked ready to press the button.

"The fifteenth," Bernita said.

After several stops of people entering and exiting the elevator finally stopped on the fifteenth floor and they stepped off. In the lobby they noticed a well-dressed middle-aged woman sitting at a large round desk in front of an oval shaped window. Her smile was very welcoming.

"Good morning," the woman said pleasantly.

They chorused, "Good morning."

Bernita said, "We're here to see Paul Domingues."

"May I have your name?" the receptionist asked while picking up the phone.

"My name is Bernita Haynes."

"Please have a seat and I will inform Mr. Domingues that you're here."

Janet plopped down in a chair next to a big plant. Trying to camouflage her nervousness, she had never been in an attorney's office before. She sat back and observed the elegant atmosphere. *Mr. Domingues must be doing well for himself*, she thought.

"You may help yourselves to some coffee and pastries," the receptionist offered as she directed them over to the table with her head.

A few moments later Paul entered the room. He was a huge man with a receding hairline.

"Hello, Bernita." They embraced.

"Hi Paul, it's nice to see you again. It's been a long time."

"How's Terry?"

"Fine, just fine."

"So, who do we have here?" Paul asked, staring directly at Trevor.

"This is Trevor, my godson, and this is his Aunt Janet—Janet Price."

Janet waved from behind a large leaf. When she was able to stand to greet him, he shook her hand and then instructed the receptionist to hold his calls for a half an hour. As she acknowledged his request, he beckoned them to follow him to his office.

The office was enormous and elegantly decorated. Janet's eyes glowed. She was now impressed and felt like Trevor was in good hands. She admired the cherry wood desk and matching cabinets and a bookshelf that housed hundreds of books. The view was magnificent and the Washington Monument and the tip of the Capitol could be seen from the oval shaped glass window.

"Ladies have a seat."

He directed them to sit in the plush black leather chairs in front of his desk.

"Trevor, you come and sit by me."

Paul took a yellow legal pad from his desk and positioned himself to take notes. He began slowly with caution asking Trevor questions, and as before, Trevor repeated the same story again. Paul nodded as he took notes carefully. The array of questions was asked and Trevor quickly responded without hesitation. During the last round of questions Trevor started crying.

"Feeling rotten, huh?" Paul asked.

Trevor nodded and wiped the tears away, trying his hardest to control them. But they seemed to have a mind of their own and just kept flowing. After the meeting, Paul ushered them back to the reception area and assured them that they had nothing to worry about. He gave Janet his business card and instructed her to call should she need him. Bernita and Paul embraced once again and they left the office feeling somewhat relieved.

As Bernita wheeled the car down the busy street, Trevor spotted a department store.

"Hey, Aunt Be, can we stop here and pick up some things for Alonza?"

Bernita had honestly forgotten about Alonza's situation, she accelerated and pulled into the parking lot. They browsed the store while Trevor picked up a few things he thought Alonza would like. He placed trucks, games, Uno cards, and a bag of colorful balloons in the shopping cart. Janet picked up a roll of purple yarn and a pack of black buttons and tossed them in the cart with Alonza's gifts. At the check-out stand, Bernita happily paid for the items. Back at the car, Trevor stuffed the bag of toys in the trunk, turned around and gave Bernita a big hug and then told her how much he appreciated what she did. She knew that she had temporarily made him happy and she smiled back with joy. Before arriving back at Janet's house, they stopped and had lunch at a charming deli on the corner of 15th Street and Pennsylvania Avenue. The drive through town was interesting with their bellies full and a trunk loaded with gifts for a sick little boy.

Back at Janet's house, Bernita's flight was leaving that evening so she rushed into the den to pack her belongings.

"Hey, Snook," Bernita yelled. "Come here, I would like to speak to you."

Trevor entered the den, and she closed the door behind him. She was somewhat speechless as she watched Trevor with concern. At first she didn't know what to say but she found the strength to speak.

"Snook, I'm leaving this evening and I want you to promise me that you will take care of Aunt Janet and your mother. Aunt Janet is getting old and she needs your help as much as possible."

She badly wanted to tell him about her heart problem, but didn't. She placed a blouse inside the suitcase and attempted to zip it. Trevor nodded as he helped zip her bag. Bernita placed her hands on his shoulders.

"Your mother is a very strong woman, and I know she will be all right. I know you said some things out of anger yesterday, and we wish to forget about that. If you don't remember anything else in life, just remember that your mother loves you with all her heart. Everything she does is for you. She's fighting for her life for your love. I spoke to your mother constantly and I know there's nothing that she wouldn't do for you. So, you must be strong—not only for yourself—but for Aunt Janet and your mother."

She slowly turned his body to face the mirror hanging on the wall. They both stared at the image of the slim frail boy.

She continued, "Snook, when you look in this mirror what do you see?"

He lowered his head and said, "Aunt Be I see nothing."

"You know what I see?"

She lifted his head up so he could look at his reflection in the mirror and said, "I see Ann's baby. You are the only thing she has left. Promise me you will never say your mother doesn't love you again, because we know better."

She turned him around and tilted his head toward her saying, "Don't we?"

Trevor tried to speak but she wouldn't let him.

"Uncle Terry and I are here for you anytime. If you'd like to come and visit with us for a while, let me know and we will send for you. Just remember, Snook, you're not in this alone. We feel your pain and we understand exactly what you are going through. We love you."

She finished as she took him in her arms and held him tightly. Trevor returned the embrace and laid his head on her shoulder. Then Bernita peeled him away from her and lifted his head where their eyes met and whispered.

"I love you, and don't you ever forget that."

It was obviously that the woman who was not his mother and not his real aunt would never desert him. Bernita planted a wet kiss on Trevor's cheek, leaving the impression of red lipstick on his face.

Chapter 14

Trevor couldn't wait to get to the hospital. He rushed Janet and Bernita all morning anticipating the visit with his mother, Sue, the babies, and now Alonza. Pushing them out the door to the car he smiled with joy. As Bernita drove down the crowded street they could hear rattling noises coming from the back seat.

"Trevor what are you doing?" Janet asked.

"I'm trying to decide which present I want Alonza to see first."

"Just give him the bag," she said grinning.

"No ma'am, no fun that way. I would like to hand him one at a time. Just wanna see the expression on his face. Hey Auntie, what's the yarn for?" Trevor asked, pulling it out of the bag.

"Feel like knitting, Baby."

"What are you going to knit?"

"A sweater for Ann. Maybe by the time I'm finished she will be able to wear it home."

"I hope so, Auntie," saying as he pushed the yarn back in the bag.

It had been a very busy and productive day. Bernita was becoming depressed because in a couple of hours she had to say good-bye to her dear friend. When they reached the hospital, they stopped at the gift shop and Bernita bought a card. The cashier behind the counter was smiling as she asked for a pen. She quickly wrote on the card and sealed the envelope.

"Snook do me a favor? I would like for you to read this to your mother next Sunday if she is still unable to read it for herself."

Bernita handed the envelope to Trevor; he stuffed it in his jacket pocket.

"Don't' forget, Snook."

As he zipped his pocket he stated, "No ma'am. I won't."

It was about noon when they entered Ann's room. The air was still sweet with the scent of flowers. Trevor went over to the bed and bent down and whispered in Ann's ear.

"Hello Mom. Miss you and love you." He kissed her as he always did.

Janet took a seat in her oversized chair in the corner and Bernita sat beside the bed rubbing Ann's motionless hand. The nurse entered carrying a chart. She took a reading from the machine and wrote the information down promptly. She wasn't a friendly nurse. She always spoke but that was it. As the day slipped away, Trevor read a book to Ann as Bernita listened. The relationship between Ann and Trevor was characterized not by a two-way dialogue, but maternal love. Janet was comfortable in the corner where she begun knitting the sweater. After hours of reading, Trevor was eager to see Alonza. He had become uneasy and bored and Janet could tell he was ready to go.

"I guess it's time for your visit with Alonza," Janet suggested before he could ask.

He took the card from his jacket and laid it on the corner of the nightstand next to Ann's head.

"I can't wait to see Alonza's reaction. Sure hope I make him smile today," he said as he grabbed the bag.

"Come back soon, Snook. I'll be leaving in a couple of hours."
Bernita removed the airline ticket from her purse and looked at it for several moments.

He kissed them and proceeded down the hall to room 517. Trevor stopped at the Maternity Ward to see Sue. He noticed that the baby that was very ill was gone. He asked Sue where he was. She informed him that he was transferred to Children's Hospital. Trevor couldn't wait to show Sue the gifts he had purchased for Alonza. He didn't visit long with her because he was in a hurry to see his sick little friend.

When he entered room 517, he noticed a little old woman sitting on the bed with a cane lying on the floor and no sign of Alonza.

"Excuse me," Trevor said as he peeked his head in the door. "My name is Trevor and I'm here to see Alonza."

"Oh Trevor it's nice to finally meet you. I've heard a lot about you. Have a seat and Alonza will be back in a couple of minutes."

Trevor pulled a chair closer to the bed and sat down.

"My name is Clara."

He greeted her in return.

"Where's Alonza?" he questioned while looking around his dull room.

"He had to take a test, but he should be returning soon," she said in a low tone.

"Thank you for visiting Alonza. We really appreciate this. He's a very sick little boy. Been sick all his life," she said as she rubbed her leg. "Feel sorry for the little guy. Don't have anyone but me."

"When do you think he can go home?"

"Don't know, Sugar, spends most of his time in the hospital."

Trevor dropped his head because he knew at that moment how blessed he was. Although his mother was in a coma, she was still alive.

"Have any brothers or sisters?" she asked as she tried to rise up from the bed.

"No sisters, one brother but he doesn't live with me."

"Mother and father?" she asked as she peeped from the top of her glasses.

"My mother is downstairs in room B12 and my father is deceased."

"Oh, sorry to hear that, Sugar." Clara pushed her glasses back on her face. "Hope your mother will be all right."

"Me too, Ms. Clara," Trevor said as his eyes wandered the room.

The room was bare, nothing like room B12. There were no balloons or cards. Only a small bunch of flowers that looked like they were ready for the wastebasket, rested on the nightstand.

"I brought some gifts for Alonza."

Trevor reached inside and pulled out some of the toys and showed them to her. He could tell they were poor and didn't have much. Her shoes were run down and her coat that was thrown across the chair seemed worn with several missing buttons. Her glasses had stains on the lenses and the frame was slightly bent.

"Wow, Sugar, you didn't have to do that." But in her heart she was glad he did.

The nurse wheeled Alonza back to his room, his eyes glittered. It was pure bliss for Trevor to watch him receive his new toys. Alonza couldn't choose which one to play first. It made Trevor feel good to see his sick friend so happy. Trevor knew his grandmother was thrilled too, because her enchanted smile never left her face. Trevor blew up several balloons and tied them around his bed and chairs, giving the room a festive and joyous look. He was satisfied within at all that he had done and blinked tears away. Trevor began to cultivate a relationship of friendship with Alonza. It wasn't until that moment when he realized just how exultant he had made Alonza.

Trevor returned to his mother's room, he noticed that Benita was gathering her things.

"Snook, glad you made it back in time. I'm leaving in ten minutes," she said as she glanced at her watch.

Janet wasn't sitting in the oversized chair in the corner.

"Where's Aunt Janet?" he asked.

"She went to the cafeteria to get something to eat."

Bernita never looked up as she fumbled through her bags. Trevor walked over to Ann and shared his day with her. He would break from talking once and a while, smile and then continued to talk about Alonza. Moments later Janet strolled back in the room with a bag in her hand.

"Hi Baby," she said as she placed the bag on the tray. "Are you hungry?" She removed a sandwich and handed it to him.

"No ma'am. Can't eat right now."

Trevor was so excited about his day; he knew his stomach couldn't digest any food for the moment.

"How's Alonza?" Janet asked as she put the sandwich back in the bag.

"Auntie I never felt better in my life," he said with complete confidence. "The little fellow was so excited about his gifts and his grandmother thanked me."

A brief pause. "You know Auntie," Trevor said as he looked at the sweater she had started. "Today, Alonza made me realize how blessed I am. I have so many people who love me. Yes, it may seem like I have lost a lot, but I still have a lot. I have more love than most kids."

Janet looked surprised because she had no idea what had come over him.

"Yeah, Baby, you're so right. Your mother worked hard for you and she will continue as soon as she gets better. She loves you. We love you and that's the way it is."

"I know Auntie, I know."

Trevor grinned and walked over to Ann's bed and bent down and kissed her eyes, nose, and mouth. Being constantly bombarded with the terror that he had to endure, today his eyes were opened to the truth. Trevor realized he was a blessed young boy. William made it to the hospital before Bernita's departure. As he entered the room, Bernita was standing over Ann, staring at her without blinking, without any words.

"Hi ladies, and how's my favorite nephew?"

William walked over to Trevor and lightly tapped him on his back. Janet had just demolished the sandwich and wiped her mouth before greeting him. Bernita didn't acknowledge him. She continued staring at Ann.

"It's time for takeoff," she said as she looked at her watch again. "Let's say a prayer."

Bernita motioned everyone to come near. As she prayed, she couldn't hold back her emotions any longer and began to weep. She tried to continued, but her voice began breaking up. Trevor noticed the difficulties she was having so he took over and finished the prayer. Janet blushed with gratitude as Trevor took charge again. Bernita continued to sob wiping her swollen eyes with a tissue. After the prayer Trevor walked over to Bernita and held her close and politely whispered in her ear.

"Aunt Be its okay, Mom will be just fine. I know this from the bottom of my heart, and just like as you said earlier, I have to take care of her and Aunt Janet. Everything is in God's hands," he added.

Bernita wiped her last teardrops. She composed herself, combed her hair, put on some lipstick and went over to Ann speaking gently.

"Ann, I'm not going to say good-bye." She caressed her hand and said, "Farewell for now my beloved friend. I'll see you soon."

She then leaned over her and placed a warm firm kiss on the bandage on her forehead. The imprint of red lip stick was visible and everyone began to chuckle. Bernita was a true friend and she was leaving reluctantly. Janet, William, and Trevor escorted her to the lobby and they exchanged long hugs and kisses. They waited in the lobby and watched until Bernita's rental car sped off.

Chapter 15

The weather was changing and so was Trevor. Janet noticed a difference in his attitude. She was awakened some nights finding him pacing the hall carrying on a two-way conversation. Confused and paranoid, she didn't know what to do. Some nights she would lie there, pretending to be asleep because her fear for him wouldn't let her face his pain. She knew her heart had gotten weaker as she tried to understand all that had happened, and she could tell that Trevor's mind was weak also. But deep down tucked away in his soul, his heart was still beating strong for Ann.

The daily visits to the hospital began to take a toll on the family. No matter what pain they had to suffer, they found the will to keep going for Ann's sake. Trevor continued visiting Sue, the babies, and Alonza while Janet sat in the oversize chair careful knitting with loving attention. Ann had been living on borrowed time for several weeks now. There was no change in her health condition. Some days Trevor would jabber all day and other days, he was sad and had little to say.

With Thanksgiving quickly approaching Janet tried to prepare herself. Traditionally they spent Thanksgiving at Ann's house. With little money and no resources to get more, her retirement income wasn't enough. The church and neighbors helped, but still she struggled. Trevor never knew how bad her financial situation was because she always made what little she had work. The pots and pans were always full and their clothes were clean. Only Janet knew her dilemma and she kept them all to herself.

Janet was watching Oprah as Trevor relaxed in the den. During commercial breaks, she slipped into the den and checked on him. At that moment, the phone began ringing.

"I'll get that, Auntie," Trevor said as he reached for it. He answered and then handed Janet the phone. Janet plopped down beside Trevor and started muttering under her breath. She let out a big sigh and replied, "Hold on William."

She handed Trevor the phone and asked him to hang it up once she got to her room. Trevor took the receiver from Janet's hand and watched as she wobbled into her bedroom and waited for the okay.

"Janet are you sitting down?" William asked.

"No, do I need to?" she said firmly.

"I think so Sis."

Janet sat on the edge of the bed and resumed talking.

"William, what's the problem?" fearing something had happened to Ann; she waited for him to spill his beans.

"Detective Brown called me today."

"Who is that?" she snarled.

"He's the detective that was at the house the night of the incident."

"What does he want now?" she asked angrily, as her memory was quickly restored.

"He wants me to bring Trevor to his office for a meeting."

"A meeting! Nonsense," she mumbled. *He just wants to torture him*, she thought.

"Janet we have to get it over with sooner or later. We have been putting it off long enough. Have Trevor ready by 9:00 tomorrow morning and I will pick him up."

There was silence between them and then Janet finally said, "If you insist William," letting out a heavy sigh.

"Thanks Sis. See you tomorrow."

The next morning William arrived bright and early. The sun was hot but the air was brisk. Trevor was in the shower and Janet was sitting at the dining room table sipping on a cup of hot coffee.

"Hi Sis," he said as he poured a cup for himself. "Where's Trevor?"

"He's taking a shower," she replied never looking at him.

Janet was upset and he could tell she didn't want anything to do with the conversation. William sat quietly on the sofa and sipped his coffee. When Trevor entered the living room, he was dressed to the nine, wearing a pair of *Tommy Hilfiger* jeans and a matching top. His hair was brushed neatly and he wore a big smile.

"Good morning, Unc."

"Are you ready to go?" William asked as he placed the empty mug in the sink.

Trevor smiled. He took them by surprise. They had no idea going to the police station would be that easy. Janet, William, and Trevor walked out the building toward William's car as a family and at that moment everything seemed normal.

During the drive to the Third Precinct, Trevor asked William to turn on the radio. Amazed that he wanted to listen to music, William quickly pressed the on button.

"What station?" he asked as he turned the dial.

Trevor heard a song by the Back Street Boys and William automatically stopped. Trevor hummed to himself and beat to the tune on the seat with his hand. When they pulled up to the fifty-year old brick building, Janet began to get nervous. She didn't know what to think. In less than a month, she's been in the hospital, to an attorney office, and now the police station. *What's next she thought?*

When they arrived at the police station the detective was nowhere to be seen. The building was packed and everyone seemed busy. This was an experience Janet didn't want. Several people were being booked as others were released. Women of the night were sitting on a bench; they smiled at Trevor as he passed by. Discombobulated and lost, they stopped and asked an officer talking to a man in handcuffs for help. He pointed in the direction of the front desk. They proceeded to the desk and asked for Detective Brown. An arrogant officer spoke up and told them to have a seat over in the corner. Two empty seats were on the other side of the room. They spotted them quickly and sat down. William stood beside Trevor and watched the action coming down the hall. A drunken loud mouth man was yelling ruthless profanity to the officer walking beside him. As William watched, an officer noticed them and came to their aid. He escorted them to a tiny discolored room with a huge table in the middle of the floor, surrounded by six chairs. Approximately five minutes later, two officers walked in. One was Detective Brown, the other they didn't recognize.

"Hello Mr. Jones," Detective Brown said as he stuck out his hand. "This is Detective Powell. He'll be assisting me today."

William acknowledged both of them. Powell civilly waved.

"This is Janet Price," Detective Brown said as he turned in her direction.

Janet barely opened her mouth to speak, remembering him from the hospital.

"Hello, Son," he said as he sat down beside him.

Trevor leaned forward, greeted him warmly and sat back in his chair.

"Before we get started would you like something to drink?"

Trevor politely declined. The meeting was awkward at first with a great deal of silence and many sidelong nervous stares. Then the interrogation began slowly.

"This is a very informal meeting, just a couple of questions and you can be on your way," he said as he smiled at Trevor. "How's your mother?" he asked as he took out his note pad.

"She' fine," he answered uneasily.

He waited for the barrage of questions, but only received silence; then came the first one.

"What's your full name?"

"Trevor Edward Sanford."

"How old are you?"

"I'm eleven, sir."

Janet was surprised by how refined Trevor was. William watched as the detective scribbled on the note pad, while Powell stared with blankness.

"When is your birthday?"

"March third, nineteen eighty-eight."

"What's your address," he asked as he turned the page?"

"1550 Fair Court Lane Leesburg, Virginia."

Janet cleared her throat as she thought the questions were silly.

"Can you tell me exactly what happened on October 22, 1999?"

Trevor sat up straight and began to tell his story. The detective quickly took notes trying to keep up.

"What happened after you came in the second time?" he said quickly interrupting him.

"The second time when I came in the house?" he repeated making sure he understood the question.

"Yes the second time," the detective repeated.

"I went to the kitchen to get some juice. I called for my mother again and she didn't answer. I went to her room, but the door was locked so I phoned my Aunt Janet. I spoke to Aunt Janet for a minute; then I went back outside to ride my bike."

"Where did you go?"

"I rode up and down the street and then I went to the park."

"What happened next?"

"The sun was going down so I decided to go in. I parked my bike in the garage and went upstairs. I yelled for my mother again, but she didn't answer so I went to my room and put on a CD."

"So let me get this straight." the detective stated. "You checked the door, but the door was locked."

"Yes sir," Trevor said as he folded his arms.

"How did the knife get on the floor?" he asked as he flipped back several pages.

Trevor was trying to stay calm, but the more questions he asked the harder it was to answer them. The detective could tell he was becoming uncomfortable.

"No need to be nervous, take your time and tell the truth."

The detective looked at Trevor with a smile.

"I went searching for a knife."

"Where did you get the knife from?"

"In the kitchen—from the knife stand."

"What did you do with the knife?"

"I tried to pry the door opened but I couldn't so I dropped the knife on the floor and phoned Aunt Janet."

Trevor looked over in her direction. Janet was resting her head in her hands.

"Now tell me about the phone call?"

"Well," he said as he cleared his throat, "I went back in my room and lay across the bed. I was listening to one of my CD's. Then I started to cry. Don't ask me why, because I couldn't tell you. The next thing I remember, the phone started ringing. I turned down my CD because it was kinda loud," he said with a grin. "A lady asked to speak to my mother and I told her she wasn't at home."

"Wait just a minute, Trevor."

Detective Brown put his hand up in the air to stop him from speaking. Then the room became deathly quiet as everyone focused their attention on the vulgar noise coming from the hallway. Seconds later there was a knock at the door. Detective Brown stood up and went to the door, disappearing out of sight. Janet grabbed Trevor's hand and told him he was doing a fine job. Detective Powell and William were making small talk in the corner.

"Not as bad as I thought," Janet mumbled.

Trevor agreed. The detective re-entered and continued his questioning.

"Sorry for the delay Trevor," he said as he sat down.

"Let's see—where were we?" After a pause the detective continued. "What did the lady on the phone say?"

"She asked for Mom; I told her that my mother wasn't home and she told me to go to my mother's room because she needed me as soon as possible. I rushed to her room and tried to push the door open. That's when I went to the kitchen for the knife."

Trevor placed both elbows on the table to rest his face.

"Son, let's elaborate on the phone call."

Brown closed his note pad. He leaned back in his chair and stared at Trevor. Trevor knew this was a problem for the officer because there were no records indicating that such a call was made. He glanced at Janet and she clutched her purse.

"What kind of voice did she have?"

"It was a very soft, sweet, voice."

"If you heard it again, would you be able to recognize it?"

"Sure," Trevor said with confidence.

"Who do you think it was?"

"Sir, I really don't know. I never heard that voice before and I've been wracking my brain everyday trying to figure this out. I can't sleep at night—constantly thinking about it. It's always on my mind."

Trevor's eyes began to well up because he knew this information was extremely important and he couldn't offer any assistance. The detective could tell this was getting difficult for Trevor, so he called for a short break. As the detectives passed Trevor, they patted him on his shoulder. Janet rushed over to Trevor, trying to help console him.

"Getting a little rough, Baby?" she asked as she wiped his face.

He nodded holding his face up so she could wipe away every tear.

Why couldn't this be me? She thought.

"Why does Trevor have to go through this torment?" she whispered to William.

"I know, Sis, it's breaking my heart too," he nodded as he left the room.

Moments later both detectives and William returned. Detective Brown walked over to Trevor and asked if he was ready to continue.

He nodded yes as he looked at Janet, knowing that she wanted this to be over. The sooner they finished the better it would be for all of them.

"Trevor I really need you to think for me. Can you do that?" he asked with persistence. "Does your mother have any enemies?"

"Enemies," he mumbled glaring at William.

He became silent. The detective repeated the question.

"Was there anyone who your mother didn't get along with?"

Trevor feebly sat and stared at the door. He said nothing for several minutes. The detective started to ask the question again when Trevor interrupted him.

"Sir, I'm thinking," he blankly stated.

It was a hard question because he knew that his mother was a well-liked person.

"Hum," he said as he lifted his hands from under the table. He tapped his temple with his finger and frowned mildly, then added.

"The only person I know that didn't get along with my mother was Tyler's mother."

"Who's Tyler?" the detective asked surprisingly.

"Tyler is my little brother."

"Where is he?" Detective Brown asked, while re-opening his note pad.

"He lives with his mother in Virginia Beach."

"When was the last time you saw him?"

"About eight months ago. After his dad died, he went to live with his mother."

"How did your mother feel about that?"

"It made her sad. She wanted him to stay."

"How did you feel about him going to live with his mother?"

This new information quickly caught the detective's attention as he looked stunned.

"It made me sad too. We love him and when he moved back to Virginia Beach we felt lost."

"Do you know Tyler's mother's first name?"

"Yes. Her name is Barbara Sanford."

Talking about Tyler played heavy on Trevor's heart. He loved his brother and thinking about him he realized how much he was missed. The detective handed Trevor a piece of paper and asked him to write down Barbara's number. Trevor took the paper and began to write wildly.

"Thanks Trevor for the information, this is some very important stuff. You did great, Son."

He said smiling at him. Janet breathed out a deep, long sigh of relief. The detective studied his notes with a puzzled look on his face. After several minutes of silence he informed them that the meeting was over. He thanked them for coming, looking at Trevor, as he made comments on how well he did and complimented him on his candor. As they were standing to leave, William and Janet's eyes lit with great satisfaction, thankful Trevor showed his bravery.

"Is it over?" William asked as he took a cigarette from his pocket. He so desperately needed a smoke.

"For now Mr. Jones. If I have any more questions, I know how to find you," Detective Brown said, smiling.

Janet was so happy it was finished; she quickly grabbed her coat and headed toward the exit sign. William stopped the detective in the hall and asked about the suicide note.

"I don't think this is a good time. The note is very deep and to be honest with you, I don't think Trevor can handle it at this time, bring him back in a week or so to read it. This will give you enough time to prepare him for it."

William agreed. Janet, William, and Trevor rushed out of the musty old building. Hoping Ann would open her eyes and reveal the secret that she held deeply in her heart.

Chapter 16

Glad the questioning was over William lit a cigarette as soon as he reached the fresh air. As they crossed the boulevard, Trevor noticed the beautiful clouds in the sky. The nightmare they dreaded was finished for the moment. Now they could focus on Ann and her recovery. Enroute to the hospital they stopped at a Seven-Eleven to purchase some gas. William pumped, while Trevor and Janet browsed inside the store. Trevor saw a red heart shaped balloon with the words *I LOVE YOU* printed in white letters.

"Hey Auntie, can I get this for Mom?"

He held it in the air. Knowing she only had a few dollars, she agreed, trying not to disappoint him for his courage he showed at the police station earlier. The visit to the hospital was a joyous one. Janet felt relieved as she settled in the oversized chair in the corner and continued to knit the sweater. Trevor went over to Ann's bed and completed his normal kissing routine. He slid a card aside on the nightstand and placed his balloon by her head. William turned on the TV, pretending to watch it. Trevor relaxed on the edge of the bed talking peacefully to Ann and every chance he got, he glanced at the picture tube. He sniffed the beautiful assortments of flowers and read some of the many cards that surrounded the room.

Trevor laid his head on Ann's chest and kissed her again. This was his life after all. He admiringly gazed at his mother, hoping she would awaken. As he stared at Janet, William, and his mother, suddenly he realized they were family and that their love had conquered all.

Trevor rushed down the hall headed toward room 517 stopping briefly for a refreshing sip of water from the fountain. As he wiped his mouth, he heard a weird voice.

"Come here, Lad."

From inside one of the rooms was the hoarsest voice he had ever heard. He turned in the direction of the faint intonation and looked through the door noticing a frail old man with a white beard and white mustache. He was sitting in a wheel chair.

"Sir, are you talking to me?" Trevor asked pointing to his chest.

"Yes," the old man answered calmly waving him in. "Will you get my glasses for me, they rolled under the bed?"

The old man removed his hand from under the blanket that covered him and pointed in the path to which they rolled. Trevor scooted down on his hands and knees and found them.

"Here you go, Sir," he said as he stood and brushed the dust off his jeans.

The old man put the glasses on, and then stuffed his hands back under the blanket.

"What are you up to Lad?"

"Nothing—I'm on my way to visit a friend."

"Where are your parents?"

"My mother is downstairs."

He didn't want to tell him she was sick—wasn't in the mood to discuss it.

"Don't get lost."

He straightened himself up. He seemed to be shrinking as he slumped in the chair. Trevor sensed that the old man was lonely and wanted someone to talk to.

"Mind if I sit down?" Trevor asked while moving a chair near.

"Help yourself. It gets kinda boring some days. What's your name?"

"My name is Trevor."

He sticks out his youthful hand and shakes the old man's wrinkled hand.

"Trevor, ah, that's a nice name. Don't think I know anyone by that name."

The old man said as he rubbed his tiny acorn shaped head.

"My name is Lt. John Fitzpatrick."

Trevor and Mr. Fitzpatrick talked for several minutes when he realized Alonza was waiting.

"Lt. Fitzpatrick, it's nice to have met you. Would you like for me to come and visit soon?"

"I would like that," he said as he pulled the blanket up to his shoulders.

"Are you cold?"

Trevor helped tuck the man in.

"It's always cold in her," Mr. Fitzpatrick said as he shivered. "I guess you get used to it after a while."

"They say coldness kills germs," Trevor stated as he tucked the blanket around his feet.

"Smart young Lad," he murmured. "Come back soon so we can talk."

"I will."

With a good-bye he disappeared down the hall.

Alonza was sitting in a chair playing with his truck when Trevor walked in.

"Hey Alonza."

Trevor smiled at him. Alonza reminded him of Tyler. He thought of Tyler whenever he looked at him. He often wondered how he would react if this was his little brother.

"Hi Trevor," Alonza said, looking up with gleaming eyes. "I've been waiting a long time to see you."

"Yeah, sorry, I know but I had to go the police station this morning."

"Wow!" his eyes got brighter. "That's cool."

"Where's your grandmother?"

"Down the hall. She should be back soon."

"How are you feeling today?" he asked hoping for good news as he raced the car up and down the table.

"Today I feel fine. Some days are better than others."

Trevor noticed the balloons were still flying high in the air and a few games were thrown around the floor.

117

"Think you can go home for Thanksgiving?"

The car fell off the table and slammed against the floor.

"Don't know, Grands said she'll try to have me released for a few hours."

"Maybe you and your grandmother can come over to my Aunt Janet's house for dinner."

His eyes brightened, "I'd like that, Trevor."

The sound of a dragging cane could be heard hitting the floor rumbling throughout the hall. Clara walked in the room as Trevor watched the smiling lady drag her cane. It shocked Trevor to see her like that and he wondered what was wrong with her leg.

"Hello, Trevor," she said as she plopped down allowing the cane to fall to the floor next to her leg, releasing in a loud thump.

"Hi, Ms. Clara," he said, trying not to stare.

"Alonza had been asking for you all day?"

"I know. Sorry I was late. We had something important to do this morning. How are you feeling today?"

Trevor immediately changed the subject; in fear of her asking what he had to do that was so important.

"Fine, Sugar. How's your mother?"

"The same. Thanks for asking."

"Grands did you speak to the doctor about me leaving for a couple of hours on Thanksgiving?"

Alonza interrupted, hoping the doctor had said yes.

"I just left his office. He'll let me know by tomorrow."

"Do you think we can go over Trevor's aunt's house for a while?" he asked as his bottom lip began trembling, fearing the answer *no*.

"Please," Trevor begged as he leaned toward her.

"Let me think about it. I don't know what we have planned yet."

Trevor knew they didn't have anything planned. He knew she was just saying that so they wouldn't look so desperate.

"My family would really like to have you over," Trevor said gleefully trying to reassure them.

Alonza smiled at his remark. He was pleased and happy that he found a friend who didn't take his illness as such a problem. He believed Trevor accepted him the way he was sick and all. They continued to play until it was time for Alonza to rest.

Trevor strolled back to section B12. Upon walking into the room, he noticed Janet gazing out the window. Trevor hopped up on the edge of the bed swinging his legs. Janet acknowledged him and continued to stare out the window. She had slipped into a quiet daze. Trevor could tell she was daydreaming; her body was motionless as she stood there barely breathing.

"Where's Unc?"

"He's taking a smoke." Janet replied, never looking up.

"Auntie, what's wrong?" Trevor asked, trying to get her attention by clapping his hands.

Every muscle in her body jumped when she heard the sound of Trevor's clapping hands. He successfully broke her concentration and within seconds she snapped back to reality.

"Oh, I'm sorry. My mind went blank for a moment. How's Alonza?" she said as she returned to her oversized chair in the corner.

"He's fine. Auntie, can Alonza and his grandmother have dinner with us on Thanksgiving?" he asked excitedly.

"Sure, Baby, I would like that."

Janet smiled showing her pearly white dentures. She never refused company. Although she was raised in the country and moved to the city, she still had her Southern country ways.

"I know, Auntie, having them over is going to be nice, but the one person who will be missing—is my mother."

He leaped off the edge of the bed, walked up to Ann, kissed her according to his custom. Trevor laid his head on Ann's chest, closed his eyes and finished with a silent prayer.

Chapter 17

Trevor lay in the bed admiring his silhouette on the wall while his mind rushed like mad with respect to his mother. This was the first Thanksgiving he has ever spent without her. He felt strangely sad. He could hear Janet in the kitchen preparing the meal. The water was running in the sink and pots and pans clinging against each other. He was so tired, from lack of sleep and he wished he could roll over and sleep for a few more hours. He tried to cheer himself up before seeing Janet, not wanting to spoil her day.

After several days of preparation she did her best to make this day in particular, successful. Trevor wanted to focus and think of happy thoughts but his mind always ricochet back to his mother. He wished she were there with him. He prayed that she would come out of her coma soon. The ringing of the phone silenced his dreary thoughts.

"Trevor are you up?" Janet yelled from the kitchen. "Pick up the phone."

He rolled toward the end of the bed, dragging the blanket with him and answered.

"Hello, Happy Thanksgiving," the squeaky voice on the phone said.

"Tyler," Trevor shouted as his smile expanded. "Is this really you? How are you little brother?"

Trevor was so happy to hear from him as he jabbered continuously. Tyler barely got a word in. He told Tyler about Ann's condition and his new friend Alonza. Trevor had a speed round of questions. After Tyler's response, he was more excited than he had been in a long time. They talked and giggled for several minutes, just like old times. After the call ended, Trevor felt like a new person. He now had energy and dashed into the bathroom to take a shower. He dressed in a nice sweater and pair of jeans. He vacuumed the floor and dusted the coffee and end tables. Janet was happy that Trevor took charge saving her some work. One call from Tyler had made him happy just for the time being.

Trevor greeted each guest with a friendly hello and smiled as he took their coats and offered them something to drink. There was plenty of food and people were scattered around in the tiny two-bedroom apartment. The men settled in the den watching football. The women gossiped as they prepared the food and set the table. Janet carved the turkey and ham while Mae sliced cakes and pies and placed them on platters. The other ladies placed the food in serving dishes and decorated the table with a variety of dishes. Trevor didn't know where to fit in. He spent the majority of the day in Janet's bedroom in solitude, thinking about his mother. He pretended to watch football with the men but felt uncomfortable, plus William had the room clouded with cigarette smoke. His mind wasn't in the mood for the Dallas Cowboys or turkey. All he wanted was his mother—to see, touch, talk, and hold him in the way he was accustomed to.

At dinnertime, Janet called everyone into the dining room. They crammed around the table. Janet asked them to hold hands while she said grace. A short prayer followed. The Price family tradition that had been carried from generation to generation was that everyone had to say why he or she was thankful for that year. Janet chose to skip it this time. She didn't want Trevor to get sad, thinking about all the tragedy that had happened to their family.

They ate, danced, and listened to music. The crowd tried to enjoy the day, but they knew something or someone was missing. They packed up the desserts and loaded the cars. Everyone in the apartment agreed that Thanksgiving was a day to give thanks and they felt that there was no better way to end their thankful day but at the hospital with Ann.

Outside the clouds were thickening as Trevor thought about his life. It was hard to imagine that Thanksgiving was just one week ago. Janet was, as usual, busy knitting away on the sweater when William walked into the room. He knew that this was the only thing that kept Janet's mind occupied. Today, she was in a different world.

"Hello," William said as he took off his coat and laid it across a chair.

Trevor greeted him and Janet waved her hands quickly trying not to lose her groove. A third of the sweater was completed as she steadily knitted daily. The bandage that was wrapped around Ann's head had been removed, displaying two patches placed on both sides of her temples. Janet styled her hair making her look very pretty. She simply looked as though she was in a peaceful sleep. William was amazed that the bandages had been removed and he kissed her for the first time. Prior to this, he was afraid to touch her. After finding her in the terrible condition, the fact that she looked normal made his visit easier.

Visitors never stopped coming, and Ann's room was always decorated so nicely with balloons, flowers, and cards. Janet, William, and Trevor spent so much time at the hospital, the staff knew them personally but Trevor was their favorite. Their hearts bled for the quiet, polite little boy who showed his dedication and steadfast love for his mother. During the day, the nurses would stop in to talk to them or bring them food from the cafeteria and drinks out the vending machines, making their visit pleasurable. Since Alonza's disease was becoming progressively worse, Trevor hung around the room most of the time. Alonza was always asleep when he went to visit him. Later that evening Trevor decided to see if Alonza felt like playing. He walked down the corridor, stopping from time-to-time to talk to the staff when he recognized a familiar face. Trevor looked in the room and noticed the same tiny old man, whom he helped to locate his glasses.

"Hello Lt. John Fitzpatrick." Trevor thought. *How could you forget a name like that?*

"How have you been Lad?"

He was sitting in the same position the last time Trevor saw him.

"Fine Sir, I see you're still here."

"Where have you been?" he asked as he snuggled under the blanket.

"I've been staying close to my mother lately. My friend is not feeling well these days, so I don't get a chance to play with him much."

Trevor plopped down on the empty bed. The old man nodded his head as Trevor spoke.

"Where are your glasses?"

He noticed they were not on his face.

"I'm afraid I've lost them again, and I have no clue where I placed them."

Trevor leaped off the bed and looked underneath.

"Well they are not under there," he said as he hopped back on the bed.

"Can you see?" Trevor asked as he looked into his grayish dim eyes.

The old man leaned forward in the chair and spoke to Trevor in a low tone.

"Lad, I see clearly; better than most people," he added. "Tell me about your mother."

"What do you want to know?"

"How's the recovery coming?"

"No change yet, the same thing every day, stiff as a board."

"Lad, do you believe in miracles?"

"I guess I do." Trevor responded while jumping off the bed and moved closer to him.

"Do you believe in God?"

It was incredibly quiet for a moment then Trevor blurted out. "Of course I do."

He stood up straight and glared at the old man slouched in the chair.

"Do you repent?"

He heard that word before and asked faintly, "Repent, "what's that?"

"Repent is when you pray to God and ask Him for forgiveness of your sins."

"I guess I've never done that," Trevor said looking frightened.

123

"Tonight I want you to repent?"

"Repent for what?" Trevor asked confused.

"I don't know, Lad, just do it," the old man commanded as his voice rose. He struggled to sit up straight. Trevor didn't know the man had the strength in him. He seemed to raise taller in the chair.

"Well I should be leaving now."

He walked over to the man and shook his hand. He held Trevor's hand tightly not letting go.

"Take care, Lad, and God bless you."

Trevor smiled and proceeded to Room 517.

When Trevor stepped inside Alonza's room he was awake. He could tell he was weak and tired so he tried to keep his excitement down. They were happy to see each other and it was obvious Alonza wasn't in the mood to play, so he didn't ask him to. He quoted some verses from the Bible and they were both excited, singing *Jesus loves the little children*. Alonza smiled trying to sing along with him. His voice was crackly and barely above a whisper but he refused to give up and did his best to stay in tone. What could be sweeter than two lost and sick little boys singing or the special bond of friendship they were creating? Words were not needed to communicate their enjoyment of each other's company as they listened to their melodic voices fill the air. Although they couldn't play they were happy just being together.

After Trevor's visit with Alonza he walked the hospital halls thinking about how abnormal his life had become. Trevor was the true combatant against himself. Anguish, sorrow, and despair had overshadowed him. He had not attended school in a while, but was able to maintain good grades. William faithfully went to his school each week to drop off his assignments, returning with the new ones. He didn't mind that he had to miss school or not sleep in his own bed; all he wanted was for his mother to come home so he could be a happy boy. Though he rarely showed it, he just wanted to be a kid again. He realized he had fears. What if his mother didn't make it? What if she died not knowing how much he loves her? Or what if, God forbid, she remained in a coma for the rest of her life. Whatever consequences life had in store for him, he was willing to deal with it. All he could think about for the moment was his mother. Trevor stopped at the doorway and spoke to God before he entered her room.

Pastor Getrite was standing over Ann praying and Mae was silently weeping. Trevor couldn't take the weeping so he quietly slipped out of the room and went to visit the nurses. He chatted for a while before deciding to return to the room. By that time, the Pastor was gone and so were the tears. He greeted Mae with a kiss and sat beside William to watch TV. Janet and Mae sat in the corner talking as Janet continued to knit.

William was more talkative than usual. During the conversation, he began to share a lot of his feelings. This felt awkward to Trevor, knowing this was out of the ordinary. William was a quiet man and it was hard for Trevor to believe that they were actually sharing a deep conversation. William stared at Trevor for a second and then asked a favor of him.

"Son, I need you to be strong again. Can you do that?"

"I think I can. What do I need to be strong for?" he asked as he watched Janet's hands rapidly knitting not missing her momentum.

"I need you to go back to the police station to read a note."

"A note. What kind of note?" Trevor asked with a sullen look.

William swallowed hard and replied, "A note your mother left for you. Can you do that?"

There was a long pause but Trevor nodded slowly. He had a pitiful look on his face, but he knew that reading the note was something that needed to be done. Maybe the note could help him find peace. After preparing Trevor for his latest unwelcomed adventure, they both continued to talk, while watching the tube. Janet and Mae were absorbed in their conversation. Trevor didn't know what they were gossiping about, but it kept a smile on their faces and a giggle from time to time.

Chapter 18

Detective Brown was standing in the hallway when Janet, William, and Trevor approached him. He led them down a different hall. They followed him, full of trepidation and uncertainty. They entered a dingy office with a desk, a few chairs and an overflowing file cabinet. He sat them at the far end of the table and left the room. Once Trevor sat down, he glanced around the sloppy office. The desk was littered with papers. The wastebasket was full of several days old trash. A foul odor permeated the room. A picture of the detective and his family hung crookedly on the wall beside an enormous stuffed fish that hung over his desk. Trevor could tell that the detective spent a lot of time there. Janet stood in the corner staring out the glass door. William sat in a chair beside Trevor as they patiently waited for the detective's return. Detective Brown entered the office carrying a package in his hand.

"Thanks for coming back," he said warmly as he sat down.

Janet turned her full attention to him with a dreaded heart.

"Trevor, I guess you know why you're here?"

He nodded yes.

"Are you sure you want to do this?" the detective asked.

Trevor slowly nodded again while fiddling with his collar. The detective handed him the package. Mentally he was reaching for it but his body refused to let him touch it. William took the package for him, noticing the perfectly typed suicide note in the clear plastic bag that was labeled Ann Sanford Case number 66. The white tag attached to the corner read evidence number four. They were all motionless and no one seemed to breathe or move. Aware of their fears, the detective cleared his throat and spoke up.

"People we really don't have to do this now."

William looked at Janet first, then Trevor and said, "Son, would you like me to read the letter to you?"

Trevor dropped his head and nodded yes, sat back, and gripped the edge of the chair. He closed his eyes as though he were taking off on a roller coaster ride, fearing the worst. Trevor nodded for William to start. William held the paper up close to his eyes and began reading aloud.

To my precious Son:

If you are reading this letter, I have accomplished what I set out to do. My life has been wonderful with you. You have brought me more love and joy that few mothers would ever know. You are the perfect child, my angel. A mother couldn't ask for much more. I am worthless now. I have dwindled down to nothing. I'm lifeless, just a big empty shell. My heart and soul have been drained from grief. As I watch you sleep at night I can't help but wish I could be the mother I used to be. Unconditional love is what you ought to have and deserve to have, but I know I can't supply that to you anymore. I'm leaving you in good hands. Aunt Janet will make sure you are taken care of and give you the love you deservedly need. Janet I know you're there with Trevor. I now pass you the baton. Run girl for I know you will finish what I have started. Don't feel sorry for me and don't make any excuses for my behavior. This is what I chose. I guess you may say I was a coward. But facing life and hurting my son, I just can't handle it any longer.

William began to cry as he tried to continue the alarming letter. Janet dropped her face into her hands. Now Trevor was in a deep thought, and grinding his teeth. Trevor just stared blankly as he tried to digest every word. The tears started to flow.

Don't weep for me Son. Shed tears for my love we used to share and not the pain you had to endure. I'm giving you a better life. Go on and make Janet proud. I love you my precious Jewell. Remember me the way I used to be and not the sadness I've shown you the past several months. I was just buying time.

Janet take care of my baby for me, and William, they need your love and support too. It's going to take everyone's strength to help

127

Trevor overcome this. And to you Trevor, my precious gem, I'm leaving you a big kiss and a bear hug. Take it and hold it close to your heart forever. I'm sorry my beloved, Mom.

Janet was in the corner praying out loud. She was dabbing her eyes, trying to stop her free flowing tears. Trevor couldn't take any more. Then he broke, placing his hands over his ears as he tried to suffocate her words. He rocked back and forth and sobbed like a baby. It was such a horrific cry; his voice roared like nothing they had ever heard before.

"Stop! Please stop," he yelled at the top of his lungs. He rose abruptly and dashed out the room.

Janet and William thought about the suicide note all the way home. Trevor was still weeping. His face was buried in the back seat. Janet read her Bible trying to keep her mind occupied because Trevor's expression of grief disturbed her and yet touched her heart at the same time. William speeded through the traffic as he listened to Trevor's distress. Upon arriving at Janet's house, Trevor's shirt was soaking wet from the abundance of tears. Janet was baffled. She didn't know how to handle the situation. Trevor ran into her bedroom and plopped across the bed. His eyes were red and puffy from weeping.

"Baby," she said airily as she walked over to him. "Come here."

Janet held him close to her. She pulled the blanket back, took off his sneakers and tenderly laid him across the bed. As she lay with him, she cuddled him close until he drifted off to sleep.

At the Third Precinct, Detective Brown worked conscientiously researching the new information that Trevor had given him on Barbara Sanford. He went to the courthouse to pull their marriage certificate and divorce decree. He called Ed's attorney to request a copy of his last will and testament. He pulled credit report and bank account statements. Once all the documents were collected, he placed them in a folder and wrote Ann Sanford Case number 66 on the outside. As he considered the new information he tried to find a clue to help him with the case. He propped his feet up on his desk and meditated on the papers.

"Good morning, Detective Brown," a male voice said as he passed his office.

"Good morning."

He never looked up. His mind was preoccupied on every word, every sentence and each paragraph contained in the new folder he had just assembled. But he knew the voice belonged to Captain Wilson.

Detective Brown was a very tall, thin man. His demeanor and attitude always portrayed as one of a gentleman. He was married with twin boys. It could be said he was married to his job. He would arrive early and leave late, and was the top detective at the Precinct. The many awards and medals proved it. He worked in the Homicide Department for ten years and he was good.

As Detective Brown scanned the documents, he noticed something that caught his attention. Jumping to his feet, he promptly proceeded to the Captain's office. The Captain was reading a report from Internal Affairs when Brown tapped on the door.

"Excuse me, Sir; may I speak to you for a moment?"

He placed the report on his desk and beckoned him in.

"What can I do for you Detective?"

"Captain, I'm working on the Sanford's case and I would like permission to go to Virginia Beach to do some further investigation and research."

"The Ann Sanford case," he mumbled as he tried to remember.

"I'm sorry, Detective but that case is not familiar to me. Which case is that?" he asked as he looked on his unsolved case log.

"The suicide victim found shot in the head."

He spotted the case on his report and frowned.

"Why do you need to go to Virginia Beach?"

"I would like to investigate some new information and interview a young lady. She's a person of interest."

"Interview whom?" He stood up and placed his hands in his pockets.

"Her name is Barbara Stanford."

"Any relation to the victim?" he asked as he jiggled his change.

"No relation, she was once married to Ann's late husband Ed."

"Detective, why are you wasting your time on this case? I thought we discussed this several weeks ago and decided to rule it as an attempted suicide." The tone of his voice became aggressive.

"Well sir." The detective took a deep swallow while trying to keep his voice controlled. "I feel strongly that this lady didn't commit suicide. After thoroughly investigating, I feel something is out of place and there is no indication of such an act. The victim was participating in weekly counseling sessions. She had a successful business, a nice home, and plenty of money in the bank. I don't see the traits of a suicide victim."

"Do you have any new evidence to back up this allegation?"

"No I don't," he said as his head dropped slightly.

"Why don't you close this case and proceed to the next one?" The Captain took his hands out his pockets.

"Sir, I've tried, but something keeps pulling me back. My intuition is telling me to investigate this matter further. I just want to do my job that's all. But before I can close this case, I must be positive that she did try to kill herself."

His persistence paid off and the captain could see the passion in his eyes. After a brief pause the captain spoke with authority.

"If you must, Detective, but I'm only releasing you to go on your day off. So if you want to work on your day off that's your business."

He sat in his chair and retrieved the report from his desk and continued to read it.

"I'll phone the captain of that jurisdiction and inform him that you will be visiting the precinct in a couple of days. When do you expect to leave?"

"I plan to report to his office in two weeks," Detective Brown said with relief.

"That's final. I really think you are wasting your time, but if you insist, you have my permission. Find something or move this off your plate."

With a thank you the detective strolled out the captain's office and gathered all the data and documents he had collected and placed them in the folder and stuffed them in his briefcase. He was happy that the captain had given him the opportunity to take this investigation to the next level. He knew at some point if he didn't find the shooter he would have to rule the case as an attempted suicide, close the case and move on.

Trevor rubbed the sleep from his red, swollen eyes. He listened for Janet, who had awakened earlier; scanned the room, noticing that she had tidied up a bit when his eyes fell on a note left on the nightstand. He yawned as he reached for the note. He read it in silence and continued to lie across the bed, awaiting her return. He looked at the time and realized it was noon.

Must get ready to see my mother, he thought.

He darted into the bathroom to wash his face and brush his teeth. He was gargling when he heard his aunt come into the house yelling his name. Following her voice he entered the living room; there he saw the tallest and the prettiest Christmas tree he had ever seen. Janet was holding the tree while William tried to secure it in its stand. The fresh pine fragrance and its glistening bristles made him smile. Janet could see the sparkle in his eyes as she motioned for his assistance. He held one side of the tree and Janet held the other. William positioned the tree in the stand and secured it with the bolts. After the tree was firmly latched in the stand, Janet played Christmas carols on the stereo and started dancing. Anything to help Trevor forget about the events that took place earlier that day was foremost in her mind. They hummed to the carols as they decorated the tree together happily.

As Ann laid there unconscious the changing seasons took on a new meaning. Janet, William, and Trevor continued to visit Ann daily. Trevor had become withdrawn. His eyes were always filled with sadness. He stopped doing the things he loved. Lately, he had trouble meeting his academic requirements. His schoolwork had begun suffering a major setback because his focus had vaporized. He didn't visit Sue, Alonza, or Lt. John Fitzpatrick much anymore. He only wanted to be near his mother. During his visits, he would just stare at her for hours, wishing that she was well and praying to God that she would be healed. It was obvious he was depressed and Janet was so concerned about his health that she began to forsaken her own steadily declining heart condition.

Janet tried everything to cheer him up. She cooked his favorite foods. She brought him books and CD's and still nothing seemed to work. In her opinion, reading the suicide note was a major mistake and setback for the family. Since the reading of the note, Trevor hadn't been the same. He slept less and less and at night he cried. He began losing weight and stayed to himself most of the time. Some mornings he would awaken nauseated, standing over the toilet for hours. Janet watched him as long as she could and finally made an appointment to take him to see his doctor. The doctor was concerned about his health and emotional state. It was apparent he was depressed. The doctor advised Janet to schedule an appointment to see a Therapist. Janet declined. She knew Trevor would never go for that. The only thing that would cure him of this depression would be for Ann to open her eyes. Janet and Trevor left the doctor's office with a prescription for vitamins.

Unbeknown to the rest, Janet's worries in addition to Ann now included Trevor's health and his emotional state along with her own health issues. As the days passed she had become weaker. Janet managed to hide her illness but the tightness in her chest was getting unbearable and appeared more frequently. One visit to her doctor and she was informed the surgery was needed as soon as possible, before it was too late. She agreed to have the operation after the holidays, hoping Trevor would be strong again. She continued to monitor his behavior and health knowing he wouldn't get better until the day Ann awakened from her deep sleep. He desperately needed his mother to reassure him of the love that he was craving.

Chapter 19

It was cold and rainy this particular Wednesday evening but that did not prevent Detective Brown from packing and preparing for what he thought was a very important trip. He wanted to be at the station bright and early so he could get a fresh start on his research and investigation.

Around midnight, he kissed his wife and kids, quietly slipped out of the house, got into his car and drove off. After driving a while, he realized that it was much too quiet and he needed a boost of energy so he decided to stop at an all-night diner and get a cup of coffee and a candy bar. The caffeine and sugar would keep him alert during his desolate and disquietly drive. The early morning ride was lonely. His boys occupied his thoughts as he traveled on, making excellent time. Then he saw the sign that said *Welcome to Virginia Beach*. Driving to the beach in the wintertime was not thrilling to him at all. The highways were deserted. All the hotels had vacancy signs and the majority of the shops and restaurants were closed for the season. He had no problem finding a hotel so he decided to go for the gusto and he selected a room that offered an ocean front view. After checking in at the front desk, he dragged his body to his room. Once inside he laid across the bed to relax and settle down from the long drive. His mind began to ease as he started to review some of the documents. Before long he fell asleep with the papers lying beside him.

The sun shining through the balcony window was luminous, along with the squawking of the seagulls awakened him. He groggily got off the bed and walked over to the balcony, slid the door open and stepped out. He felt completely rejuvenated after taking a long deep breath of the wintry morning air. He watched joggers run down the boardwalk and a few couples held hands as they casually strolled on the white sand beach. The ocean waves were pounding the shoreline with a loud roaring swoosh. Not many people were there and he felt alienated. Noticing the time, he showered, dressed, and drove directly to Virginia Beach's Fifteenth Precinct.

When he pulled up to the precinct he couldn't help but notice how nice the building was. It was complete opposite of his station building. This one was newly painted. The carpet that covered the floors was vacuumed and the whiff of fresh brewed coffee drifted throughout the hallway. Everyone seemed nice and pleasant. He asked an officer at the front desk for Captain Haywood. The officer escorted him to the captain's office and left with a smile. Captain Haywood was reading the Daily Newspaper when he heard the knock at the door.

When the detective crossed the threshold, he said, "Good morning Captain Haywood. My name is Detective Brown from the Third Precinct in Leesburg."

"Nice to meet you, Detective," Captain Haywood said, while extending his hand. "Come in and have a seat. You're early."

He folded the paper and placed it on his desk.

"Captain Wilson indicated that you were coming but he said that you wouldn't be here until later this afternoon."

"I know, I left around midnight and checked into a hotel this morning so I could get started bright and early. I have a lot of work to do and I only have two days to complete my assignment."

Detective Brown admired how clean and tidy the captain's office was. He sat down in a chair across from the captain and crossed his legs. The captain's desk was well organized. Papers were stacked neatly in several piles. There was a coat rack in the corner and certificates covered his wall.

"What can I do for you, Detective?" he asked as he offered him a cup of coffee.

"Captain, I'm here to investigate an attempted suicide."

He took his briefcase and laid it on his desk and propped the locks open.

"If your case is attempted suicide, why are you investigating it?" The captain asked.

"I have reasons to believe that this may not be a suicide case."

"What evidence do you have to prove that Detective?"

He watched him pour some sugar in his cup and stir it slowly.

The detective shared the case and the documents he brought with him. The captain listened attentively. When Detective Brown finished, the captain nodded in agreement with him.

"I think we may be able to assist you with your suspicions."

Captain Wilson picked up the phone. He dialed several numbers and spoke to someone briefly.

"I will send one of my men to escort you," he said as he hung up the phone. "His name is Bill Patterson."

The detective uncrossed his legs and thanked the captain. He gathered up his papers and placed them back into his briefcase. Moments later Patterson entered the captain's office, he introduces them and they left together.

Detective Brown updated Officer Patterson on the case as he showed him the documents. They nonchalantly chatted and then discussed the case in detail. Officer Patterson was happy to volunteer his services. He knew Detective Brown was the top detective at the Third Precinct and he wanted to learn from the best as he looked and listened with anticipation. Officer Patterson felt that going with Detective Brown was a great opportunity to observe a pro in action, and Detective Brown felt he needed the assistance. The two men walked out the precinct together as though they had been friends for years and proceeded to Barbara Sanford's house to talk with her. It would be an informal visit, as they had no evidence to tie her to the shooting.

Officer Patterson drove the squad car while Brown studied the road. He circled the block, going north on Atlantic Avenue and drove ten blocks and turned right. Eventually they arrived at a house, with several large oak trees in front, stretching out their majestic canopies. The squad car stopped in front of a brick colonial with an attached two-car garage. A Lexus truck was parked in the driveway. Detective Brown was impressed that she could afford such luxury. They strolled up the sidewalk that led to the front door. A very attractive woman came to the door. Her face was radiant with well-defined features, high cheek bones and long black hair.

"Hello," she said after opening the heavy wooden door.

"Hi," they responded.

"We're here to see Barbara Sanford."

"I'm Barbara," she said as her eyes widened. "What can I do for you?" Her tone was somewhat chilly.

"Do you have a moment we would like to talk to you?" Detective Brown offered.

"And may I ask you what this is pertaining to?" She barely got the words out.

"Do you have a son named Tyler?"

This question quickly sparked her attention.

"Is there anything wrong with my son?" She cracked the glass door and waited for the reply.

"No, Ms. Sanford, we need to talk to you about Ann."

At that moment she knew they were there to discuss Ann Sanford. She hesitated before speaking.

"Ann who?" pretending she didn't know her.

"Ann Sanford," Detective Brown clearly repeated.

"Oh her," she said with a sneer.

"There's nothing I want to discuss with you about her."

"Do you mind if we ask you a few questions?"

She paused momentarily at Detective Brown's request but yet she cautiously opened the glass door. She led them to a sunken family room where the fireplace burned invitingly. She offered them a seat on the plush sofa and she sat in a chair across from them.

"Where's Tyler?" Detective Brown asked as they looked around the large stylish room.

They were impressed with her taste and decorating style. The house was warm and charming.

"He's still at school. Listen officers, can we hurry up and get whatever you came here for over before he comes home?" Her eyes were discerning.

136

Officer Patterson could tell she was frustrated and didn't want them there.

"Yes, of course, Ms. Sanford," Detective Brown said as he took out his note pad from the pocket of his blazer.

"What can you tell me about Ann?"

"Before we get started, I would like to know what this is all about. I may need legal advice before I speak to you."

She rubbed her palms together as she angrily stared at the two of them.

"No ma'am I assure you this is an informal visit. We're just investigating why she would attempt suicide. It's just normal police procedures."

"Because she's crazy," she mumbled under her breath.

"Excuse me Ms. Sanford, what did you say?" Detective Brown asked.

He thought she said the word crazy but he wasn't sure.

"Oh nothing," she mumbled refusing to repeat her last statement.

Suddenly they could tell that there was no love lost between the two of them. She definitely didn't like Ann and it was obvious.

"My name is Detective Brown and that's Officer Patterson, sorry for being so impolite."

Happy that she had agreed to speak to them, they didn't want to say anything to annoy her. So they carefully chose their line of questioning. She noticed their warmth and relaxed and participated with ease. Then Detective Brown charged in.

"Where do you work?"

"I work for the telephone company."

"The phone company huh. What's your title there?"

He stared at his notepad and flipped pages while reading his notes.

"I'm a supervisor."

"How long have you worked for the phone company?"

She thought for a while before she responded, "Uh, about three years."

"What are your work hours?"

"My hours vary."

Then it hit Detective Brown like a brick in the face. The telephone call that Trevor received; did she make the call and erase the data? *Is that possible?* He thought as he continued to ask questions, taking notes and watching her carefully.

"What was your relation to Ann?"

"Relation," she rudely responded. "There is no relation."

"I meant Ms. Sanford," trying to keep his tone polite, "How do you feel about her?"

For a moment, the only sounds they could hear were the wood crackling in the fireplace still blazing brightly on the hearth. He kept leaning forward as he listened, itching for new information.

"Well," she said as she stood up. She walked over to the bar and poured a glass of bottled water. "To be quite honest with you, I don't like her at all."

Officer Patterson thought she felt the same about them because she didn't offer them a drink. She stood at the bar and her attitude began to change.

"Why is that?" Detective Brown continued as Officer Patterson looked on.

"I just don't," she responded furiously as she took a sip of water.

"How did your son feel about her?"

Her expression changed again for the worst as she took another sip. "I guess he liked her. He lived with them for three years."

They studied her movement for a while, pretending not to notice her body language.

"Ms. Sanford is it true that your son loved her and didn't want to move back to Virginia Beach?"

This question pissed her off and she instantly snapped.

"Where are you getting your information from?" she said as she rolled her eyes. "Did you speak to my son without my permission?"

"No Ms. Sanford," they chorused.

"Ms. Sanford you must be honest with us. We are not here to point fingers or to blame you for not liking her—we're just here to investigate an attempted suicide or attempted murder."

The detective locked eyes and continued to watch her motions. Again, the detective asked if it was true that her son loved Ann and didn't want to move back with her, but she refused to answer. She stared at her half empty glass without a word.

"How did you feel about Ann taking you to court for custody?" Detective Brown asked as he took more notes.

"A waste of my time and a waste of her money," she said fighting not to smile.

"Did that make you angry?" He continued to scribble.

"Nope, it didn't make me angry. It just showed me how stupid she was. And if you didn't notice—I won." She said with a smirk.

"I don't think she's stupid. I just think she loves your son very much." Officer Patterson finally spoke as he watched her demeanor closely.

Her eyes shot upward and she said, "Yeah right—like I said stupid."

"Ms. Sanford did you know your ex-husband left Tyler a trust fund?"

This question really enraged her, knowing that Ann went to court and convince the judge to hold the proceeds until his twenty-first birthday. The smirk on her face instantly turned to a frown.

"Yeah, I am aware of that."

She took another sip of water. Her hands were now shaking rapidly and she spilled a few drops on the bar, but chose to ignore it.

"I have plenty of my own money for my son and me. I don't—I mean we don't need her stinky money." She then wiped water from her lips and shirt and it wasn't ladylike. "We don't need their money," she repeated angrily.

They could tell she had enough so Detective Brown changed the subject.

"Nice house Ms. Sanford. How long have you been living here?"

"We just moved in about three months ago."

"Where did you live before moving here?"

Officer Patterson quietly observed as Detective Brown did all the talking. He was impressed that he could get her to answer so many questions without a subpoena. *I guess that's why he's one of the top detectives*, he thought.

"That's none of your business," she snapped again. "I thought we were here to discuss Lady Ann."

She looked at her watch and said, "I think the two of you need to get going."

"Before we leave I have one last question?" Detective Brown closed his note pad and locked eyes with her. "Where were you on October 22, 1999?"

She paused, thinking about the question. Then she picked up a calendar that was lying on the coffee table and after reviewing it she said with irritation, "I was attending a seminar for my job at the Hyatt Hotel all day."

She looked genuinely uncomfortable now. She harshly plopped her glass on the table and stomped her foot.

"That's it! No more questions. Just because I don't like the woman doesn't mean I tried to kill her. So don't look through my windows for answers. You need to check out her walls."

"What do you mean by that remark Ms. Sanford?" Detective Brown asked curiously.

"What I mean is—it's time for you to go."

She looked into their eyes with purpose pausing as she shook her head.

"No more questions without my attorney."

She jerked her head towards the door, leading them as they followed. They stepped over the threshold and on to the porch, the door was slammed.

"Thank you for your time Ms. Sanford," the detective yelled through the glass door.

The temperature had dropped and hovered in the low forties creating a cool mosquito-killing frost. Officer Patterson turned on the heat as they sat in the squad car.

"Nice lady huh," Officer Patterson said jokingly.

"If looks could kill we would be two dead cops right now," Detective Brown said as he laughed.

"What's her problem?" Patterson asked as he drove away from the curb.

"Man, I don't know. But I think she was jealous of Ann and Ed's relationship. And the fact that her son lived with them and called her Mom and adored her—didn't make it easier."

Detective Brown pulled out his note pad and began to study his sloppy handwriting. He leaned his head to the side and stared absentmindedly.

"How can she afford a house like that? Patterson asked while turning the corner.

"Tyler is receiving his father's Social Security benefits."

"Detective do you think she had something to do with her ex-husband's death and the shooting to get her son back for the money?"

"I don't know, Patterson, but I intend to find out," he said with confidence.

After quietly riding for some time, Officer Patterson asked, "What's wrong, Detective?" He could tell he was in a deep thought.

"I'm puzzled?"

"Puzzled. Why are you puzzled?" The officer studied his expression for a moment.

"Her employment."

"And—what about her employment?"

He wanted in on the brainstorming.

"She's employed at the telephone company."

"And?" Patterson said while yielding at a sign.

"Trevor reported a strange telephone call from a lady the day of the incident and he was told to go to his mother's room because she needed his help as soon as possible. When I investigated the phone call there were no records. I checked the caller ID and no such call appeared."

"What do you mean there is no record of a call?"

His eyes widened almost instantly. Now Officer Patterson wore a puzzled look on his face.

"I called the telephone company from the scene of the incident and I was told that there was no data found."

"Man this is weird. Do you think she made the call and then erased the data? Is that possible, Detective? Does she have the ability to do that?"

They were concentrating on her job as Officer Patterson continued driving.

"We can check this information out once we get back to the precinct," the officer stated.

"Yeah, and I also need to find out if they had a seminar at the Hyatt on the twenty-second of October. I need the itinerary along with the names of every person who attended."

"No problem, detective. I can research that for you."

He was delighted to work with a veteran on this case. Detective Brown didn't respond.

"Do you mind, sir?" Officer Patterson asked as though he needed his permission to assist him.

"Oh no, I don't mind at all. Thanks for your help today and if you ever need me for anything, just call. I'll be more than happy to help you."

He continued to review his notes, pausing momentarily to gaze out the window at the passing traffic from time to time. He smiled while turning into the parking lot of the precinct. Officer Patterson parked the car in a space marked reserved. The detective's remark made him feel important because he knew he was one of the finest detectives in the business.

He stopped by his office and opened the file that Detective Brown had given him. It wasn't much but he was eager to help. Officer

Paterson offered his assistance by calling and speaking to the manager of the Hyatt and requested a copy of the itinerary and a copy of the attendance record for the seminars that were held at the facility on October twenty-second. The manager promptly faxed both copies of the requested documents. He then placed a call to the telephone company and spoke with the general manager. As he pulled all the information together, he went to see Detective Brown who was working in one of their empty offices across the hall. He sat down in the chair across from him, not wanting to reveal his findings.

"Detective I've finished the research for you."

He took the report that he had written along with the faxed pages from the folder and handed them to him. After Detective Brown read the report, his voice dropped in a hushed tone.

"Good job Officer Patterson."

He flashed a smile, and realized there was no need to continue the investigation in Virginia Beach. The unsetting news was not what he had hoped for. Being investigated did not automatic mean a person was guilty. It only meant there were things in one's background which had to be examined, cleared up, and verified. The detective packed his briefcase with the new information. Detective Brown took Captain Wilson's advice. He decided to rule Ann Sanford case number 66 as attempted suicide, close it and go home.

Chapter 20

There were less than three weeks until Christmas. The streets were decorated with colorful and bright lights. The majority of people were happier and friendlier during this time of the year. Janet decked her house with Christmas candles, wreaths, and poinsettias. Trevor was still moping around and continued to have sleepless nights. Bernita phoned regularly. She was concerned about Janet's health and Ann's condition. Janet didn't breathe a word to her about Trevor seeing a doctor. She didn't want people to think she was failing and not doing a good job while he was in her care.

They continued to have their daily visits to the hospital. There was no change in Ann's medical condition. The gold cross that Bernita placed above her bed was glowing as it dangled above her head. Janet always kept her hair neatly groomed. It looked as though she was asleep. As the days passed, it apparently became more difficult for Trevor. His life was plunging to earth in a dizzy fall. Alonza had become very ill with pneumonia and Trevor wasn't allowed to visit him for two weeks. Some days he would walk the halls alone or talk to the staff and others, or he would simply stay in the room with Janet and his mother. Janet sat in the same chair in the corner, knitting and humming to herself. The sweater was coming together nicely as she delicately connected each loop as every stitch was woven together perfectly.

On this particular day, Trevor aimlessly stroll the halls. He knew Alonza could not entertain visitors so he decided to visit Lt. Fitzpatrick. He really wasn't in the mood to talk to the Lieutenant, but he was bored out of his mind. Before entering his room, Trevor peeped in the door and noticed that the room was empty. He quickly got the attention of a nurse coming out the room next door and she informed him that he had been released several days ago.

"Are you a friend?" the nurse asked as she faked a smile. "Well you know the strangest thing happened. The day he checked out, we couldn't find his glasses. We looked everywhere. He had them the day before. I clearly remember because when I went to give him some medication, they were on his face and I cleaned them for him."

Trevor remembered finding the glasses under the bed and asked, "Mind if I go into the room to look for them?"

"Go ahead, knock yourself out."

She left him standing there and dashed into the room across the hall. Trevor went into the room and looked under the bed at the exact spot where he found them the first time. After diligently searching to no avail, he stood up. While standing in the room, he glanced down and noticed a note on the nightstand. The words "To Lad" were written on the cover. Trevor knew the note was for him because that's what the Lieutenant called him. Without hesitation, he walked over to the nightstand and picked up the note. He slowly read it.

"*Hello Lad: Did you repent yet?*"

Trevor froze and stood there dumbfounded, quickly closing the note, stuffing it inside his pants pocket and left the room.

The night air was windy, cold, and vicious, but you couldn't tell as Janet's house was warm and peaceful. After placing the last few pies in the oven, she settled herself in the living room to take a short break. The ringing of the phone broke her reverie and it scared her. She winced. Sitting on the sofa, she was in deep thought about Ann, Trevor and her own health. After the third ring, she got back up and limped to the kitchen.

"Hello Aunt Janet," said the unfamiliar masculine voice on the other end.

"Who is this?"

"This is Anthony."

Her face lightened with surprise.

"Anthony, where are you?"

"I'm in London—on my way to your house."

"You're coming home?"

Janet was filled with glee as she watched the lights twinkled on the Christmas tree.

"Yes, ma'am, I should be there tomorrow morning. Where's Trevor?"

The bad connection was causing his voice to fade in and out.

"He's sleeping but I can wake him."

"No, please don't. I want to surprise him."

"Oh Anthony he would love that."

"How's Ann?" The tone in his voice switched to sadness.

"Ann's condition hasn't changed. Anthony, I can't wait to see you. We miss you, son."

Janet's voice switched too but she tried to response cheerfully.

"I miss you too, Auntie."

"How long can you stay?"

"I have to leave the day after Christmas."

"Well son, it doesn't matter. I'm just so happy you can make it home."

"How's Uncle William?"

"He's fine."

"Oh, Baby I still can't believe you're coming home. I'm so happy."

"So am I, Auntie," he said in a tone that was bitter sweet.

The static in the phone was making it hard to hear.

"I should hang up now, before we're disconnected. Take care and I'll see you in the morning. Good-bye, Auntie."

"What did you say?" she yelled through the phone.

"Good-bye, Auntie."

With a click he was gone.

Janet was so excited she wanted to wake Trevor and share the good news. She raced into her room and found him sleeping peacefully. His head was hanging off the bed. She gently rolled him in the middle of the bed and slithered out the room and then telephoned William. They spoke for several minutes before their conversation ended. Janet pranced back in the kitchen and placed the last cake in the oven with a big smile covering her face.

Christmas morning and the house was cheerful and merry. The sky was a dark gray to nearly white and several flat, hazy, stratus clouds floated about. As Janet opened the curtain she noticed the featureless clouds and prayed for a white Christmas. She rushed into the kitchen to prepare Christmas breakfast as Trevor slept tossing and turning. She always made oyster stew on Christmas morning. As she was preparing the stew, there was a knock at the door. She rushed to open it hoping it was Anthony. He stood proudly and tall with a perfect smile on his face. They embraced for several minutes. She was so overjoyed with happiness that her eyes welled up and a tear rolled down her face. Anthony had a brown suitcase, a bag of presents, and a dozen red roses. He took the presents and placed them neatly under the tree and handed Janet the roses. He kissed her on the check and thanked her for caring for Trevor. They chatted for a while and then he put on a Christmas CD by the Temptations. They danced and sang as if they were the only two people in the world.

Anthony was Ann's only sibling. He was tall and handsome with perfect white teeth. When he enlisted in the military, he was only eighteen. He and Ann were very close and it broke her heart when he left home. Anthony never married and focused on his career that allow him to travel the world. Her brother, who was one year older than her, was in the Secret Service. He was on assignment in South Africa and had been deployed for a year. Ann and Anthony were close and with him gone Trevor was her pride and joy.

Anthony went into Janet's bedroom to see if Trevor was awake. Trevor had finally settled down in a comfortable position in his flannel pajamas with his eyes shut tight. Instinctively, he opened them and when he saw his Uncle Anthony, he leaped out of the bed into his arms. He clung tightly around his neck. Not wanting to let go. Anthony carried Trevor into the living room and they continued the celebration. Trevor, Janet, and Anthony danced and sang Christmas carols all morning. Trevor's eyes exuded more happiness than they had been in several months. Janet's heart was at ease because she could see the joy on Trevor's face.

The phone rang off the hook all morning. Family and friends called to wish them a Merry Christmas. Janet continued to cook as Anthony and Trevor played Uno and chatted.

"Dinner will be served at 4:00," Janet said with a big smile.

"Will you fellows set the table for me?" she asked while wiping her hands on a dish towel.

They carefully placed the china and silverware on the table for eight and used the roses as a centerpiece. Anthony and Trevor eagerly assisted her with the preparation of dinner. After helping Janet they resumed their card game. One-by-one the guests arrived. William was the first. He was extremely happy to see Anthony and after placing his presents under the tree, he joined them in the card game. Mae entered with an arm full of pies and a few presents. She placed them on the counter and helped Janet in the kitchen. Trevor tried to keep his mind off his mother but a deep sadness still gripped his heart. There was a soft, almost unnoticeable knock at the door. Trevor rushed to open it and Michael was standing there holding beautifully wrapped presents. Trevor's eyes stirred.

"Where's Mom?" he whispered.

"She's in the kitchen."

Michael tiptoed quietly into the house with his finger over his lips. Both William and Anthony were astonished and yet happy to see how well he looked. He tipped past with noiseless steps and waved silently. Janet was basting the turkey when she looked up and saw him. She froze in her movement and began to weep. She hugged and kissed him and told him how much she loved and missed him.

They ate, rejoiced, and opened their gifts. Michael was the life of the celebration. Everyone could see that he had changed. He spoke constantly of the love of God. He told them that he joined church and was singing in the male choir. Janet was so proud of him—that he had finally grown up—got it together. It boosted her spirits to see the change in him. They listened as he spoke about how God changed his life. He preached about how he was a sinner and was lost with no way to break free. After his speech, he apologized to Janet for not being the son he should have been and kissed her. Janet wept. Just seeing her son like this made her whole. She knew God had answered one of her prayers. She only had two left. One was for Ann to come out of her coma and the other was for Trevor to be a happy little boy again. As for her, she knew she was going to be just fine.

Everyone pitched in clearing the dishes from the table after the delicious meal Janet had prepared. They put the gifts addressed to Ann in a shopping bag. Janet took the eggnog from the refrigerator and packed it in her purse along with some plastic cups. Trevor went into Janet's room to retrieve their coats. His eyes became pure and innocent. As he glanced out the window he yelled, "It's snowing." They smiled with much giggles and left for Riverside County Hospital.

The drive to the hospital took longer than usual, due to the icy roads and heavy snowfall. They continued to celebrate as Michael led them in *Silent Night*. The singing resonated so loud that passengers in traveling cars smiled upon their approach. The loud celebration ceased once they entered section B12. Trevor was the first to enter Ann's room. He wished his mother a Merry Christmas and kissed her on her eyes, nose, and mouth. Janet followed, as she spoke softly to Ann before moving to her oversized chair in the corner. William proceeded to her side and kissed her on the forehead. Mae entered with a God bless you and a smile. Michael followed with a prayer.

Anthony was the last to go in. As he came near everyone was silent. He looked intently at her petite, motionless body and dropped to his knees. He tried to talk for a moment but the words would not leave his lips. He tenderly took hold of her frigid hand and placed it against his warm face.

"Sister Girl," he whispered, "I know you can hear me. I'm here."

He soothingly stroked his face with her hand, guiding it across his eyes, nose, mouth, and checks.

"Remember the game we used to play when we were kids? Pretending we couldn't see and we had to use our other senses to identify items. Well, let's play it now."

He paused still guiding her hand across his face.

"What do you feel? Do you feel the love in this room? Do you feel the love in my heart? If you can feel these things, Sister Girl, then I know you will get well and come home soon."

He winced as he spoke, for every word was painful.

"I miss you and I love you. Please wake up and stop playing the game. I don't want to play anymore. I want my Sister Girl back," he pleaded.

"Please come back to us. We need you and your little boy's heart is breaking because of the load that has been placed upon him. Hear me Lord, I pray to you. Set my Sister Girl free through your love, grace, and mercy."

As he spoke everyone in the room stared sadly. He spoke quietly to her and God. Trevor began to weep. Automatically, he knelt down on his knees beside Anthony and he began to pray. He noticed a tear dripping from Anthony's cheek. With passion he took Ann's hand and softly wiped away Anthony's tears.

"Mom," he whispered with hopelessness, "Can you feel the tears? They belong to Uncle Anthony."

Then he took her other hand and wiped his tears and said, "And Mom these tears belong to me. Please wake up. Open your eyes and give me the best Christmas present in the whole wide world. I know you can hear us. Please, I'm begging you."

Trevor's words slurred as he tried to speak. Janet turned her face, grief-stricken by his extravagant emotional plea. As Mae, William, and Michael watched with their hearts breaking, they joined Trevor and Anthony on their knees, linking hands as they prayed together.

Chapter 21

It was a dreadful ride home. The joy displayed earlier had disappeared. Trevor tried to sing but no one joined in. As they turned into the parking lot of Janet's building, Trevor showed his chivalry once again.

"I would like to make a toast?" he stated.

"A toast! How can you make a toast without something to drink?" Janet commented.

Then she remembered the eggnog and cups she placed in her purse earlier. She pulled out the eggnog and cups and handed each of them a cup. She poured the eggnog in their cups, looked at Trevor, smiled.

"Now you can make your toast, Baby."

As they held their cup up in the air Trevor began.

"To Uncle Michael, thank you for choosing God and changing your life, we miss you and love you. To Uncle Anthony thanks for being the best uncle in the world. Thanks for coming home. We also miss and love you. To Aunt Mae thanks for accepting my family as your family."

Everyone directly stared at him when he addressed them.

"To Uncle William thanks for your love and support. To Aunt Janet thanks for loving me unconditionally. To my wonderful mother may peace be with you. I love you and please get well soon and come back to us—and finally to Jesus, Happy birthday."

Their voices were speechless as their eyes filled with tears. Janet finally responded with a joyous Merry Christmas. They continued to sit in the car under the glowing streetlight, drinking their eggnog and watching the large fluffy snowflakes float through the air.

The snow glistened as the sun rose. Janet wanted the joy to last, but when the crowd vanished, so did Trevor's smile. The house was now empty and immediately their minds raced back to Ann. Christmas was over and they wanted Ann to recover before the New Year. As Trevor sat in the den reminiscing about his life, he started to weep. Janet walked into the room and sat beside him. She placed his hands across his shoulders and cradled them.

"Auntie," he said as he wiped his tears. "I'm scared."

He looked at her warily.

"Why are you scared?" asked Janet as she squeezed him tight.

"What if my mother doesn't make it out of her coma? What will happen to her? Will she stay like that for the rest of her life?"

"Baby, don't have such thoughts. I know your mother will get better."

"But Auntie how do you know that?"

He stood up and walked toward the window.

"I know this because of my faith. Do you have faith?" she asked as she went to the window to be close to him.

"Yes ma'am I do, but nothing has changed. She's been like that for over two months and now I'm scared. Auntie, can she feel anything—is there any pain?"

"No, there isn't pain. It's just like she's sleeping. Have you ever seen the movie *Sleeping Beauty?* Well that's your mother. She's sleepy beauty."

"When she awakes, will she remember me?"

She didn't know the answer to that question but taking a guess she smiled and said, "Sure Baby, she'll know you. How can she forget her baby?"

He appreciated her vote of confidence, but that was typical for her. The telephone rang which brought their conversation to a halt. Janet was relieved as she rushed to answer it. When she hung up the phone, she asked Trevor to get dressed. She walked out of the den, leaving with a million dollar smile. An hour later a knock was heard at the door, Janet asked Trevor to answer it. He trotted to the door and looked through the peephole. He didn't see anyone.

"Who is it?" he asked.

No one answered. He asked again. He cracked the door to take a peek and the biggest smile came to his face. Tyler was standing at the door holding two teddy bears. He rushed in, giving him a hug, almost knocking him down, as his excitement was overpowering.

"Little brother, are you going to stay with us?"

The words came out faster than his lips would allow. Tyler responded with a resounding yes, as he tightly held him around his neck. Barbara entered and spoke pleasantly to Janet for a while. She kissed Tyler and left.

"Aunt Janet did you know Tyler was coming?" he asked as he took his suitcase and placed it in the closet.

"Yes, Baby, his mother called earlier and asked if it was okay for him to stay with us for a week."

Trevor remembered the telephone call that brought happiness to her face earlier and now it all came together. He took his little brother's hand and led him into the den. Janet smiled and returned to her bedroom. The sounds of children's laughter lingered in the apartment for hours. Janet was pleased as she lay across her bed reading the newspaper. Tyler and Trevor played a while and then they talked about old times. Tyler asked with emphasis.

"How's Mother Ann?"

Trevor closed his eyes trying to sound cheerful.

"She's the same Tyler," he said as he held back tears.

"When can I see her?"

"Today."

They continued to talk and play. They never mentioned Ann again. The time came and they dressed by putting on their snow boots, scarves, coats, and hats. Both Tyler and Trevor held Janet's hand while escorting her down the icy sidewalk and through the snow. William was happy to see Tyler as he leaped into the front seat. Janet and Trevor took their place in the back. Tyler talked all the way to the hospital, and they enjoyed his company, knowing it was only temporary. But they appreciated him just the same.

The hospital staff was tremendously busy today. They passed several crowds and Trevor grabbed Tyler's hand. When they reached section B12, as usual there was a group gathered outside Ann's room, waiting to visit her. Trevor pulled Tyler to the front of the bed as he leaned over and kissed her in his usual way. Tyler moved to the end of the bed staring in mesmerized horror. Trevor noticed the fear in his eyes as he slowly approached.

"Tyler," he whispered, "Don't be afraid. She's not going to harm you. Come follow me."

He took his hand and directed him back to the front. Tyler didn't expect to see Ann this way and was suddenly frightened and speechless as he stood there clutching his teddy-bear.

"Mother Ann," his tiny voice said, "Hello Mother Ann, I brought you something."

He placed the teddy bear in the bed close to her heart. It was a white bear with a red ribbon wrapped around its neck with a necklace that read. *Get well soon, Love Tyler.*

As the day passed, Tyler became more comfortable with her appearance and began to communicate to her. Trevor and Tyler took turns talking and reading all afternoon. Janet was knitting as William was in and out of the room for cigarette breaks. Trevor couldn't wait to take Tyler to see his friend Alonza. On the way, they stopped by the Maternity Ward to see Sue and the babies. He introduced Sue to Tyler and then proceeded to room 517. When they entered Alonza was laying still in his bed asleep. While his grandmother relaxed in a chair watching TV.

"Hello, Sugar," she said as she waved at them and smiled at Tyler. "Who's the cutie with you?"

"This is my little brother, Tyler."

"Oh, Sugar, it's nice to meet you. Trevor speaks about you all the time."

Tyler spoke briefly as he stared at Alonza.

"Hey Trevor, what's wrong with your friend?" he whispered.

"He's sick. I'll explain it to you later."

With a nod he continued to stare.

"How's your mother?" Alonza's grandmother asked as she tried to lift herself out of the chair. Trevor instinctively went to help her, answering, "She's fine—about the same."

"How long will you be here? I need to go to the gift shop for a minute."

They agreed to stay until her return. She took her cane and left the room dragging her right leg. Trevor and Tyler played with one of his games on the floor as Alonza slept. Alonza peeled opened his eyes and he saw his friend sitting on the floor at his feet.

"Hello Trevor," Alonza groaned as he tried to wake up.

"Hey Alonza. How are you, my friend?"

"I'm okay, a little weak today," he answered with a cough.

"I brought someone to meet you. Tyler—come," saying as he used his fingers to shrug him. "This is my little brother Tyler. Tyler this is Alonza."

They spoke in an awkward tone and stared each other down. Trevor was glad to see Alonza feeling better and that Tyler was by his side. They continued visiting for an hour and then left after his grandmother returned.

William stopped at McDonalds' on the way back to Janet's house. Everyone was tired of eating leftover turkey and ham, nor was Janet in the mood to cook. Trevor and Tyler retired to the den and demolished their Happy Meals. Janet retreated in her bedroom. Worn out from their busy day of play and visiting Ann, the rosy-cheeked boys were already asleep as Janet tucked them into bed. Several hours later the house became solemnly quiet as she fell off to sleep.

Trevor realized how quickly the week had passed and Tyler will be leaving tomorrow. They were inseparable for the six days. They ate, slept, walked, ran, laughed, and played together the entire time. The wintery weather caused them to stay indoors most of the time. Fortunately, they didn't mind, just being together was enough for them.

The sun was warm and bright, the heat rays began turning the snow into mush. As the snow slowly melted away, Tyler wanted to go outside and ride Trevor's bike. Trevor wasn't in the mood, but he would do anything for his little brother. Plus he was the only one he allowed to ride it. After breakfast they hurried to dress and headed outside. Trevor carried the bike downstairs as Tyler walked behind him.

While the boys played, Janet used that time to do some much needed laundry. She collected the dirty clothes from the hamper and headed to the laundry room on the second floor. The wash finished and she began to fold Tyler's clean clothes and placed them in a basket. She hummed while smiling from the boy's laughter from the playground. After folding the rest of the wash she went back into the apartment. Moments later there was a loud bang at the door and Janet hurried to answer it. Tyler was standing in horror, screaming for help. He was exhausted and his breathing was labored.

"What's wrong?" Janet asked as she grabbed her slippers.

"It's Trevor, Aunt Janet."

"What's wrong with Trevor?"

Her heart began to throb and the look of desperation spread across her tried old face.

"He's fighting."

"Fighting! What in the world is going on?"

Janet ran out the door down the stairs to find a large crowd of children standing in a circle. She pushed her way through the yelling kids and noticed Trevor straddling a boy and whaling on him like he was a stationary punching bag.

"Take it back, take it back," Trevor shouted.

The little boy was howling and crying. Janet grabbed Trevor's coat, snatching him off with vigor and ordered him into the house. She helped the little boy off the ground, wiped his bloody nose and asked him if he was okay. She trotted quickly upstairs to find Trevor in hysterics. Trevor was pacing the floor, repeating the words over and over.

"I'll kill him. I'll kill him."

She forcefully grabbed him trying to get his attention but he wouldn't calm down.

"Listen to me, Baby, what's wrong, why were you fighting?"

Trevor's eyes were blood shot red and smoke was coming from his nostrils. Like a possessed person he had transformed into a person she didn't recognize. Tyler stood in the corner sobbing and hyperventilating as he watched Trevor's bizarre behavior. Janet tried to soothe Tyler then she turned her attention back to Trevor. Stuck in the middle of a disaster, she felt bewildered and frustrated. When she turned her attention back to Tyler, his cries became louder.

"Why is this happening to us?" she yelped.

"Trevor," Janet screamed as she watched him pacing back and forth repeating those dreadful words. "What's wrong? Stop it now and talk to me?"

Trevor continued to pace back and forth, mumbling to himself. She embraced Tyler and held him tight.

"Baby, tell me what happened outside?"

Tyler tried to speak between gasps while catching his breath but Janet couldn't understand his whimpering words. Finally she threw her hand up in the air and shrieked, "Help me Jesus."

Suddenly Trevor relaxed. She could tell he was genuinely upset. She looked at him with sad puppy dog eyes and asked what happened.

"Auntie, I don't feel like talking about it right now. I want to lie down for a while."

Trevor jogged out the room into the den and plopped across the sofa. Tyler was still crying when Janet approached him.

"Let's get some rest and we can talk about it later."

He nodded and they retired to her bedroom. Moments later a knock was heard at the door and Janet rushed to answer it. Charles was standing in the hallway with Trevor's bike. Charles placed the bike in the dining room. Janet thanked him. She returned to her room and lay across her bed and prayed until she fell asleep.

When Janet awakened, she noticed that Trevor had joined them in bed. She watched him intently; thinking about his quandary that took place outside earlier and thought, *what would cause him to behave this way?* He was changing in front of her and she didn't know what to do.

As she crept out of bed, trying not to awaken them, she went into the kitchen and telephoned William. Whispering into the phone, Janet began telling William that Trevor got in a fight and beat-up a little boy. In the midst of her conversation, she began to weep.

"William my heart can't take much more," Janet said as she wiped her tears. "Why is this happening to us? In the same hospital where Ed died Ann is fighting for her life. And now this. When will I wake up from this nightmare?"

William listened to her grief and finally asked if she wanted him to pick Trevor up to spend a couple of days with him. Janet remembered the words of Ann's suicide note and declined. As she was hanging up the phone, there she saw Trevor standing in the doorway. He glanced at Janet moving his face in a silent apology.

"Aunt Janet, I'm sorry for fighting today. I didn't mean to upset you."

His apology was drenching with embarrassment. He held her tightly around her waist.

"Trevor, promise me you will not get yourself in a situation like that again."

She took his hands and held them passionately.

"Baby next time walk away and come in the house if you feel you must fight."

Janet went to the cabinet grabbed a glass and filled it with water.

"Now tell me what happened?"

Trevor took the glass of water, raised his eyebrow and began by saying, "Tyler was riding the bike and I was running beside him. Philip made a joke about my mother."

"What kind of joke?"

"He asked how many bullets it takes to kill a mother."

"I said, excuse me," and he repeated the question.

"Another little boy answered 'one' and he responded 'no dummy, it takes two.' When I heard them laugh I wanted to hurt both of them. They made me so angry. I couldn't believe they would laugh about something as serious as that."

Janet was stunned at what the boys said and it made her upset.

"Baby, I will go talk to Philip's parents and tell them what happened. But for now you must promise me you will be smarter than them. If you hear jokes or comments about your mother, turn away. Sometimes kids don't think before they speak."

Janet knew the joke was wrong and that it hurt him badly, because it hurt her. Presented with such a dramatic situation she tried to hide her pain. Trevor handed her the empty glass and revealed a crooked smile as he headed toward the bathroom. Tyler was standing in the doorway of the bathroom watching Trevor wash his face and hands. Trevor noticed him.

"Hey, little brother, did you sleep well?"

Tyler nodded yes, rubbing his eyes.

"Sorry about today."

Trevor bent down and kissed him on the forehead.

"Do you forgive me?"

He nodded again and they proceeded to the dining room to eat dinner together.

Trevor and Tyler were savoring the last few hours together. They did not want to separate. Trevor packed Tyler's suitcase and placed the teddy bear he had given him on the bed. They played until they heard the tap at the door. Janet called for Tyler. The two young boys walked slowly into the room, holding hands. Barbara was standing in the hallway.

"Bye Trevor," Tyler said sadly.

"Good-bye, little brother—I hope to see you soon. Take care and be good."

Tyler hugged and kissed Janet. Then he rushed into Trevor's arms. The grip was so tight Trevor could tell he didn't want to go.

"I love you and I'll be in touch," Trevor said with a gloomy look.

Tyler nodded and walked out the door. He looked up as he swayed down the stairs and in his ingenuous voice yelled, "Kiss Mother Ann for me."

Janet and Trevor stood at the door listening until the footsteps subsided and they disappeared into the darkness.

Chapter 22

The holidays ended as quickly as they started. Janet and Trevor brought in the New Year at church. The late night service was long, but they enjoyed every minute. For the past several months their feelings remained the same. While Ann's recovery dragged on, she continued to receive daily visits. Trevor was coping, but he hardly went outside to play. His friend Charles would visit from time to time to check on him. Alonza's condition had worsened and he was moved to Children's hospital. William took him to visit occasionally. Life for all of them was abnormal, but they did their best to adjust.

Detective Brown closed the Ann Sanford case and was working on a drive-by shooting case. Trying to get organized for the New Year, he cleaned his desk. He straightened the picture on the wall. He emptied out his file cabinets and piled the papers on his desk. Then he placed each document alphabetically to re-file them. He removed the scattered papers from his desk, reviewing each one destined for the wastebasket or the file cabinet. Under stacks of papers, he noticed Ann's suicide note.

How did I forget to take this back to the evidence room? He thought.

His desk was always messy; it was easy to miss. He sat at his desk, reviewing the sad note. He read the note again and again, shaking his head in disgust. All of a sudden it hit him. The note was clear of blood. As he studied the note closely, wondering how that could have happened. He leaped from his chair and he went to the evidence room and requested document number two and three. He signed the release form and proceeded back to his office. The detective carefully looked at the evidence marked number two which was the ashtray. He noticed blood spatters on the rim and his eyes brightened. He picked up evidence marked number three, which was the picture, and there were blood spatters on it also. Looking somewhat embarrassed he moaned, *how he could have missed that.* He went to the evidence room to retrieve 'Ann Sanford-Case number 66.' As he reviewed the document, he looked at his old report and notes from the night of the incident. According to the report, the suicide note and picture were on the left side and the ashtray was on the right.

Why wasn't blood splattered on the suicide note?

He reviewed the information that William had given him that night, remembering that he stated he didn't touch or move anything. He picked up the suicide note, turning it over. Then he noticed the small blood spatters at the bottom. By trying to answer his own questions, his mind went blank. He was confounded; there was only one possible answer. Did the firemen move the evidence?

He paced back and forth in his office, trying to collect his thoughts and figure out this odd finding. *Why* h*adn't I paid attention to this earlier,* he thought?

Suddenly his mind race back to the night of the incident. He could clearly picture the crime scene like a picture on a picture tube, remembering where her body lay and where the evidence was placed. He was in deep thought when Captain Wilson entered. He spoke and took a seat.

"How's the drive-by case?"

He glanced down at the cluttered desk and then he noticed the documents inscribed the 'Sanford Case' then he asked.

"What are you doing?" He stood up and picked up the suicide note. "And why are you still working on this closed case Detective?"

His tone was quite sharp.

"Captain, I'm not working on this case. I was getting ready to take it back to the evidence room when something caught my attention."

He handed the captain the evidence and asked for his opinion.

"Captain, what do you see?"

After reviewing the evidence, the Captain said, "I see an ashtray, a picture, and a suicide note."

"I know that, Captain," Detective Brown said as he faked a smile. "What do you see on them?"

The captain held up the picture, he carefully reviewed it, turning it over. He placed the picture on the desk and picked up the ashtray. After observing the ashtray, he placed it on the desk. Then he reviewed the note and looked up and his eyes were sharp and probing.

"Why isn't there blood on top of the note?" he asked as he picked up the ashtray and picture again.

"My thoughts exactly, Captain. According to my report and notes, none of the evidence was moved. But now, Captain, take a look at this."

He took the suicide note and turned it over.

"There's small blood spats on the back on the bottom," he said while pointing to them.

The captain smiled because he knew they were on to something.

"Good job, Detective." He patted him on the shoulder with a slight smile on his bearded face. "How did we miss this?"

"Sir I don't know, but I always felt this was not a suicide case."

"Do you have any suspects?"

"No I don't."

Detective sat with disgust while the captain studied his report.

"Barbara Sanford had an alibi and I don't have a clue where to start. But apparently I missed something. All crime scenes tell a story and if this woman didn't attempt suicide there's got to be blood outside of that room. The end depends on the beginning. Whoever pulled the trigger had to carry blood out of that room. If I can locate a blood trail then I will find the shooter."

The detective knew he finally had the captain's attention and asked with emphasis.

"Captain I would like permission to re-open this case."

The captain stared at the ceiling scarcely and managed to raise his eyes but finally gave him his approval. He exited the office looking dazed.

It was less than twenty-four hours since the captain had given him permission to re-open the case. Detective Brown arrived at his office and opened the Ann's Sanford file. He reviewed the information that William had given him. It wasn't much but the little scrap of information was enough for him to get started. Glancing at his watch, he decided to take a ride to the Sanford's home, since he had nothing on his schedule that morning. As he sat in rush hour traffic, he studied his notes, reviewed the pictures and thought about the evidence.

When he arrived at the house, the yard had just been landscaped. There were piles of dead flowers and bags full of weeds stacked along the sidewalk. He parked his car in the driveway and proceeded up the sidewalk to the house. The tape that once labeled the door was removed and the house look well maintained. He knocked on the door holding his camera bag, and was greeted by a large woman with a pointy nose and full lips.

"Good morning, Sir," she said as she looked surprised, "What can I do for you?"

The detective flashed his badge and said, "Hello, Miss, I've been assigned to the Ann Sanford case. Do you mind if I come in to investigate and look around?"

She opened the door and welcomed him in.

"My name is Detective Brown."

"My name is Sally. I'm the housekeeper."

She led him into the foyer and closed the door. As he looked around, he took notice of the immaculate house. The smell of dried blood no longer lingered in the air and the hardwoods floors were shining with such a glow; he could see his reflection from them. She steered him to the family room and offered him something to drink but he declined. She continued toward the bedrooms and he went into the den and took out his report, a note pad and an ink pen.

He noticed a computer on top of an antique cherry wood desk so he turned it on and began to search for the suicide note. The detective searched the majority of all the documents on the computer but no note was found. He even went to the desktop to check the recycle bin, but still no note. Looking befuddled, he continued on and opened every document stored on the computer, he was unable to locate the suicide note.

Where can this note be stored? I can't locate it on the computer.

The detective went into the kitchen and examined the knife stand. He noticed that a knife was missing. Then he proceeded toward Ann's bedroom. After stopping momentarily to examine the door, he witnessed small-ridged scratch marks around the lock. He retrieved his camera from his camera bag and took several pictures.

When he entered her bedroom, he noticed that the carpet had been replaced. He glanced at the spot where Ann's bloody body was found. The walls had been freshly painted and the fresh smell of wet paint loitered. As he scanned the room, looking behind and under everything and every item, he was disappointed that the room had been totally redone. Sally entered asking if he needed help. Surprised to see her standing there, he asked her if he could ask her some questions.

"No," she said. "I don't mind at all."

She took off her apron. He placed his camera and bag on the night table and took his note pad out his jacket's pocket and began to write.

"What's your full name?"

"Sally Campbell."

"How long have you been employed by Ms. Sanford?"

"About one year."

She smiled as she dusted off the dresser with her apron.

"How many days do you work a week?"

She answered quickly, "I clean twice a week—Mondays and Saturdays."

"When did you hear about Ann's incident?"

"The next day, after it happened. I came to the house and an officer stopped me. He told me I couldn't come in—that I needed to speak to a family member to get any information. I paged her uncle; he told me what had happened. I asked him if they still needed my services, and I was told to keep in touch and they would let me know when I could return."

"When did you report back to work Ms. Campbell?

"About five weeks ago."

"Do you know anything about the carpet?" he asked while still taking notes.

"What carpet, sir?"

"This carpet," he said while pointing downward.

"Sorry but I don't. The carpet had already been installed when I came back."

"What about the walls Ms. Campbell, were they also painted?"

"Yes," she answered rapidly and began to look unnerved.

"What can you tell me about Ann?"

She sat on the edge of the bed and tilted her head toward the floor. Her body expression changed distractedly because discussing Ann was painful.

"Sir, this family was my best client. Ann, Ed, Tyler, and Trevor were always so nice to me. They treated me like part of their family. I loved them and I enjoyed coming to work for them."

She took a deep breath and then continued.

"I remember when I first came to work, my mother became very ill and I had to take some time off and fly to California. I had little money and I didn't know if I would have the opportunity to see her. They donated the airplane tickets and Mr. Sanford was nice enough to drive me to and from the airport. I never had any problems with them."

By then her voice was almost as soft as a whisper.

"How did Ann treat you after the death of her husband?"

"This was a very hard period for her and the boys. They were so much in love. When he died, a part of her was buried with him. She was always sad and depressed. She would stay to herself, locked in her room for days. It got so bad she stopped eating. On several occasions, I cooked dinner for Trevor because I felt she wasn't feeding him properly. There was nothing I wouldn't do for them."

This new information shocked the detective because he was told Ann was such a good mother. Now he's finding out there was a secret she was keeping from her family.

"What can you tell me about the last time you saw her?"

"Well," a short pause and then she stood up.

"I remember clearly. It was the six-month anniversary of Ed's death. Ann had been crying all day. She tried to smile for me, but I could see her pain through her tears. I began talking to her and prepared some hot tea. We sat in the kitchen and she went on and on about her life."

"What were some of the things she discussed with you?" The detective asked as he followed her around the room.

"She told me that she thought she was failing as a mother. She stated that her pain was much too great and that she couldn't bear it any longer. I knew she wanted help and I tried my best to accommodate her, but the real strength had to come from her. I asked her what did she want out of life and she told me she wanted to move on and give her son the love he deserved. She also said she was tired of being tired and hurting her son and she would do anything to make him happy again."

"Did you believe her?"

"Absolutely. She needed time to grieve and once that period was over her heart would lighten and she would come back around. One thing you must remember detective as you continue to investigate this case. Ann loved her son and there was nothing that she wouldn't do for him. I have never seen the love of a mother as strong as Ann's."

Sally became sad as she continued to speak about Ann and the detective could tell, but he continued to question her.

"What can you tell me about her son Trevor?"

Now she blushed. "Trevor was a good child, very humble and shy."

"How did he react after Ed's death?"

"He was heart stricken, and the day Tyler moved back with his mother, he became very withdrawn. He shut the world out completely. He never went outside to play. He started spending most of his time in his room and milk and cereal became his diet."

167

Detective Brown continued to follow her as his eyes narrowed. His voice grew indistinct towards the end of the questioning. He still had one last question to ask.

"Ms. Campbell, do you think she tried to kill herself?"
She froze in her steps and looked at the detective as though she was looking right through him.

"No way—no way," she said shaking her head. "Ann wanted to live for her son's sake, if not for anything else."

The detective was stunned by her final response. He believed every word but for now he needed to find some evidence to prove this theory. He still didn't rule out that she was a suspect though. Everyone in his eyes was a suspect until the case was solved. He smiled with a slight sparkle in his eyes as he stared at his notes. He had no more questions for her and tranquility settled in the room.

"I'm leaving now. Please lock-up for me," she said as she walked toward the door swinging her apron. She looked back at him with a flirtatious smile as she exited the room.

The detective continued to comb the house, inspecting every room for a clue.

"If someone was in this room they left with blood on them," he murmured.

He pulled out his old crime scene photos and examined each one for any footprints. The photos didn't assist him. He went into Trevor's room and searched it throughout. He looked under the bed, the mattress, and in his dressers. He opened the closet and looked inside. He found nothing. As he started to leave the room, he noticed a big brown chest on top of his desk. He opened the chest to review the contents within. It contained baseball cards, a necklace with a heart shaped charm that read *To Trevor, Love Mom.*

He looked at a piece of white paper, which appeared to be a map. As he studied the map and realized it led to a secret hiding place close to the house. He clipped the small piece of paper to his note pad and placed the note pad on the desk. From the corner of his eye he saw a baseball cap hanging on top of a trophy. The detective picked up the cap and

168

noticed an unidentified stain. The cap was placed in a plastic bag. After thoroughly searching the room he left headed outside to check the windows and doors. There was no evidence of forced entry.

If Ann didn't commit suicide, the person who did attempt this murder had access to her house. They either used forced entry, came in with a key, or she let them in without suspicion, he thought.

The detective examined the windows and doors. He looked throughout the bushes and trees seeking any evidence to lead him to the shooter. Although he knew the landscapers were there, he was hoping to find anything out the ordinary. He gathered the information quickly and returned to the family room. The two-way radio bleeped. It was the captain; he spoke to him as he continued to comb the house. It was getting late and they needed his help back at the station. He flicked off the lights and locked the door. The car was packed with the computer, cap, camera, and the small piece of paper. As he drove away, he looked back at the large dark empty house, wondering to himself what happened in this peaceful loving house to cause such paralyzing terror on October twenty-second.

Chapter 23

William drove through the Sunday morning traffic. They rode in silence for a long time. Blocks away from the hospital, Janet finally asked a question.

"Trevor you're going to have a birthday in a week. What gift would you like?"

Trevor glanced out the window, and then spoke with such coldness in his voice.

"I want my mother back—nothing else." He said bluntly.

His reply boomeranged and split her heart in two. Janet hesitated before replying.

"Yeah, Baby I know, but if that didn't happen what else do you want?"

Sadly, Trevor never spoke another word. Janet had been anticipating this, and now it had finally come. She had stepped knee deep into a cesspool and she didn't know how to dig herself out. Taking on Trevor was more than she had bargained for; she stared out the window refusing to speak another word, too.

Another week passed and it was a very foggy Sunday morning. As Janet awakened, she reached for Trevor, but all she found was a blanket, pillow, and an empty space. She jumped out of bed as quickly as her aging body would allow and rushed through the house. She looked in the den and then walked to the living room. Trevor was lying on the floor under the window reading his Bible by the sunlight that beamed through the window. She smiled when she noticed him. His mind was engrossed by the words he was reading and he didn't notice his aunt standing behind him. She shuffled back into her bedroom without disturbing him. The birthday present that she had purchased some weeks ago was buried in her closet. After digging through the clutter she spotted the wrapped box, which was surrounded by old clothes. A smile grew on her tired, worried face at the very sight of the present. She was barely able to lift the present out of the closet because it was extremely heavy but she managed. As she slowly walked down the hallway with the heavy present in her arms, she sang happy birthday.

Trevor smiled brightly as she walked over to him with the gift. It was the kind of smile that sent chills through her body. He was still grinning while he unwrapped the present when they heard a knock at the door. Janet opened the door; William entered carrying a present and wearing a small grin.

"Happy birthday Trev."

He placed the present on the floor next to the gift Janet had given him. Trevor showed more happiness than he had shown in months.

"Hey, Trevor," Janet said as cheerful as she could muster.

"Take your shower we're going on a trip."

"A trip! Where?" Trevor asked wide eyed.

"It's a surprise. Now hurry," she said as she clapped her hands.

Trevor didn't ask any more questions. He grabbed a towel and tossed it over his right shoulder. He dashed off to the bathroom for a quick shower, while Janet and William waited for him in the living room.

William stood and put his jacket on when Trevor entered the living room. Charles stood by the door holding a balloon with white lettering that displayed the words *Happy Birthday*. Charles wished him a happy birthday and handed the balloon to him. Trevor didn't know what was going on, and had no clue as to where they were going. He wore a huge smile as he walked down the stairs because he knew that wherever they were headed was a big surprise.

Everyone settled in the car and William drove out of the parking lot onto Main Street. He continued on Main Street, turning left on Central Avenue. Trevor knew they were not going to the hospital because the hospital was in the opposite direction. He tried to keep an eye on which route they were traveling, but Charles kept him busy and he finally lost his sense of direction completely. Two hours later they reached their destination.

After looking up, Trevor began smiling vibrantly. There set the mountain that he had been daydreaming about directly in front of him. This was the biggest mountain he had ever seen. It appeared to stretch high into the sky—the tip was covered by white fluffy clouds. Trevor stole a quick glance at both Janet and William. He realized that he was a blessed little boy.

Up the mountain they went, high in the sky, away from fog and pollution, where the air was crisp and the only fragrance that filled their nostrils was the sweet fluorescent smell of pine needles, honey combs and freshly cut grass. They walked for hours. At the end of the trail was a horse stable. Charles had only seen horses on television and nothing prepared him for their size and beauty. He ran excitedly to a stallion and gently rubbed his large head. The horse's long black mane was gorgeous. Charles placed an apple in his hand and the horse gently grabbed it, making him giggle. The horse-handler was polite to the boys and offered them a ride around the fenced yard. William and Janet watched as the boys trotted back and forth on horseback. They rode and laughed for about an hour. Even when their small feet hit the ground, the laughter continued. After a full day of hiking, horseback riding, exploring the mountain, and leading William and Janet from one adventure to another Trevor and Charles were exhausted. Everyone was exceedingly glad and satisfied that Trevor enjoyed his birthday. This is the first birthday he had ever spent without his mother.

On the ride back home, they stopped at an ice cream parlor and William treated everyone to their favorite flavor. Upon reaching the city limits, Trevor suddenly became quiet and sad again. The happy evening abruptly ended when they walked into the hospital. Trevor's eyes widened when he entered his mother's room. The staff at the hospital had decorated Ann's room and filled it with presents and balloons. A table was placed in the corner where Janet normally sat. It was beautifully decorated and a cake set on top. The brown and white football shaped cake had the words *Happy Birthday Trevor. We love you* written on it in white letters. Sue lit the candles as they sang happy birthday to him. He closed his eyes and made a wish. The wish was lengthy and everyone could tell it was for his mother by the expression on his face. He blew out the twelve burning candles, glancing back at his mother with a sympathetic stare as a tear rolled down his cheek.

Chapter 24

The seasons seemed to have changed rapidly. Winter was shaken off and erupted into an explosion of trees and flowers budding, ushering in spring. Looking at this seemingly unchangeable and long term situation of Ann's condition, but that didn't stop their daily visits to the hospital. Trevor was moody most of the time mainly due to the fact his mother's medical state was at a standstill. His happy times became few and far between. Janet was scheduled to have surgery in a month because the strength of her heart had weakened. Bernita agreed to come and stay with Trevor during this time. Life in the tiny apartment was the same and Janet managed to keep her physical condition a secret from Trevor.

Three months after re-opening the Ann Sanford case number 66, Detective Brown continued working vigorously. He devoted many hours to it, spending less time with his family. His wife knew this case was important to him, so she kept herself and the boys busy. He came home late at night and left early in the mornings. He investigated Sally the housekeeper again and again, nothing surfaced. The detective checked Trevor's alibi. He visited the neighborhood and spoke to several kids and they remembered seeing him riding his bike on that day. After speaking to his teacher he ruled Trevor out as a suspect. He ate, slept, and breathed the Sanford's case. There were so many missing pieces to the puzzle and he simply could not tie it together until his first big break came.

The detective was working late in the office reviewing his notes from Sally when it dawned on him. According to Sally's words, Trevor never went outside to play. He had completely shut the world out after Tyler moved back with his mother. He also recalled that both William and Trevor stated that Trevor was outside riding his bike and playing with the neighborhood kids. *Why today* he thought. The detective scratched his head while looking intently at the picture of his wife and kids as he continued to think.

Why did Trevor go outside to play that day? What made this day special and why would he leave the house if his mother had promised to take him shopping to buy him some new sneakers?

The detective sat at his desk and the letters started to blur before his eyes. He had been over the reports a thousand times in the past months, but the story didn't add up. Continuing to work late into the night, he retrieved the piece of paper he found in Trevor's chest and began to digest it. The design made no sense to him. He roused from his desk and left the office and proceeded to the evidence room. All was quiet in the building. Most of the cops had left for the night. The late shift officers were busy booking criminals. When he entered the evidence room, the night duty policeman was on the phone. He interrupted by asking for the Ann Sanford's file case. The officer placed the call on hold and searched for the box. The officer laid the box on the counter beside the log-out sheet. The detective signed the log and the officer resumed his telephone conversation.

Detective Brown rushed into his office and opened the box. First he read the report over and over, producing a merciless smile. The detective muttered to himself as he looked out the window at the glowing streetlights. He placed the report back inside the box and grabbed the suicide note, studying the note as if he was preparing to take an exam.

"Wait. Wait," he mumbled.

"If Ann typed this note why couldn't I find it on the computer? And how do we know she typed it? Anyone could have typed it, forcing her to sign it and placed it beside her. Maybe that's why there was no blood on the front of the note," he continued. "Perhaps the note was placed there after the shooting."

The detective felt his stomach tighten. In spite of all the evidence he had before him, none of it made sense. He took a yellow legal pad from his desk drawer and drew a line down the middle of the page. On top of the page on the left-hand side he scribbled in big letters, EVIDENCE and on the right-hand side he wrote the word STATUS.

Under the evidence heading he wrote the words, alleged phone call. Next to it he wrote cannot locate call. He skipped a line and wrote the words, suicide note. Next to it he wrote unable to locate on computer, no blood spatters on front of note. Small spatters on back of note were written in bold letters.

He scratched his head again as he stared at his handwriting and said, "If I can explain the phone call and the suicide note then I know I can solve this case."

This situation was a puzzle to him and it must be solved.

"This crime scene was staged," he whispered to himself. The more he stared at his words the more he felt in his heart that Ann didn't attempt to kill herself.

After hours of reviewing the notes from Sally, William, and Trevor's statements, he continued to write on the legal pad. The detective wrote word after word trying to connect the puzzle. Much time had passed since he began his investigation and it had gotten late. He decided to go home and spend the rest of the evening with his family. He clicked off the light switch, closed the door and walked out of the building in the direction of the parking lot.

Several weeks had passed as spring welcomed in summer. There was an excitement in the air as the neighborhood kids were preparing and making plans for their summer break. Trevor had no plans and wished summer would fly by quickly. He knew he had too much time to muse over his mother. There was still no change in Ann's medical condition as she lay peacefully in the same position through winter, spring, and now heading for summer. Her room always remained the same. It was decorated with beautiful vivid plants and the flowery aroma saturated the air.

As the days turned into weeks and the weeks turned into months, Janet's heart condition was at its weakest point. But she kept a smile on her face attempting to fool the little boy who needed her now more than anyone in the world. She had to make a decision to have the operation before it was too late. She placed a call to her doctor and waited for him to call her back.

Some days the visit for Trevor was fun and other days he wished he was lying on the beach, taking in the rays from the sun and watching the waves crushing against the ocean. As he lay across the sofa reminiscing about his life and the wonderful mother he so desperately missed, he began to cry. The guilt of not having a mother for such a long time began to disturb him. He became grumpy and snapped at Janet from time to time. Janet would ignore his behavior because she knew he was under a lot of stress dealing with his terrible ordeal. Janet did everything her seventy-plus year old body would allow to keep a smile on his face, all the while praying for Ann's recovery.

Chapter 25

The stain found on Trevor's baseball cap was tested for Ann's blood. One day while sitting in his office the forensic report was handed to Detective Brown. The DNA conclusively matched Ann's blood. Surprisingly all evidenced pointed to one person and one person only. The investigation had unfolded and hit its moment of truth. After months of investigating Ann Sanford's case the detective had enough evidence to finally issue an arrest warrant. He placed the yellow legal pad on his tidy desk and his eyes glazed with sadness. The detective didn't want to make this arrest but he had to do his job and many months and hours of hard work finally came to an end. As he lingered over the yellow pad drafting an affidavit to support an arrest warrant he began to weep loudly.

"Why, why did he do such a horrible thing?"

It didn't make sense to him, but in his mind his job was finished. It's now up the prosecution to do theirs. After he completed the affidavit, he signed it and slowly placed it in his briefcase. His next assignment was to get the judge's signature and then make the actual arrest. Captain Wilson walked down the hall heading towards Detective Brown's office. He noticed him staring in a daze.

"Good evening Detective," speaking as he passed.

He waved, not wanting the Captain to see the tears in his eyes. This case touched him like no other as he thought about his wife and sons. As he walked slowly to the door he paused and stared at the picture of his family on the wall. He clicked off the light and closed the door.

The early morning sunlight streaked through the detective's window as he drove out the parking lot toward the apartment. The junior cop who accompanied him sat in silence. Detective Brown didn't say a word until they reached their destiny. He turned toward the officer, stared in his eyes and sighed.

"We're here."

It was as though he had to push the words from his lips. He parked the car along the curb and they proceeded up the sidewalk that led to the three-story brick apartment building. They rushed up the stairs to the third floor, anxious to get this very hard task over. The two stood quietly at the door. Then finally Detective Brown let out another sigh and pounded on the door with his hand, generating a loud thump. They waited patiently for someone to open the door. Slowly the door was cracked as brown eyes peeked out. Janet stood behind the protective barrier in her bathrobe.

"Good morning, Ms. Price."

Detective Brown flung opened the door. She quickly tied her robe and then spoke in a stern tone.

"What can I do for you this morning, Detective?"

She noticed the tall lean officer with an ample mustache standing beside him. The officer had an emotionless look on his face with a firm frown.

"We're here to see Trevor," Detective Brown said raspingly.

Janet led them in, wondering why they wanted to see Trevor so early.

"I think he's still asleep. May I ask why you are here to see him? Did something happen to his mother?"

"No, we just need to see him now."

Janet could tell that this was important by the punitive tone of the detective's voice.

"I'll get him for you, wait one second."

As Janet turned toward the direction of the bedroom, the detective intercepted her.

"No Ms. Price," he said rudely. "Take me to him."

By this time Trevor had awakened from the loud bang and talking in the living room. He crept walked down the hall, wearing his blue pajamas. Everyone looked up, very much aware of him standing there wiping the sleep from his eyes.

"Good morning, Sir," Trevor said politely.

Trevor realized something was wrong when he entered the room. The junior officer spoke up when he noticed Trevor approaching.

"Are you Trevor Edward Sanford?"

"Yes," he answered as he yawned, placing his hand over his mouth.

"Trevor Edward Sanford, we have a warrant for your arrest. You must come with us."

He walked quickly over to Trevor and yanked him by the arm.

Janet's jaw went slack, her eyes dilated as she moved to stand beside Trevor to block the officer from him.

"Wait a darn moment," she yelled. "What in the H…E… double hockey sticks is going on?"

Detective Brown gently grabbed Janet and moved her out the way. The junior officer proceeded to handcuff Trevor as Detective Brown held Janet back. Trevor was trembling visibly as he was handcuffed. Then the words that Janet was afraid to hear escaped from the junior officer's small thin lips.

"Trevor Edward Sanford you are under arrest for attempted murder. You have the right to remain silent, if you choose to give up that right; anything you say may be used against you."

Trevor stood there in complete shock with a blank, pitiful expression on his face.

"What do you mean arrest for attempted murder?" Janet screamed. "Why are you doing this to my family?"

Trevor looked at Janet and began to weep. As his breathing sped up, so did Janet's.

"Aunt Janet, tell them to leave me alone. I didn't do anything."

Janet pulled herself from the detective and flung across the room directly in front of Trevor. She burst into tears and hugged him tightly. For several moments she was petrified and quite baffled. She stared at him while holding him in her arms. Her grip was so tight it took both officers several attempts to break them apart.

"No, no, let us be," Janet yelled. Her voice was louder now, harsher. "You're making a big mistake. Trevor didn't harm anyone," Janet begged repeatedly as she let out a long-suffering sigh.

"Ms. Price, please do not make this any harder than it already is. I'm sorry, but we have to do our job." The detective spoke meekly.

By then, Trevor was shaking out of control as the junior officer tried to separate them.

"Aunt Janet, help me, don't let them take me. I didn't do anything wrong. Please help," he yelled over and over again.

"Please stop," Janet pleaded as her face tightened angrily.

"He's only a little boy, and who in the world did he try to murder? Please I'm begging you, let him go."

Janet was practically out of her bathrobe and nearly dragging Trevor. Janet and Trevor were both crying out of control as the junior officer finally managed to separate them. The officer proceeded to shove Trevor toward the door. Detective Brown held Janet as he tried to calm her down.

"Wait, I'm going with you," Janet said as she finally broke free from the detective.

"No you can't Ms. Price. You can come down to the precinct later. But we must take him with us, alone."

Detective Brown tried to be gentle with her. He spoke to her as easy as he could muster because he knew this was hard on her and she was not a young woman. His emotions surprised her because she always thought of him as a cold, heartless man. Trevor was sobbing and fighting as the officer used force to remove him from the apartment. Janet could see the terror that had overcome him. His fear and fury was obvious. Janet was *pissed*.

"Please, Aunt Janet don't let them take me. I'm scared and I don't want to go." His tiny voice was hoarse and strained with sadness.

"I didn't do anything wrong?"

The junior officer pushed Trevor through the hallway and down the stairs while Janet followed in her bare feet.

"Trevor listen to me? I will get you out I promise. Don't say a word until you speak to your attorney. You hear me?"

She repeated those words as she jogged beside him. Trevor nodded as he was pushed along the sidewalk. The look on his face said it all. His face was red and puffy-covered with tears and pain. Detective Brown opened the patrol car door as the officer pushed Trevor into the back seat.

"Trevor, I'm on my way, remember what I told you. Don't say a word and remember I love you. Everything will be cleared up as soon as possible. Baby, don't be afraid and stay strong."

She looked at Trevor with accusing eyes. Those were the last words he was able to hear as the car door slammed in his face. Janet stood barefoot on the dirty sidewalk and watched Trevor in the back seat of the patrol car shivering with fear. He peered out the window of the car at Janet as they pulled out the parking lot onto the street. Janet looked back at Trevor. He looked more nervous than anything, he had grown feeble. Time seemed suspended during those few moments as Janet watched the patrol car turn the corner. A hint of panic snaked its way into Janet's heart and it was beating fast and hard as a sharp tingle shot up and down her spine. She sprinted up the stairs as quickly as her tired ailing body would allow and began to pace the living room floor appearing dizzy. Fear had seized her and she collapsed onto the floor with continual weeping. She was in pure agony as the words of the junior officer rung in her ears. She could hear the ringing sound and those words being repeated like the howling of a strong powerful wind. She clamped her hands over her ears wishing the ringing would stop. Sorrow, anguish, and pain had taken over her like a woman in labor. She telephoned William and tried to explain to him what had just happened, but she couldn't find the right words to say. William could tell by her tone that she was in a considerable amount of agony. Janet hung up the phone and started to cry.

Fifteen minutes later, there was a knock at the door. She opened the locked door and was greeted with a hug. She leaned over and buried her face on William's shoulder. She was afraid for Trevor and as the hours slipped away it was getting difficult to conceal the terror she had endured.

Chapter 26

Paul Domingues rushed to the Juvenile Detention Court once he received the call from William. When Trevor entered the dimly lit room, a smile broke across his lips. Finally he saw a face that he recognized. He had already been logged in, fingerprinted, searched, and photographed. Paul was sitting in a brown swing-around chair. He was wearing a black double-breasted suit with a bright red tie. When the guard relieved Trevor of the handcuffs, he rubbed his wrist temporarily and greeted Paul with a handshake. There were three empty chairs stacked around the table. Trevor noticed a seat closest to Paul. As he plopped down in the chair next to the large man his body began to relax.

The room was dull and gloomy, and the masculine smell of Paul's cologne, which dawdled in the air didn't make it easier to breathe. Paul encouraged the little frightened boy. He further instructed him that everything was going to be okay. He began explaining to Trevor what had just happened to him. The more he talked the sadder Trevor became. Finally interrupted him Trevor spoke in his naïve childlike state.

"What's going to happen to me Mr. Domingues?"

Paul removed a legal pad and some documents from his briefcase and continued to speak. He sat up in the chair, looked at Trevor seriously and explained what was going on and how the legal system worked.

"Trevor, do you know why you are here?" he asked as he reviewed his notes from their first meeting.

"No, sir," Trevor answered quickly as he looked intently at the husky guard who stood quietly in the corner.

"You're here for attempted murder. According to the state of Virginia, they say they have proof that you tried to kill your mother."

There was a deathly quietness in the room before Trevor gathered up the courage to speak.

"Kill my mother!" he screamed out in a high-pitched sound. "I didn't do such an awful thing. I love my mother and I wish she was here with me now."

He placed his hands over his face and began to weep. He was paralyzed with fear, he knew he didn't belong there, but how was he going to convince the state that they had the wrong person. Paul tried to keep his voice steady as he spoke gently to him. He asked Trevor questions about his whereabouts, watching him closely as he spoke. Trevor's answers were convincing as he stared directly into Paul's eyes. At the end of the questions Paul instructed him to dry his tears, handing him a handkerchief from his pocket.

"Trevor we have to go in front of the judge for the bond hearing." Paul announced as he glanced at his notes.

"What's a bond hearing?" Trevor asked as he handed Paul back his soiled handkerchief.

"A bond hearing is when you go in front of a judge to find out how much it will cost to release you until the trail date. Do you understand son."

Paul spoke with a crooked smile. Trevor slowly shook his head, acknowledging his response.

"The arraignment is scheduled for today at 2:00 don't talk to anyone regarding this case except for me. Understand?" Paul ordered with authority.

Trevor nodded again as he watched Paul place the documents back into his briefcase.

"I brought you some clothes from home for the hearing." Paul added coolly and exchanged a stare.

"Trevor I need you to stay composed and look neatly as possible when you go in front of the judge. Can you do that?"

Trevor nodded yes.

"Remember, son everything will be okay. I will try my best to have you home for dinner."

His comment eased Trevor's slim worried face. They shared a private smile before Paul left the room.

Meanwhile back at Janet's small apartment, she and William waited for the phone call from Paul. Janet was in the bathroom when the call came. William answered, fearing the worst. Janet knew he was speaking to Paul when she entered the kitchen.

"Okay, Paul I understand," he nodded as he held the phone in his right hand while reaching for Janet's hand with his left hand. They clasped hands and Janet listened closely.

"We'll be there," William said as he hung up the phone.

"What's going on William?" Janet asked as she let loose his hand and waited for the news.

Speaking in a nervous stutter, William said, "The arraignment is scheduled at 2:00 today in the Juvenile Detention Court."

"What's an arraignment hearing?" Janet asked lowering her head and sighing.

"It's when the attorney announces an innocence or guilty plea for the defendant and the judge sets the bail."

Janet threw up her arms in the air, struggling to speak and replied, "I guess I need to find something to wear—can't show up in court wearing this ragged old robe huh."

Janet and William raced to the Juvenile Courthouse. It was a short drive, as they rode in silence, lost in their own thoughts. Once inside the swarming halls, they pushed their way through the crowd. They stopped at the directory and then asked an officer standing nearby for directions.

"This way, Janet," he said as he grabbed her hand and escorted her down the hall.

When they reached the designated room, Janet stopped cold before she entered. After getting herself together, they slowly proceeded through the swinging doors. The courtroom was packed; William's eyes scanned the room, spotting an empty seat on the second row. While holding her Bible close to her heart and whispering a silent prayer, Janet followed close behind. They sat down on the hard bench. Knowing how hard this must be for her, William held Janet's hand as they waited patiently for Trevor to enter the crammed full room. In the short time

Janet had last seen Trevor, he had be processed through the legal system. Janet felt a big sigh of relief as a strong surge raced through her body when she spotted him coming through the side door. Trevor was crying but tried to hide his tears when he entered the room. His tears eased up when he looked up and saw Janet. His face was swollen, his tiny lips were dry and his eyes were tearing. As the guard unlocked his handcuffs, he made eye contact with Janet. She winked at him, which caused him to smile. The blue pajamas she remembered him wearing had been replaced with a freshly pressed white collar shirt, a pair of blue slacks and a pair of black loafers. He was no longer Trevor Edward Sanford, an innocent young boy. According to the state his new identity was inmate number 55669.

It took everything within her to remain seated and not reach out to hold him. While staring at the back of Trevor's small oval shape head, she wished that this was just a dream—and with a quick blink of her eyes, the terrible nightmare would be over and they would be enjoying lunch in her tiny two-bedroom apartment or sitting in the hospital with Ann.

The bailiff who stood in the corner strolled over to the front the podium and watched as the courtroom continued to fill up with people and attorneys. Everyone was waiting for their case to be called. Janet was sweating profusely, glancing around the room watching the fear on the other faces. The arresting officer sauntered down the aisle towards the front of the judge's bench, showing off his tall, lanky body. When Janet looked at him, she gripped her Bible firmly in her hand, forcing her body into a numb state. As time drew near she sat as transfixed looking at the large clock on the wall. From time-to-time she would angrily glance at the officer. Once they exchanged a quick look but she hastily turned her head. Sitting quietly still and clutching her Bible, she thought of Ann's suicide note. To the state that note seemed nonexistent.

At exactly 2:00 the bailiff spoke. "All rise. Court is now in session. The Honorable Judge Hewitt Vance now presiding."

Janet struggled to her feet. Her legs were weak from fear and her heart was beating rapidly. When the judge entered, everyone in the room became completely still.

He was an old wrinkled man with thinning grayish hair. The black robe he wore was accompanied with a white shirt and black tie. The round gold-framed glasses that straddled his aging face sat on the bridge of his nose. When he finally spoke, his voice was deep and powerful. Each syllable carried a thunderous sound that sent chills down your spin and put fear in your heart.

The bailiff returned to his original corner and watched the judge read the rules of court. Janet stared at the judge, trying to listen to his words. She could see his lips moving but a sound didn't register.

Please Lord, she thought, *I want this to end once and for all.*

Her tiny comfy apartment crossed her mind and she wished she was there now while her eyes roamed the room. Everything was happening so swiftly.

When Trevor's case was finally called, Janet quickly sat up straight and stared at the judge with apprehension, closed her eyes and muttered a prayer. She could tell Trevor had begun to cry again by the fluttering of his eye lids. As Paul addressed the judge, Trevor struggled to sit contently with his head tucked in his hands. Janet felt her heart beating wildly while listening to Paul's plea of not guilty and his argument. His performance was brilliant and now she could see how he could afford such a luxury office. At that moment she realized he was good at his job. The judge was very stern and seemed reluctant to set bail. He looked at his records and read his notes through the glasses that barely sat on his face. He glanced at Paul, Trevor, and the Prosecutor and spoke in an authoritative reasonable tone.

"Since the defendant has never been in trouble with the law, bail is set for two hundred and fifty thousand dollars."

He rapped the gravel against the desk. Janet and William sat engrossed and did not speak because they were both overcome with so much fear and anxiety that words simply would not come out. William tried to be calm as he swept away a sickening feeling. His body began to shake when the dollar amount was announced.

"Two hundred and fifty thousand dollars," he whispered. "Where in the world are we going to get that kind of money from?"

Janet didn't comment knowing she didn't have a dime to offer. Trevor was handcuffed and removed from the courtroom. She tried to get a glimpse of his face before the door slammed behind him. Neither Janet nor William could move. They sat shocked and dazed by the words of the judge. A gentle tap on the shoulder by Paul snapped their attention back in the courtroom. They followed him out the courtroom up the hall toward the exit. The long day wore Janet down. She was feeling a bit fatigued by the time they reached the end of the hall. She began to feel pains in her chest and her breathing became complex. She noticed a lobby at the end of the hallway and asked if she could rest a bit. Paul and William grabbed her arms and escorted her to a chair by the window. While she tried to regain her composure, Paul raced over to a nearby deli to get her some water. When he disappeared around the corner Janet, struggling to breathe, looked at her brother and managed to say, "William what are we going to do?" After a long silence she continued. "Where are we going to get the money to bail Trevor out of jail? We can't leave him in this horrible place. He's only a baby. What would Ann do if she knew this was happening to him?"

William watched his mother-like sister struggling to speak and breathe normally.

"Why William? Why did God place this great burden upon our family?"

She paused and gazed at William and began sobbing even harder. *Nothing seemed fair anymore*, Janet thought as she let out a heavy gulp.

William turned his face away from her and began crying quietly. Each tear that rolled down his face meant something to him. He cried for Trevor, Ann, Janet, and the tragedy that had unfortunately attacked their happy family. Sitting across from Janet, William saw the misery in her eyes and he didn't know how to respond. He scooted his chair closer, gripped his sister's hand and said with a scowl.

"Cheer up Janet. God did not place more upon us than we can bear. He'll make a way and we'll come up with the money. We must place this, as everything else, in His hands and leave it there."

Janet listened as William spoke. His soothing responds brought an ingenious smile upon her face. He didn't talk much but when he did, what he said always made a lot of sense. His confidence reassured her.

"You're right, William. Why am I testing my faith? What appears wrong now will turn out right later."

She wiped her tears and smiled with a loving nod. In her heart she did understand. William and Janet continued chatting in a low-key manner until Paul returned carrying a bottle of spring water.

Chapter 27

The guard transferred Trevor to a holding cell. As they rushed down the long bright corridor, Trevor knew this horrible place would be his home until they could get the money to bail him out. After making a quick left turn at the end of the hall, they stopped in front of a tiny grimy cell. The guard removed the handcuffs from his right wrist and signaled for the door to be opened at the same time. Trevor stood in silence, trying not to panic. Once the handcuffs were removed he looked subdued. When the door opened the guard gestured Trevor inside. He walked into the cell with fear. The cell door closed behind him with a loud clang, and now he was in solitary. The cell was dark and clammy. The moldy smell in the air was an undesirable scent. As he stood in the nasty cell he was afraid to touch anything and move. From the corner of his eye, he saw a round tarnished sink, a single rusty toilet and a defiled twin mattress. He stared upward toward the ceiling, trying to distract himself from the tragedy that had befallen him since morning. There was no place for him to go but where he was.

Unable to control his fear any longer he lay on the stale mattress, buried his face in his arms and began to weep. Tears were streaking down his cheeks. After a while, Trevor tried to stop himself from shivering from the moist chill that hung in the air. His arms and legs were numb from the dampness and his breathing began to suffer from the harsh smells. His heart was racing and he thought he was having a panic attack. He had never been this frightened and cold in his life as he was right now. He tried to keep himself warm by briskly rubbing the goose bumps that covered his arms and legs. He looked around the room for a blanket but there was none.

As he lay across the old lumpy mattress, he gripped his stomach, feeling a billow of nausea coming forth. He placed his hand over his mouth, jumped from the mattress and ran to the filthy toilet. After several minutes ejecting the contents of his stomach, he splashed his face with cold water and returned to the hard uncomfortable mattress. He tossed and turned, trying to find a comfortable spot.

Trevor lay curled up like a new born baby and positioned himself close to the wall. He unwillingly cried even louder than before and could not stop shivering from the cold. He rocked back and forth, moaning. After being alone for several hours it was now dark in the room except for a dim light that came from a square shaped window high above his head. He wished he could have fallen asleep as soon as his body hit the mattress but he found it hard. Instead, he flipped back and forth and the moaning and weeping continued most of the night until falling off into an uninterrupted sleep.

The thoughts of Trevor arrested for murder tortured Janet's troubled mind, keeping her up most of the night. When sleep finally paid her a visit, she awoke in a cold sweat. She instinctively reached for the clock beside her bed and was stunned when she saw that it was 7:00 in the morning. Although she had been asleep for several hours, it felt like days. She dashed into the bathroom to dry her soggy face, gently stroking herself with the hand towel that was lying on the sink. She tried to keep busy the remainder of the morning. On impulse she grabbed her knitting bag and began working on the sweater she was knitting for Ann. At this point, doing anything to keep her mind off Trevor and Ann's predicament was much needed. While knitting, she would glance at the clock and wonder if Trevor was okay.

Deciding to take a short break from the task of knitting, she walked to the 4th Street deli to get a newspaper. When Mr. Chan saw her, he hurried over to assist. Janet's greeting to him was barely a whisper and she utilized a lot of strength just to do that. She shuffled back to her apartment because it was blazing hot. At noon, the temperature had hit a record breaking high of 101 degrees.

At home, she began to prepare a smoked turkey sandwich. After removing the turkey from the refrigerator and two slices of bread from the breadbox, the telephone rang. It was a collect call from the Juvenile

Detention Center. She accepted the call, knowing it was Trevor. Janet waited for the recording to stop.

"Trevor, is this you?"

"Yes ma'am."

"How are you, Baby?"

"Aunt Janet, I'm scared and it's so cold in here." He grunted.

Janet could hear the affliction in his voice and it cut into her heart. For a second she was afraid to speak for fear of letting him down, not knowing what he was facing while being locked up.

"Can you bring me my white long johns and sneakers?"

"Where are your sneakers?" Janet asked as she piled the turkey on the bread.

"They're in the closet in the den." Trevor's top lip quivered as he asked about his mother.

"Your mother is the same."

"Can you kiss her for me?" he asked as he choked on a lump in his throat.

"I will, Baby, as soon as I see her," she replied as cheerful as she could.

"Aunt Janet, when do you think I can come home?"

"Soon—Uncle William is at a bondsman's office as we speak, trying to get the money to bail you out. Can you hold on until he gets the money?"

Again there was silence. He sighed and answered the question to end the long hush that had fallen between them.

"How long will I have to stay here?" His lips barely moved as he spoke due to his fears. "I'm scared and at night it gets extremely cold. Last night was one of the worst nights of my life. I got sick and the food they serve is awful—it's worse than hospital food."

Trevor paused. "My body was so cold and I could not get warm. I can't take this another night."

His heart saddened and depression set in at the thought of spending another night in that appalling place. Trevor took a deep breath, hoping that he wouldn't break down and cry.

"Trevor listen to me, you must hold on and keep your faith. You'll be home before you know it."

"Aunt Janet why do they think I tried to kill my…?"

She interrupted him before he could finish the sentence.

"Trevor, I know you didn't do this and the Lord knows," she said a bit hesitantly. "What you're going through is temporary. It's just a big misunderstanding," Janet said. "With Paul's help and our faith, everything will work out."

"Auntie, please help me! I can't do this. The secret is too hard."

"What secret," Janet repeated.

After a brief pause he said, "Never mind."

His secret was his mother's secret—though it appeared not to be a prevalent one with Trevor. Janet listened with great concern but it was much too hard to understand his fears, as she had never experienced anything like this before. She felt helpless even to the point where she could not control the tears that dripped down her face.

"Wait a minute," Janet said mildly. "There's nothing placed before us that is too hard for us to handle. We will get through this—do you hear me?"

Her voice was frantic as she swabbed away her tears.

"Trevor this is life and sometimes life isn't fair, but you cannot be afraid to face it."

She could feel the misfortune that was tearing at Trevor's heart. Again there was silence and then Trevor softly said, "Well Auntie I have to hang up now."

"Okay take care of yourself and do everything they tell you. You have your whole life before you and everything will be fine."

"When will I see you again?"

"You will see my pretty face tomorrow."

Trevor tried to stifle a chuckle but a deep laugh managed to work its way from his mouth.

"I'm grateful to you, Aunt Janet. Thanks for believing in me."

Janet grinned because she was happy that she was able to make him laugh.

"I love you, Baby and I'll see you tomorrow."

The beep that disconnected his voice abruptly ended. Suddenly Trevor wasn't afraid anymore. Though he could neither see nor touch her; the love that resonated over the phone was strong. Janet placed the receiver on the cradle and found herself unwillingly sprawled on the kitchen floor. She broke down in tears letting out several gulps as her heart skipped a beat. After her sobbing heartache she carefully arose and wiped her face with her hands. Janet managed to smile, overwhelmed by the heart-warming love that flowed through her. For now she had lost her appetite. She wrapped the sandwich in foil and placed it in the refrigerator on the bottom rack.

Just as Janet had gotten herself together, William telephoned. They spoke briefly about Trevor's bond. William listened intently as Janet told him about their conversation. They ended the call. Janet retreated to her bedroom to read the newspaper, hoping tomorrow will bring better results for Trevor's situation. As she lay across her bed with the paper scattered about, she realized she wasn't even interested in reading the news today. She neatly folded the paper and laid it on the nightstand. Janet's mind began to wander and she allowed it to do so. Then she remembered her promise to Trevor. She went into the den to retrieve the long johns and sneakers he had requested. Janet began to hum while she searched the closet for the items. She looked in the clothes hamper and in all the drawers but was unsuccessful.

"Now where can they be?" she mumbled under her breath as she searched every room of the apartment.

Twenty minutes had passed and it was apparent that the long johns were not there.

I'll just have to buy him a new pair, she thought.

Upon re-entering the closet in the den, she fanned away hanging clothes from her view and then spotted the sneakers tucked away in the corner. When she bent down to grab the sneakers, a big smile came across her face, for she knew then she was going to see Trevor in the morning to deliver his things. As she lifted the sneakers from the floor, the floorboard popped loose.

"I must fix this before someone gets hurt," she said aloud.

She sprinted to the hall closet for her toolbox, retrieved a nail and hammer, and returned to the den. After she removed articles of clothing obstructing her view, she bent down on her knees with the nail and hammer in her hand. While preparing to insert the nail into the wood, she spotted an item sticking up from under the damaged wood.

"What is this?"

She lifted the wood and pulled the foreign object from its place. As she glanced at the strange article she wondered what it was and to whom it belonged. She carefully examined the outside and finally realized it was a book.

Why would a book be here? She thought.

Tossing the book on the sofa, she reattached the floorboard and slowly lifted her aging body. She brushed her aching knees with her hand and returned the hammer to the toolbox.

Janet was lonely but now she had something to focus on. It took one call by Trevor to set her mind in the right direction and she had to follow his request to the end. Knowing she had to go to the store to purchase the long johns, she ironed a sleeveless summer dress and then took a bath. She quickly dressed and combed her hair.

The sun was scorching, as the temperature had risen to 104 degrees. Janet didn't want to leave her cool comfy apartment but she had to do this for Trevor. *A little heat doesn't hurt anybody*, she groaned to herself as she grabbed her purse. When she found her wallet, she emptied the money out into her hand as she made a quick tally. Despair settled upon her face when she realized that she only had two dollars and twenty-five cents. Janet rushed to her bedroom to collect the change jar that she had hidden underneath her bed. As she poured the change onto the bed, she slowly counted three dollars and seventy-five cents. Scooping the change, she placed it in her wallet. She had used the change from time-to-time to make ends meet but she had no clue that this was all that remained.

Janet grabbed the phone to call Mae. As she waited for Mae to answer, she could feel her blood surge throughout her body. The answering machine came on, so she hung up feeling a bit sad.

"Where am I going to get the money to buy Trevor's long johns?"

She moaned because she knew six dollars wasn't enough. Janet paced back and forth in the kitchen. She knew a call to William was not warranted because all the money he had was tied up for Trevor's bail. As she continued to pace her heart was breaking because she wanted so desperately to see his smile in the morning. Janet paced and prayed. Then she walked into the living room and plopped down on the sofa, praying fast now that she would not let him down. The thought of him being cold another night and frightened made her break out in a sweat. She knew she had to buy him a pair of long johns one way or the other.

She dragged her body into the kitchen to get a glass of water to cool down. As she stood over the sink imbibing the cold water, she felt piercing pains in her chest.

"Lord not now," she said, as she grabbed her chest and leaned against the counter.

Heart, please don't fail me. She thought.

Janet eased over to the dining room table and sat down. Sharp pains shot through her body and she began to weep.

"I can't let him down. I will not let him freeze another night in that pit."

Janet spoke to herself as she continued to hold her chest trying to sooth the rapidly firing pain. The pain eased up tremendously and the thought of going to a pawnshop popped in her mind. Jenkins pawnshop was several blocks away. She stood slowly to her feet, realizing that the pawnshop was her only alternative. She raced into the living room to check to see if she had anything of value. After searching the living room she was sadder now because she had nothing to pawn. Janet went into the bedroom and emptied the contents of her jewelry box on the dresser. She had several pieces of costume jewelry, a silver bracelet, one broken watch and a black velvet sack.

"This junk is worthless," she mumbled.

She placed the items back in the box except for the black velvet sack. As she dropped the contents of the pouch in her hand, a beautiful pearl necklace fell out. Her eyes opened wide bringing a smile to her face. Janet had worn the pearl necklace only twice and she remembered the day she received it. Ann, Ed, Trevor, and Tyler had given her the gorgeous necklace for a Christmas present three years ago.

"My necklace. But I can't pawn this precious gem. It means so much to me."

She placed the necklace back into the sack and dropped the velvet sack in her purse. She continued to search for something—anything of value. Janet was now beat-up and exhausted but she refused to give up. While pacing her bedroom she knew this was it. She didn't have any money, or anything of value to pawn. Up to now Janet didn't realize she was poor and this realization made Janet afraid and angry. She picked up her pillow from off the bed and hurled it across the room. Recognizing all the years she had lived—her life came down to six dollars—and a turkey sandwich on the bottom rack of the refrigerator. Janet couldn't help but break down and cry for herself. The sounds of her sobs were very loud because in her heart she had let the little boy down she vowed to protect. Then a little smirk escaped her trembling lips because she realized she would see his face in the morning whether she had a pair of long johns or not. She decided to undress, removing her dress to reveal her slip. As she walked over to the hall closet to hang up her dress, she looked up and there she saw a box.

It's not over yet, Janet thought as she reached for the box and pulled it from the top shelf. She rushed to her bedroom reached for the Bible that lay opened by her nightstand and grabbed the white envelope taped to the last page. She quickly dressed again and whispered, "Hallelujah."

Chapter 28

Janet locked the door and hurried as best she could to Jenkins'
pawnshop in the thick, palpable heat. Up Pine Street, and turned left onto
Main Street, proceeding at a snail pace. As the summer's heat hit its
peak, Janet was eager to shop for Trevor. She didn't mind the terrible
humidity. Finally, after walking two more blocks, she spotted the
pawnshop and glanced at the door, afraid to go on. Several minutes later,
she took a deep breath and went inside.

The store was tidy and merchandise was neatly displayed. The
furnishings were old but elegant. She rushed to the counter trying not to
bump into anything as a dark-skinned woman approached her and
greeted her with a smile.

"Miss, do you need any help?" She asked kindly.

Janet panted for air because she wanted to turn around and go
home.

"Yes," Janet began slowly, as she reached into her purse and
handed her a box. "I would like to pawn these."

The woman laid the box on the counter, handling it with care.
When she opened the box, a small laugh broke across her lips.

"Napkins," she responded. "Miss, these napkins are beautiful but
I'm sorry I cannot accept them. We only accept things of value."

Janet stood in the middle of the floor. She was more afraid now
than before. As she looked closely at the woman, she took another deep
breath and then spoke clearly and slowly.

"But they are worth something. These napkins have been in my
family for over a hundred years."

Obviously the woman was getting upset now, grinning in a
maddening way.

"Listen, Miss, my boss would fire me for accepting them." She quickly closed the box and handed it to Janet. "Do you have anything else—like jewelry?"

The woman asked staring at Janet's watch. Janet remembered the pearl necklace that lay at the bottom of her purse, but she knew she could not let that go. She tried her best to act as though she knew what she was doing, but her body expression betrayed her real actions of fear.

"Wait! Listen to me."

Janet stepped back, standing in disarray. Sweat rolled down her forehead.

"Miss," she began quietly, "these napkins are worth something. These napkins are the most valuable thing to me outside of my family. You see these napkins once laid on the table of President Abraham Lincoln."

Janet cleared her throat as she felt her mouth drying.

"My great grandmother was a cook of Abraham Lincoln and they were given to her by President Lincoln himself," Janet added.

"Look!"

She opened the box and pointed to the initials AL engraved in each corner. The woman's eyes opened wild with enthusiasm.

"What are you saying?" the woman demanded.

There was a long pause. Janet looked up towards the ceiling and said, "Miss, I'm telling you the truth. I do not want to pawn them but I need the money and I don't have any other choice. These napkins have been in my family for generations and they mean so much to me."

Janet turned her focus on the lady while trying to remain calm. Letting go of the napkins would be extremely hard for her. She tried to conceal her emotions when she reminisced about the time when Trevor asked her what the initials 'AL' meant. She remembered telling him that they stood for Auntie's Love. Janet looked directly into the woman's eyes, unable to move, frozen. Though she didn't show it, Janet was nervous and wanted to leave that very moment. Suddenly she reached into her purse and pulled out a document in an envelope wrapped in plastic and handed it to the woman. There it was right in her hand, the official certificate of authenticity. The woman looked at Janet and realized that she was serious. As she held the certificate of authenticity she realized Janet's napkins were the real deal.

"Miss, I'm sorry for not believing in you but we get all kinds of characters in here, if you know what I mean."

The woman was visibly embarrassed. Within a few minutes she was behind the counter writing a receipt. She handed twenty-five dollars and the receipt to Janet, grinning joyously.

"I need to keep the certificate so I can show my boss if you don't mind."

Janet smiled at the woman and the woman smiled back. She agreed with happiness because she now had the money to purchase Trevor's long johns. As she moved swiftly out the building stuffing the receipt and twenty-five dollars in her purse, a haze of humility smacked her in the face. A heat wave had moved in and didn't budge. She wiped the sweat that had accumulated from her forehead as she realized that the heat was becoming too much for her. From the corner of her eye she noticed a jewelry shop. She wanted to stop in and inquire about shortening her pearl necklace and making two bracelets from the remaining links. When she opened the door, the bell rang and a salesman appeared. She beamed happily at him. As she retrieved the black velvet sack from her purse and explained to him what she wanted, he nodded in understanding. The cost to separate the pearls was affordable but she realized she didn't have enough money to make two bracelets from the remaining strand. For now, the necklace was fine with her.

Janet stepped away from the salesman and sat by the door enjoying the cool air blowing out of the air conditioner. She glanced at the table and picked up a magazine to read while waiting for the necklace. The salesman waved Janet over to him.

"I'm finished Miss."

Janet inspected the necklace and to her it looked lovely. She quickly placed the necklace and the two links back into the black velvet sack and carefully put them in her purse and paid the bill.

"Come back anytime to get the bracelets fixed," the salesman said as he handed her the receipt and a business card.

She nodded with a smile and left.

Janet entered her chilly, cozy apartment, pleased with herself. Her day had been hectic with all the things she felt she needed to complete before her visit with Trevor the next morning. She was still afraid for him, but at least she was happy that she didn't have to let him down. Today had begun as a nightmare but turned out okay. Janet finally finished everything with more than an hour of daylight left to spare. She sunk into a chair trying to regain her strength from the long walk in the scorching heat. Remembering the turkey sandwich she had earlier, she entered the kitchen and demolished it within a few bites.

Several minutes later, her body began to relax so she flipped on the TV to watch the evening news. Janet yawned sleepily and before she knew it, she had slipped into a peaceful sleep. As she napped, the TV continued to blast away. The phone awakened her. She rushed into the kitchen and grabbed it but the caller had already hung-up. All was dark in the apartment except for the light from the TV casting a gray illumination. Realizing that it was 8:30, she hurried into the bathroom and turned on the faucet to prepare her bath. She undressed, throwing her clothes on the floor. When Janet finished her bath, she donned her silk pajamas. The house was very quiet and dark as she realized she was going to be spending another night alone. She walked around the living room and closed all the curtains. Then she made sure the apartment was secure. She entered the den and pulled down the shades. She grabbed the sneakers and tossed them in the bag with the long johns, scooping up the book as she headed for her bedroom to call it a night. As she sat on the edge of her bed, with inquisitiveness she opened the book. What she was about to read—no one or nothing could have prepared her for it.

Chapter 29

Janet stared closely at the book, realizing that it was not a book, but a diary.

"Whose is this?" She mumbled the words under her breath as though someone would answer. Then she saw the handwriting and recognized that it belonged to Trevor. She hesitated for a moment, turned to the first page and begun to read.

Dear Diary,

Today is Monday. It's been three months since the death of my stepfather Ed. Today at school my teacher yelled at me for not paying attention. I was daydreaming about my mother. She's in the hospital and I miss her. Hopefully she will be home this week. I can't wait to see her. Must go now. Aunt Be is calling for me. Will write later.

She read in silence in the mutedly lit room. As the dark hour of the night enclosed her bedroom, she continued to read.

Dear Diary,

Today is Friday. It's been four months since the death of my stepfather Ed and I miss him so much. My mother is still depressed and sad. My mother, Tyler, and I will be leaving this weekend for our seven-day cruise. I'm looking forward to it so that we can take a break from this house and the sadness that has moved in. That's it for now. Will write later.

Janet was stunned as her mouth flew opened. All this time, she had no idea Trevor was keeping a journal. She wanted to close the book, but her heart and mind pushed her to keep reading. She continued reading seemingly without breathing. As she read, the sounds of loud music coming from a car in the parking lot reached her apartment. She ignored the music and kept reading to herself. Her mind was so intrigued with Trevor's writings she couldn't put it down.

Dear Diary,

It's been five months since the death of my stepfather. My mother is sadder than ever. I cooked her breakfast and brought it to her in bed. She looks a mess. Her hair is mangled to her head and heavy rings around her eyes prove that she is not getting enough rest. My mother has been in and out of court, fighting for Tyler and finally she lost. He's been gone two weeks now and I miss him dearly. Our life will never be the same. My mother took a turn for the worst when she lost Tyler and I don't know what it will take to make her happy again. Her sadness has overcome her and it's tearing my heart to pieces. I don't know if I can take much more. Must go now, time to say my prayers and go to bed. Will write later.

Janet's heart froze as she read his words. She covered her mouth to hide her frown.

"Poor Trevor," she whispered to herself. "I had no inkling he was going through this."

Lost in her own world and concerned with Ann's welfare after losing Ed, Tyler, and the baby, she did not see his misery. As Janet continued to read she suddenly became morose and serious. Janet was flabbergasted by his words, and there was a hint of sadness in her sleepy eyes. She was not able to put the diary away; her head throbbed with a terrible headache from the constant reading. She laid the diary on the bed and went into the kitchen to get an aspirin and a glass of water. When she returned to her bedroom she reached for the diary. As she flipped the pages her eyes heightened with fear.

Dear Diary,

Today was awful. My mother has been weeping all day. Ed died on this day six months ago. She's unable to get out of bed, staying in her room all day. I would check on her from time to time. She tried her best to hide her tears from me but I could see them clearly on her worried face. I didn't sleep well last night. I tossed and turned listening to the mourning and suffering that came from her room. I can't take it any longer. I wish I didn't have to be here. I wished that I was dead, but if I left she would have nothing to live for.

Janet felt Trevor's words were a struggle for him to write. Regardless, she continued reading, captivated in her finding. She hesitated then slowly continued.

Why, did this happen to her, she didn't deserve this. She's a wonderful person who deserved the best but for now only sadness lives here. Sometimes I think about running away, but she would worry about me and that would cause her to be even sadder. Lord what can I do? Please help us and come by here now. We need you more than we ever did before. Guide me and give me strength because I am now weak and I'm only a child. Must go now. Will write later.

Janet was in a state of shock. It took a few moments for what she had just read to sink in. Intense and shaken, Janet laid stone still on the bed, staring up at the ceiling tightly gripping the diary in her right hand. Her mind worked wrathfully, trying to analyze Trevor's sentences. She closed her eyes, trying not to cry. Janet attempted to get off the bed, but her muscles had tightened so, she almost felt paralyzed. She finally pulled her body from the bed.

"My poor baby."

She blurted out as she strode across the room, still holding on to the diary. Until now she hadn't realized how serious this was. It was now midnight and she has been reading for several hours. She knew she had to get some sleep because of the long ride to the detention center. Janet felt her stomach churning as she continued combing the diary. Finally reaching the last five pages, she took a deep breath and read further.

Dear Diary,

Today my mother asked me to do something that's the most awful thing I could ever imagine. It's so bad, I can't even write it. Please God help my mother and remove that feeling. It's making me sad and I can't take it any longer. Must go now, Will try to write later.

Janet felt her heart skip a beat by reading Trevor's sentences. She wanted to quit but her heart was glued to his words.

Dear Diary,

Again my mother asked me to do it. She told me that I would have a better life with Aunt Janet and that she has failed miserably as my mother. She told me if I didn't do it, she would. She said this was the only way and that if I did it I would be setting her free. I told her no and left her room. All night I could hear her weeping. I slept on the floor of her bedroom door, praying and asking God to help her.

Janet placed the diary on the bed and raced into the kitchen to get a glass of ice. As she reached for the glass her hands was shaking and a big ball of nerves had tied a knot in her stomach. She returned to her room and located her bottle and poured a glass of liquor and quickly guzzled it down.

Dear Diary,

After weeks of my mother's crying, my heart couldn't muster it any longer. I finally gave in and told her I could help her. The biggest smile streaked her face. She scripted me on how to do it and that I had to promise never to tell anyone our secret. She told me I couldn't tell Aunt Janet, Aunt Bernita, Tyler and not even Charles. She said I had to carry this to my grave and 'that a secret is only a secret if you don't tell.' I had to promise her with the pinky finger. She kissed me and told me everything would be fine if I carried out the plan. I asked my mother why she needed me to do it and she told me that if she did it she could not repent, but if I did I could go to God and repent for my sin and God would forgive me. I know this is wrong but I love my mother and I can't live like this. My mother has the world fooled and only I really know her broken and suffering heart.

After reading those dreadful words Janet poured another drink and downed it with one big gulp. Her eyes were tired from reading and her heart rate wouldn't slow down. She closed the diary and wept silently to herself. But she knew she had to keep reading. She reopened the journal and continued reading.

Dear Diary,

After weeks of rehearsal tomorrow is the day. We have planned everything to the t. We practiced every detail. Fake the story about the mysterious phone call. My mother told me what to do and say. Each day like clock-work she would drill me, making sure nothing was missed. She told me if I practiced, when they question me they would not be able to catch me in a lie because it will be the truth. This is the plan. I would come home from school during recess and remove all my clothes, socks, and shoes and meet her in the bedroom. She would leave a pair of gloves on the dresser and after I put the gloves on I would pull the trigger. Then I would redress and place the items in a plastic bag. The stage was set and I knew exactly what and how to do it. Could I really carry out my mother's plan? Only time could tell. But I can't go on. I must leave this house and find happiness. Only sadness lives here. We have been evicted by sorrow. I pray to God every night and He has not answered my prayers and I don't know where to turn now. My heart is stricken with grief and my sleep is disturbed. I pace the halls listening to my mother's agony. I must be a man and do the right thing. I will put our plan in effect and follow it to the end. This is the only way to save us. Lord, please forgive me for what I'm about to do. I love my mother, but this is the only way she sees out. Must go now. Will write later.

Janet felt herself suddenly awaken. She clenched her jaws while flipping the pages as her eyes bulged and she continued to read.

Dear Diary,

It's over I did what my mother had asked of me to put her out of her misery. During recess I snuck away from the other kids and ran home as fast as I could. I cut through the woods to our backyard. My mother had a piece of plastic runner on the floor from the door of her room over to her body. She told me to take off my clothes, socks, and shoes so I wouldn't get blood on it. She was nude and I asked her why. She said, 'naked I came from my mother's womb, and naked I shall return.' I didn't understand her reasoning and undressed outside her bedroom. She had the 22 caliber handgun, plastic gloves and suicide note lying on her dresser. She told me to put on the gloves and then pick up the gun. She instructed me to hold the gun up to her head and after I pull the trigger, placed it on the floor by her thigh and put the note beside her other thigh. I watched her smoke a cigarette while looking at my picture and she wept as I held the gun to her head. Then I could tell by her eyes it was time. I leaned over kissed and hugged her. We exchanged our love. And then I turned my head and pulled the trigger. All the while my eyes were shut closed. I positioned the gun and note where she'd showed me. I was afraid to look so I walked out of her room and rolled the plastic runner with the gloves lying on top. I went outside and hosed myself off and dried with the towel and placed the towel in the bag with the gloves, and runner. I put back on my clothes, socks, and shoes and locked my mother's door. I hid the bag deep in the woods of our house and ran back to school as fast as I could. Then I returned to the playground and mingled with the other kids so that no one had missed me.

"My God!" Janet realized what she had just read. She found it difficult to believe this. "No, Trevor, you couldn't have done this."

But he had, according to his own written words. Janet stopped reading for a moment before continuing.

After school she told me that I had to act as if I didn't know she was home and go about if things were normal. No one could see any change in my behavior. She told me to go outside and ride my bike to give myself an alibi and come in and walk to her door and turn the knob. After that I was told to check the garage. Then she told me to make up a phone call regarding a strange lady to Aunt Janet so I could get her attention to hurry over and by the time she'd arrived she said without blinking she should be dead.

Janet's heart dropped as she read the horrible words of Trevor's diary. Her eyes became heavy with sorrow. By now she was restless and sleepy, but she couldn't go to sleep if she wanted to. She had to finish the diary if it took her all night. As she wiped her tired eyes, she relentlessly continued to read.

Dear Diary

After speaking to Aunt Janet I went outside to ride my bike. When darkness approached and the kids went inside for dinner I decided to go in also. I went to my room and turned on my CD player and laid across my bed in the darkness. I started daydreaming about what had just happened, and then I became afraid. But the strangest thing happen, the telephone rung and I picked it up and a lady told me to go help my mother. Who was this lady and how did she know. My mother told me to make up the phone call but there was actually a phone call. Now I am puzzled. Terrified by the lady's words I decided to call Janet and tell her about the mysterious call. She told me she was on her way and I rushed to the kitchen and grabbed a knife from the stand and hurried to her bedroom door hopeful of rescuing her.

Lord, I know what I have done is wrong, but was this lady trying to help me save my mother. Was she dead or alive? If she's dead like she has planned at least she's at peace. No more weeping, no more pain and no more loneliness. Now she can be happy when she joins the angels, Ed, and the baby in heaven and most of all, no more suffering. I love her that much to set her free. Doing this was extremely hard, but this was the

209

only way. No one will ever understand what I have done for her. I will love my mother forever and this is our secret. Well, I must stop writing for now. Aunt Janet is on her way. Will write later.

Janet couldn't read any more of the dreadful words and she cried out his name. When the hysterical sounds escaped her lips, she thought she was having a terrible dream. Her findings were profoundly depressing and upsetting. Janet felt sick. She didn't know how to react to the words she had just finished reading. She had to keep reading so she flipped the next page.

Dear Diary

It's been a while since I've had the courage to write. My mind is playing tricks on me. The question is did I actually receive a phone call or did I imagine it? I don't know what the truth is any longer. What have I done? My mother is barely alive living off a machine like a vegetable. This is not the way we planned it. Now what do I do? I can't tell a soul because of the promise I made to her. Why did I agree to such a ghastly thing? Why did I pull the trigger? What was I thinking? I harm the person I love more than life. My life is over. It's over. I can't write any more. There's nothing left inside of me. I am an empty shell. My unspeakable actions have evaporated every part of my being. The guilt is breaking me down and pretending that I don't know the truth has melted my soul away. The pain in my heart is deserving, how could I—and why did I. Love is not supposed to hurt. I'm passed hurt. I'm totally destroyed. The secret-the secret-the secret. This is it. No more words.

Janet began to cry out in misery. *This story isn't true*, she told herself over and over. She snapped the diary closed and flung it across the room, while yelling at the top of her lungs. She lay across her bed sobbing like she never cried before. As she laid there sniffling, she then realized Trevor's actions were not out of hatred but love. She frowned; surprised at the depth he would go for his mother. The tears were threatening again, but she felt better knowing how much he really loved her. In her mind she knew Trevor was just following orders, but the world would treat him like a ruthless criminal. After all this was Ann's request. The only person she felt she could trust to carry out this horrific crime was the person she loved the most. Within minutes there was absolute silence in the room as Janet fell asleep.

Chapter 30

At 7:30 the warm rays of the bright sunlight shinning on her face awakened Janet. The nightmare she experienced last night replayed visibly in her head. The diary was real now. Janet counted the hours before her visit to Trevor. She tried to prepare her heart to meet him, knowing what she was up against today. But she was willing to do anything to keep the secret. In Janet's mind keeping the secret was the right and only thing to do. Everything Janet did had been done for the love she had for Ann and Trevor. The fateful words in Trevor's diary made her shiver in fear.

Her watch indicated that she had only two hours to prepare before the bus left for the detention center. She showered and dressed quickly trying to erase Trevor's words. Determined to keep her mind clear of the diary, she combed her hair, pinning it up in a bun. The ringing telephone drew Janet's attention away from her deliberations. Her heart momentarily stopped beating, afraid the secret was out and Trevor would spend a long time in jail. She took a deep breath and answered as normally as she could. She was relieved to hear William's voice on the other end.

"Hello Sis," he began slowly. "I called you last night, but I didn't get an answer. Are you okay?"

He sounded very concerned about her. Janet responded dryly as though life in the apartment was normal.

"Yeah, I was a little tired yesterday so I turned in early."

"I see," he grunted. "I'm happy you were finally able to get the rest you needed."

Janet wanted so desperately to break down and tell William the secret of Trevor's diary. How she lied and didn't rest at all. And her body was yearning for the rest it deserved but yet she had no time to think about her plight because she had to protect Trevor and Ann's secret. She knew the diary held the secret of courage, closeness, and love they'd shared. She wanted to tell him but her heart wouldn't allow her. She had never considered their life a secret until now. As she fondled the telephone cord, she wanted to scream out the truth.

"Janet," William added. "I have some good news. After speaking to Paul yesterday he informed me that he had made an agreement with the District Attorney's office."

"What's that?" Janet quickly asked interrupting him sternly. Right now she needed to hear nothing but good news.

"If Ann ever comes out of the coma and confesses that she tried to commit suicide all charges would be dropped against Trevor."

Janet's eyes lit up as she said an unnoticeable prayer.

"William, that's great news, but do you think Ann will ever recover?"

He knew what she was asking, and he didn't answer immediately. He swallowed hard trying to suppress his fears.

"Oh course she will. There are too many people who need her and I don't think she would want to leave Trevor."

Janet passionately agreed with a frown, knowing the awful secret of his diary.

"William, I must go now. The bus will be here in forty minutes. I'll see you at the hospital later."

Janet picked up the diary from the floor and began ripping out the pages that she had read and the pages she didn't have the courage to read. After tossing the pages in the bathroom sink, Janet lit a match. Her eyes began to water as she tossed the flaming stick into the sink. Puff! The kindled papers blazed like a raging forest fire. She cautiously watched the torch consume every page. When the last of the charred pages had finally burned, Janet quickly turned on the faucet, letting the water run wildly until the fire was completely extinguished. Then she picked up the remaining debris and flushed it down the toilet, placing the torn diary in her purse. She grabbed the bag with the sneakers and the new long johns and left the apartment with the bag in her hand and the secret of the diary in her heart.

Janet staggered up the street heading toward the Fourteenth Street bus stop in the bright blistering sun. By the time she reached the corner she was weary and exhausted, and the heels of her feet were in pain. The driver stopped the bus rather hastily and she smiled as she climbed the few steps, thankful to be on the bus and out the flaming heat. She inserted her money into the slot and then she noticed an empty seat behind the driver and quickly sat down before the crowd behind her took it. Then she secretly slipped off her shoes and rubbed her aching feet gently. Janet felt drained as she stared out the window of the bus. The last two days had taken a toll on her and she could feel the severe pains in her chest more frequently now. She didn't have the strength to go to the detention center, but she felt she had to go for the love of Trevor.

Janet's body had stiffened a little from the elongated bumpy bus ride. They were blocks from the detention center and she began to get nervous. The closer the bus got to the gate, the faster her heart pounded.

Janet thought, *in the last few months, I had visited an attorney's office, police precinct, court room, and now jail.* All these places were foreign to her. In all her seventy-plus years they were places she had only seen to TV. There was a large barbed wired fence that surrounded the entire detention center with three guard towers. One tower stood at the entrance and the other sat in the middle of the grounds. She could see guards standing on the towers holding large riffles. She had never been inside a prison before and she was frightened. When the bus finally stopped, she felt her heart drop. The bus driver opened the door in front of the entrance. The crowd began to fall out and against her will; Janet lowered to the steps, and wiped the sweat that beaded around her neck. She slowly turned around to wave at the bus driver and he politely waved back.

The sidewalk that led to the entrance was lengthy. She took measured steps as she trailed the crowd in a single line. While waiting patiently under the overpass until the crowd dispensed, she walked over to the large guard standing at the door and entered the forbidden building. He greeted her and asked for her identification while searching her bag. He dumped the sneakers and long johns on the table and searched them thoroughly, along with her purse. She handed him her senior citizen card, allowing her eyes to glance down the long dark dungy hall. He looked at her ID quickly and checked off her name on the visitor's list. As he gave her back the ID card, he motioned her down the hall. The next stop was at the metal detector. Janet stood while a female guard swung the device around her body. She placed her keys in the tray that was provided and put her purse on the moving belt as she walked through the metal door. Once the body search was completed, she pointed her to the next wing without breaking a smile.

The detention center was filled with boys and girls talking in various clusters. Most wore smiles. On the other side of the room were the armed guards. Janet sat down in the middle of the room and waited for Trevor to enter. Her body temperature was on the rise. The over-crowed room was hot and she could feel the sweat on the palm of her hands as she briskly wiped them on her skirt. The inmates began to enter the room one at a time. Shortly Trevor entered.

Janet was relieved when she saw the trembling youth approaching her. The orange jumpsuit he wore hung loosely on his slim body and the flip flops were too large for his small feet. Seeing Trevor again since his incarceration shouldn't have been a problem for her, but it was. Trevor grinned when he noticed her. He rushed into her arms and smiled as he held her tightly.

"Hello. Aunt Janet."

He planted a long and wet kiss on her cheek as they continued to embrace. The guards watched every encounter closely. They chatted about everything except for the night of his mother's incident.

"You look great," Janet commented, giving him the sense of confidence that he needed.

Trevor couldn't stop talking. He rambled on and on, talking about any and everything that came to his mind. He had a lot to talk about in a short period of time. The majority of their conversation consisted of him being incarcerated and his mother's condition, he asked about his friend Charles and Uncle William. Janet couldn't answer his questions quick enough without him asking another. Janet watched Trevor's zest fill the room. The hours of visitation went quickly. As the time drew near Janet glanced at her watch and realized that they had only fifteen minutes remaining.

When the 'time's up' announcement came over the intercom, Trevor's demeanor changed to sadness. He knew that she would have to leave.

"Auntie," he said gloomily, "I want to thank you for being there for us. You never left my side no matter how bad things got. Thanks for always being there when I needed a mother. God has placed you over our lives to be our angel and I thank you for carrying out the task."

He cleared his throat and took a deep breath, hoping that he wouldn't break down and cry. He continued to speak — never making eye contact.

"No matter the result of this tragic situation, just remember I will always love you—and my mother. I thank God every night for you and pray that all our prayers will be answered one day."

Janet finally made eye contact and smiled at his poetic grin. Janet looked directly in Trevor's eyes and felt sorry for him and for Ann. Then speaking to him in a motherly tone she said, "Don't worry, Baby, everything will be all right. Just wait and see."

She held back tears, casually smiling at him. Her soothing words floated through him. As the crowd faded out, Janet was hesitant to leave. A guard approached and rudely informed them that their time was up. Janet rose from the chair gradually and hugged him firmly. She whispered in his ear how much she loved him. Trevor watched as she headed for the exit. One step from the threshold and she stopped short, slowly turned and called his name. Her face was the epitome of sadness, afraid for Trevor now. Trevor rushed to her side to comfort her. She reached into her purse, pulled out the dairy and handed it to him. Attached to the diary was a strand of pearls hanging freely from the inside as if it were a book marker.

His face flushed with color. The two of them exchanged a look that didn't require words. They would have plenty of time to talk about it later. They both knew with certainty that the secret he had carried for so long was out. She exited the room, leaving him standing in the middle of the floor with tears rolling down his cheeks. The truth was written all over his face. He clutched the diary in his arms as he moaned loudly, feeling sorry for himself, Janet, and the mother he loved deeply. What he did most people would view it as the unthinkable, but in his youthful heart it was done purely out of love.

Chapter 31

The heavy evening traffic began to loosen up as Janet rode in silence to the hospital. The temperature had dropped just a bit making it easier to breath. She looked out the window of the moving bus, trying to keep from thinking about Trevor. It was useless; she could still see his slim frail body every time she shut her eyes. The bus ride took a little longer because the hospital was on the other side of town. Janet stared at two young boys playing in the back of the bus, wishing that Trevor was there with her.

When Janet reached section B12, she peeped into Ann's room and Sally was the only visitor at the time. Janet greeted Sally and retired to her oversized chair in the corner. The words she had read in Trevor's diary were embedded in her heart as she listened to an approaching ambulance siren. Sally left with a jovial good-bye. Janet smiled and waved back, coming out of her daydream. The room was now deserted and her sadness was acute. Janet dragged the oversized chair close to Ann's bed and began to speak to her in a mellow tone.

"Ann, how are you? I know you can hear me. What I'm about to say is difficult, but I must tell you the truth. First, I must confess that I am very ill. I have been sick for a long time. My heart is frail and to be honest with you I don't know how much time I have left. The precious Lord had given me this day to deliver to you the truth and I come to you in sincerity and honesty. Trevor is a lost sheep with nowhere to turn. His heart yearns for your love and his soul is damaged. The only way he can break free of his guilt and shame is to know that his mother loves him and wants to live for him and not die. I can't do that for you Ann. I've tried for months and I have failed." Janet swallowed hard and cleared her throat and continued. "I know you love him and I know he loves you, but somewhere along the way, the link has been broken. I must bring the two of you back together and restore the love and desires of your hearts that you both need."

Janet spoke to Ann as thought she could hear and understand every word. Her voice was trembling as she asked, "Where did it go wrong? When did the link break—and why didn't I see it?"

Questioning herself, Janet began to weep.

"My God, Ann," she yelled out in a high-pitched scream. "Your voice is the missing link that's holding this family together. Now wake up and speak and reconnect the link. I'm begging you. You must wake up before it's too late."

The tears were flowing freely as she grabbed Ann's hand.

"I know you miss Ed, Tyler, and the unborn baby, but your son needs you now more than he ever needed anyone in his life. If you don't wake up, Trevor will spend many years in jail. Please Ann wake up and reattach the link. Show him love and comfort him through his darkest hours. Heal his heart and please — please let him be the little boy that we both love so much."

Janet lowered her head and grasped her chest.

"It's tearing at my heart knowing what you're going through and I can't do anything about it."

Janet pulled the chair closer as she attempted to speak.

"I don't know how much time I have left, but you and Trevor have the rest of your lives together. Wake up before it's too late. If something happens to me what's going to happen to you and your baby? Wake up now and reunite the love."

Janet was determined to let Ann have it. She was disappointed that Ann and Trevor's life ended this way. All this time she was clueless and now feeling guilty that she didn't see the signs. Her anger turned to Ann and she spoke forceful.

"Ann you made this mess. How could you ask Trevor to commit such a God-forbidden sin? You know his love for you is exceedingly great and he never wanted to let you down. Failure was not an option for him. You made this mess—now wake up and clean this mess up."

Janet's voice began to get stronger as she finished her soliloquy. A gloomy and feeble sensation had descended in the room. Then Janet fell to her knees and cried out in a low, squeaky voice.

"Heaven, help us."

A powerful prayer followed those words. Her heart was pounding and her joints were in pain, but she refused to get up and proceeded to pray as she held Ann's hand unable to let go. After the long prayer Janet struggled to her feet and grabbed her purse and thumbed through it quickly, the black velvet sack that contained the pearl necklace and the other link was resting on the bottom. She dumped the necklace into her hand and held it high into the sky speaking desperately.

"This pearl necklace I give to you in remembrance of our love. May the power of this gem find its way home? Home is where the heart is and there's no doubt in my mind Trevor is in your heart and you are framed in his. Come out of this coma so you and Trevor can return home."

She kissed the necklace gently and placed it around Ann's neck. As she leaned over Ann, she could feel the warmth of her body and heartbeat. She stroked her face lovingly while whispering softly into her ear.

"Ann I know the secret. What Trevor has done was out of love and not hate. The world will never see it that way. Get up and save our baby. He didn't mean it. Everything done was your request and his unconditional love. This was not the perfect crime. Somewhere you made a mistake. It might have been your plan, but it was not God's plan. Now wake up—please."

She placed a warm peck on her eyes, nose, and mouth dabbing, away the falling tears. Janet squeezed Ann's hand. After a long solemn glance, she quietly slipped out of the room.

The welcomed moment of solitude met Janet when she returned home. The first thing she noticed when she entered the kitchen was a bowl of fresh strawberries. She grabbed a handful and stuffed them into her mouth. Janet knew she had to regain whatever strength she had left so she took a hot bath and slipped into her nightgown. Janet located her knitting basket, sat in the chair by the lamp and proceeded to knit. No matter what she did, she couldn't help but think about Trevor and Ann. It was impossible to believe that the shy, frail boy that she loved so deeply had the nerve to attempt such a heinous crime. In her heart she didn't believe it was a crime of hate but an act of love. But she knew the juridical system would never see it that way. Janet continued to work diligently on the sweater as the night went on. By the time she had sewed the last black button on the sweater it was almost midnight.

Janet folded the sweater neatly and laid it on the corner of the bed. She located the pawn receipt and laid in on top the sweater. Then she was reminded of the promise she had made Trevor. The promise that by the time the sweater was finished, Ann would wear it home. Now that she had finished it, Ann was still motionless; unaware of the danger her baby was in.

She pulled the covers back and slipped into bed. Janet dozed in and out of sleep. She tossed and turned, trying to forget the horrible diary and their mind-blowing plan. Visions of Trevor pulling the trigger surfaced from the corner of her mind. Janet sat up in bed and began to weep. Unable to sleep she located her Bible on the nightstand and read it in silence. After hours of reading she was now in a tizzy. It was impossible to erase the words of Trevor's diary in her mind. Feeling guilty she didn't know what was worse, thinking about Trevor's predicament or Ann's condition. No matter which one she dwelled on, the two was about the same. It wasn't long before Janet realized that she couldn't sleep. The diminishing light that illuminated through her room gave off a meek glow. Janet struggled with her fears and frowned at the thought Trevor and Ann may never be a family again. As far as she was concerned, her life meant nothing. All she ever wanted was for Ann to come out of her coma and rescue Trevor from this crime of which he had been accused. Her last wish was for them to go home and be the loving family that they once were. She knew this was not farfetched. With the power of love, redemption, and determination, anything was possible.

Janet rose from the bed and paced her room nervously. She moved throughout the room with very little grace. Then she walked over to the recliner by the window and leaned against it. Moments later she was back by the bed. She kneeled on the floor and said a prayer. Janet locked her eyes close to what seemed rimmed with tears. With a quick gesture she clasped her hands—holding the link of pearls and began to pray as fervently as she could. Engaged in a conversation with God—her voice was edged with fear and agony. Janet continued speaking.

Back in the tiny cell Trevor had awakened from a terrible nightmare. His clothes were drenched with sweat. He had cotton mouth. It was dry and his face was covered in fresh tears. His stomach contained one big knot of anxiety. At that moment Trevor understood clearly that he had no one to blame but himself. No one would ever understand what and why he did what he did. But in his heart he felt his mother gave him no choice. Thinking about his mother and the damage he caused his family brought no pleasure to him. Trevor struggled to understand.

"What have I done?" he asked himself repeatedly. "What have I achieved and at what length I went through to destroy the person I love more than life?"

His mother's condition and his very own drama was his fault. When the verbal fight had begun, he couldn't resist feeling sorry for himself. Then without warning he started weeping. It suddenly came to Trevor's mind the word of his mother and Lt. Fitzpatrick "repent."

"I must repent before it's too late," he mumbled under his breath.

Until now he was not aware of the consequences he faced and what to expect if the court found him guilty. Leaping from the decayed mattress, his feet hit the floor like two snare drums. Forcing his emotions to cease, he positioned himself on the floor and leaned across the bed crossing his hands which sandwich the link of pearls. Closing his watery eyes, Trevor waited for a second before he began. Trevor felt his emotions speed out of control as he pleaded for forgiveness and begged God to spare his mother's life and bring her out of her coma. Janet and Trevor were resting on their knees making similar requests. With both of their hands clutched to the link of pearls. Moments later they finished their prayers simultaneously. As Janet and Trevor struggled to their feet, peace embedded their tired, worn-out hearts. They climbed into bed staring at the link of pearls and fell to sleep.

Chapter 32

The following day William rushed to the hospital, happy with himself that he almost had enough money to bail Trevor out. The bright sunrays blinded his sight as he quickly pulled down the visor to block the glare. As he drove onto the parking lot, his mind had begun wandering about the family quandary. He felt badly for Janet knowing how much she loved Ann and Trevor. The cigarette that settled on his lips was shaking and the ashes were hanging on by a thread. He put the cigarette out and entered the hospital.

William scanned the room while pulling a chair close to Ann. He crossed his leg to make himself comfortable. As he stared at Ann, he wondered if she would ever recover. William uncrossed his leg and leaned closer to Ann, still gazing at her. Leaning forward in his chair he spoke to Ann with loving-kindness.

"Ann, I need to speak to you," he began slowly. "Is that okay with you? It's time. We have waited long enough. It's time to come home and be a mother again. Your baby is in a lot of trouble and he needs your help. Janet and I are doing all that we can do, but the final decision comes from you. I don't know what happened that dreadful day and to be honest with you it doesn't really matter. What does matter is for you to wake up and be here for Trevor."

William paused for several moments. Then he continued to speak with firmness.

"Ann, I'm sorry. I'm sorry for what happened to you and I'm sorry for what happened to Trevor. I thought I had it all figured out, but I now see that I am wrong. What's more important to you? Is it important for you to lie here and die or to wake up and live? Janet and I can't make that decision for you. Only *you* can make the final choice—but I think it's time to live again."

William leaned in closer and said with authority, "Ann if your heart is telling you to get up—then do it."

His voice was demanding. William placed a moist kiss on her cheek while forcing a smile. By the time William had ended addressing Ann the nurse walked into the room.

"Hello Mr. Jones," she said gleefully.

William returned the greeting. As she punched the buttons on the machine, she beamed at him cheerfully.

"How's your sister?"

"She's fine, thanks for asking?" William replied while watching her fumble with the machine.

"You know this is the first time I can recall her not visiting since Ms. Sanford's admittance."

"As far as I know she's here," William said with a plastic smile. "She's probably at the gift shop or the cafeteria."

William shifted his eyes on Ann.

"No sir, I haven't seen her all day," the nurse said as she wrote on the chart by the bed.

"Are you sure?" William asked with concern.

"I'm positive, the staff and I were discussing this earlier. We have never encountered a family so strong and with so much love and devotion. After a while people eventually start dropping off like flies, but not this family. You guys have something real special." She shook her head happily as she spoke.

"Oh yeah, we do," William said, admiring the pearl necklace around Ann's neck.

He had not noticed the necklace before and wondered if Janet had placed it there. William was surprised that Janet didn't make it to the hospital today. Janet and William communicated daily and he couldn't understand why she didn't show up. At that moment he wasn't in the mood for more conversation.

"Excuse me," William said as he picked up the phone beside Ann's bed.

He dialed Janet's number and waited for her to answer. The phone rung several times and Janet didn't pick up. William felt his pulse race when Janet didn't answer. To refrain from thinking the worst, he dialed her number again. Still, there was no answer. William quickly rose from the chair and decided to go to the gift shop and cafeteria to see if Janet was there. William shuffled past the people in the gift shop and the cafeteria looking for Janet. He moved quiet slowly down the aisle and he scanned each area and still no Janet. William dashed out of the hospital and headed toward his car almost sprinting. When he found the car he jumped in. William concentrated on the statement by the nurse as he drove the blue Lincoln off the parking lot at high speed. A vision of Janet being in trouble was enough for him to race through town.

Seven minutes later he drove onto the parking lot of Janet's building. He dashed up the three flights of stairs and pounded on her door. William took a deep breath and opened the door using his spare key. The apartment was quiet when he stepped inside. He yelled out her name. William felt a lump in his throat when she didn't respond. He yelled out louder. By the time he had crept his way past the kitchen there was still no sign of Janet. The light from her bedroom was evidence she was in there. As he continued to inch down the hallway, he repeatedly called out her name.

A few steps away from the bedroom, William peeked around the corner and there he saw her. William froze where he stood. At first glance she looked as if she was in a restful sleep. Her skin had a glow of a walnut and her face held a smile of peacefulness. Janet was lying stone still on her back with the Bible in her right hand and a link of pearls clutched in her left. When he approached, he noticed an object lying on the corner of the bed. William glanced over and realized that she had finished the sweater. The sweater was folded neatly and the receipt from the pawnshop was lying on top.

"Janet," he said softly.

Janet didn't move. He called out her name again. When she didn't answer, William hurried to the bed and the moment he touched her, he knew that she was dead. Her body was cold and stiff.

"Janet," he groaned.

He took his hand and shook her rapidly. Her body jerked like a piece of plywood. There was no life in her and he knew it. William collapsed to one knee and began to wail. A scream rose from deep within his throat. His sobs were hysterical—sob of panic grief. After several minutes of weeping a wave of calmness came over him. There was a brief moment when he thought he heard a mellow voice speaking.

"William, no need to weep, I'm home," the angelic voice whispered. "Now get up and finish the job. There are people depending on you. You can't let them down."

The voice rang in his head as if it was speaking directly to him. William rose from the floor and kissed her gently. He laid his hand across her face, stroking it slowly; the words *God bless* you finally escaped his trembling mouth.

"Thank you, Janet for the gift of love," he murmured. William clung to her while holding her passionately in his arms.

"Sleep, my lovely sister," he said almost choking on his words.

"You may now rest in peace." His voice was barely a whisper.

Thinking about his future, William now realized that he had to spend the remainder of his life without the presence of his beloved sister, but her memories would live on forever. As he held her inflexible body with gentleness, closed his eyes, and hummed her favorite tune.

Chapter 33

William started making the arrangements for Janet's internment the next day. The weather was mostly cloudy, with a mist of rain falling late that afternoon. Michael arrived a few hours after he received the news. The telephone in the apartment rang constantly as family and friends called to express their condolences. Mae was busy in the kitchen preparing food for the visiting guests and Pastor Getrite and members of the church stopped in briefly to discuss the program.

William and Michael were in and out of the house like two busy hens, working with the staff of the funeral home, making sure everything turned out grandly. Janet was a lovely woman, and anyone who had the chance to encounter her felt that lovely presence. They wanted her burial to be as elegant as the life she lived. It wasn't long before Bernita phoned and offered her assistance. Mae assured her that they had everything under control and thanked her for calling.

In three days, the woman they loved so deeply and the link that kept the family together would be buried. It was hard for the family, but they held themselves together for the love of Janet. Michael had some free time so he decided to pay Trevor a visit to deliver the sad news. Their time was limited and it took all the strength within him to explain to Trevor that another tragedy had entered his life. Trevor took the depressing news extremely hard. As first he couldn't speak. Michael just watched as the frail, frightened little boy broke down and cried. Trevor realized Janet was gone and he didn't get a chance to say good-bye. He now knew that Janet was no longer a part of his life and his mother lay lifeless in a coma. Trevor blamed himself for everything that had happened. *If only she hadn't found the diary*, he thought. As Michael tried to console him he whimpered and said, "Uncle Michael—man you just don't understand. All of this is my fault. I killed her," he blurted out.

Trevor started with the tears again, using the cuff of his sleeve to wipe away his waterworks. Nothing seemed to console him as he cried louder and harder. Michael looked at him and felt sorry for his pain.

"Don't say that Trevor," Michael snapped. "That's ridiculous." Realizing his harsh tone, Michael smiled at him and then patted Trevor's hand.

"But Uncle Michael I did," Trevor said as he looked directly into Michael's eyes. "It's because of me she no longer lives."

Michael looked at him sorrowfully; as tears rolled down his pale face. "Trevor, didn't you know?"

"Know what?"

"About Mom's heart condition."

"What heart condition?"

"Son, I'm sorry to be the one to deliver the news, but Mom had a heart problem for over a year."

"No, she didn't," Trevor said emphatically, nodding his head in disagreement.

"Trevor, listen to me."

There was silence before he continued. "I thought you knew. Mom's heart was very weak and she needed surgery. Her doctor had already scheduled her appointment for open heart surgery, but she canceled once you landed in this trouble."

Trevor looked somewhat puzzled and frowned.

"But Uncle Michael if this is true, why didn't she tell me?"

"I guess she wanted to keep it a secret. Knowing the problems you were facing and the tragedy that our family is dealing with, she probably thought it was best that you didn't know."

Michael spoke to the little boy calmly. Trevor sat back in the swirl-around chair and covered his face with his hands. Not only were Trevor and Ann keeping a secret—today Trevor realized that Janet was keeping one also.

"Uncle Michael, I'm sorry. I wished someone had told me."

"So you see, Trevor, no one blames you. This is part of life. You live your life to the fullest and then one day you must die and enter another life. Life and death is part of God's cycle. How we fill in the gap is our choice. Don't worry she lived a long life, she lived seventy-plus years. She always said 'she stopped counting after she reached seventy and that the good Lord only promised seventy years and anything beyond that was on someone else's time.'"

"So what are you putting on the obituary for her age?" Trevor asked with sincerity.

"Seventy-plus," he said, smiling. "I've already told the Funeral Director." Michael answered with a hearty laugh.

Trevor perked up and laughed, too. He shook his head at Michael because he knew Michael was serious and crazy enough to do such a thing.

"But Mom can live forever in your heart," he continued.

Michael took Trevor's hand and placed it on his chest, close to his heart. Then he scooped Trevor into his arms and squeezed him with endearment. Trevor smiled a poetic gesture knowing the confidentiality of his diary hadn't caused Janet's death.

"Well Trevor, I must go now. I have a lot to do before the funeral."

Michael rose from the chair and hugged Trevor again this time using an extra grip. He glanced down at Trevor and there was a profound sadness about him, and it was almost impossible to say anything to cheer him up.

"Thanks Uncle Michael. Thanks for the truth, but can you do one thing for me?"

"Sure, Trevor" he said with a smile.

"Aunt Janet always treated me like a son, and by me not being able to attend her funeral can you place something in the casket close to her heart."

"I would love to Trevor. What is it?"

Looking troubled, Trevor reached into his back pocket and pulled out the journal.

"This," he said as he handed Michael the diary.

He took the diary and grinned. Trevor touched Michael's hand and smiled at him. His eyes still soaked with tears as Michael left Trevor in the dingy room. Michael rushed out the jail carrying the diary. He didn't know the significance of it. He was only delivering the wish of a little boy. Michael sped across town and stopped at the hospital to visit Ann. He didn't stay long. Back in the car heading to his mother's apartment and his heart was pounding and aching from the loss of his mother and the broken boy who didn't have the chance to say farewell. When he entered the parking lot, he slammed on brakes and the diary slid on the floor. Michael put the car in park, slowly reached down and grabbed it. When he flipped to the first page, he began to read. Engraved in Trevor's handwriting, the words were written.

"To Aunt Janet,

Thank you for your patience, guidance, and keeping the secret. I thank God that He brought such a beautiful person in my life. And most of all, thank you for your love and support. Aunt Janet, don't shed another tear for me, I'll be alright. I pray to God every night. Pleading that He would remove this pain and allow me to see my mother again. I will never forget you and stop loving you as long as I shall live. Love 4 ever. Trevor."

Michael quickly fastened the diary and wept. With closed eyes, he held the diary close to his heart. He slumped back in his seat, listening to a soothing melody on the radio. His mind was in a stupor, and mesmerized in his own thoughts, the heart-felt words of a wounded child, the mother he had just lost, and the secret she carried to her grave.

Chapter 34

In those sad dark days after Janet's death, William sat alone in his house listening to the sounds of heavy traffic in the background of his thoughts. Instinctively, he reached for the phone to call Janet. The answering machine popped on after several rings. He quickly hung up realizing that Janet would never answer again. For the first time, William was on his own. The sister who he loved so much had left him. He lingered for a moment feeling depressed, and then he took a sip of his coffee and flipped a cigarette into his mouth. Though loneliness had descended upon him like a blanket, he had to remain strong for Ann and Trevor's sake. All he needed to bail Trevor out of jail was three hundred dollars. It was possible that he could have gathered the money by now. If he had not taken time to focus on Janet's funeral.

William was sad and felt sorry for his predicament. Feeling life had dealt him a raw hand. Ann's comatose condition and finding Janet's deceased body was too much for him to handle. He banged his clenched fist against the table as hard as he could. He *knew* Janet's heart was weak and didn't offer any help to relieve her of the tremendous amount of stress that she faced every day. Janet was always the strong one in the family and she wouldn't have had it any other way. She was persistent and no one ever dared to argue with her. Everything she did was with good intentions. Snapping out of his reverie, William remembered that he had a 9:00 appointment with Paul. He drank the last bit of coffee and placed the empty mug in the sink. He moved through the house with ease and within moments he found himself settled in his car, thanking God Trevor had him to lean on.

The hospital was extremely busy today. There had been a seven-car accident on interstate 45, which kept the staff working throughout most of the night. The night duty nurses were preparing to end their long and stressful shifts, while the morning nurses had just punched in. It was six-thirty in the morning and the sun was quickly rising.

Kelly, the morning nurse, had already loaded her cart to start her rounds. Ann's room was the third one on her route. When Kelly entered, she smiled and greeted Ann like she always did for the past nine months. She walked over to the large machine that was beside Ann's bed to make sure that the device worked properly. As Kelly moved closer, a feeling overcame her that someone was watching her. She suddenly moved toward the window and peeped out the curtains, commenting how bright the sky was shining. Kelly slipped her hands between the curtains to pull them back.

"Today is a lovely day, Ann."

She pushed the curtains against the wall, revealing the bright sunlight. There was a beautiful dove nestled on the ledge of the window. Kelly acknowledged the bird, admiring its pure white color. Tapping the windowpane with the tip of her fingernail, trying to distract the bird; the small dove didn't move. After staring at the bird for a few minutes, she realized that the bird wasn't going anywhere. It seemed as if the bird had found a home for now and had contently settled in.

Just as she turned her body to face Ann, the machine made a soft buzz. Frightened, she rushed out the room to get the doctor on duty. When Kelly and the doctor returned, the machine was swiftly whirring. The doctor rushed to Ann's side and took her small wrist into his hand.

"Nurse Kelly, I think she is trying to regain consciousness."

Kelly leaned over Ann and saw her twitching eyes.

"Doctor Hurd, are you sure?" She asked excitedly.

She wanted to be positive she had heard him correctly. She stood by the doctor, surveying his every move.

"I need you to phone Dr. Garfield right away."

Kelly didn't move. She was amazed and surprised at the same time. She had never seen anyone come out of a coma and wanted to be there to observe the transformation.

"Go!" Dr. Hurd said urgently.

Kelly dashed out the room and down the hall. In the meantime, he went over to the machine for the reading.

"My God this is a miracle," he shouted! "She's coming out."

Dr. Hurd gleamed with pleasure. He smiled, flashing his teeth. Ann's chance for complete recovery was slim, but she was trying her best to pull out of this deep sleep. Several moments later the room was filled with doctors and nurses. The hospital staff was aware of the bad luck that this family had endured and many prayed that she would pull through okay. Throughout the day, different doctors took turns evaluating her. There was a specialist for every inch of her body. The news had spread quickly and it wasn't long before a crowd of people had congregated outside Ann's door. Even, Sue came down from the maternity ward to see for herself. After hearing the doctor's evaluations, Sue smiled because she was sure Ann would make it. But to what degree of damage this coma caused was still a mystery. In spite of it all, Ann was slowly regaining consciousness.

Later that day Dr. Garfield arrived. When the call came in on his cellular phone, his plane had just landed at Dulles Airport. He rushed to the hospital as soon as he could. Ann was always his prized patient. The day he performed the surgery he felt a strong presence of her wanting to live. Dr. Garfield did several routine tests. The test results were in excellent standings. Afterward, blood work was ordered and she was taken for an EKG and MRI.

Ann seemed to grow younger as the day progressed. There was radiance about her that the doctors couldn't explain. Somewhere between the incident and Ann coming out of the coma, she went through a spiritual makeover. Ann was given another chance at life and now her son had a chance, too.

When William received the news about Ann, he was on his way to visit Trevor. By the end of the conversation, William made a U-turn at the next intersection and headed for the hospital. As William approached the hospital, he screamed out a loud cry.

"Thank you Lord! I'm blessed enough that both Ann and Trevor have a second chance to be a family."

William finally reached Ann's ward, several people were gathered in the waiting room. Both Pastor Getrite and Deacon Rogers were already there. People in the waiting room were gleaming with fresh tears and continued to pray, while the staff listened with hope. There was much hugging. William stood next to the Pastor surrounded by a congregation of listeners. As he spoke to the crowd, the sniffles grew louder. William stared at their broken faces, and he was now happy knowing their tears were tears of joy and not sorrow.

After the Pastor prayed, the crowd separated. They gathered in different groups speaking amongst themselves. William disappeared down the hall to the cafeteria. Round tables with plastic red roses placed in the center were throughout the room. An empty table by the window caught his attention. Shortly after he sat down, Mae joined him. William spoke as he watched her fumble through her Bible. William never anticipated that Ann would wake up and if she did, what would happen to Trevor? William and Mae didn't have much to talk about. Mae made a happy frown when William mentioned Ann's recent recovery.

"Mae, do you think Ann will remember what happened to her?"

"I don't know," Mae replied, relieved. "Having her home and not in here anymore will be best for everyone."

At that moment, they had said a silent prayer for Ann. They didn't want to think about the outcome, and with that Mae continued to pray—keeping her eyes focused on the Bible that lay in front of her. William and Mae were not sure Ann would completely heal and if she did—what exactly would she remember? Nonetheless, it was time for Ann to live again and be the mother of a broken little boy, no matter what's the result.

Chapter 35

It had been three days since Ann came out of her coma and visitations still weren't allowed. William and Mae came to the hospital every day, hoping this would be the day that they could see her. Both the staff at the District Attorney's office and Paul had a meeting regarding Ann's condition. It was put in writing that Ann would be questioned as soon as she was strong enough. The medical staff was aware that they were to inform both offices when that time became possible. Until Ann was questioned, no one from outside could talk to or see her.

The dove arrived every morning and rested on the ledge outside of Ann's hospital window. The bird would chirp through its soft bill and would watch the activities going on in the room through its roundish black eyes. And, every evening the bird flew off the ledge about the same time. Kelly noticed the bird every day, and listened to its chirping. She smiled at the thought that the bird was building a nest.

Trevor fought sleep every night. The terrible nightmares had returned. Now, he was missing both Janet and his mother. William continued to visit, never mentioning that his mother had regained consciousness. Trevor had grown accustomed to the detention center now. It almost seemed normal to him. The cruel remarks, fighting, and the distasteful food didn't shock him as they once had. Although he was adjusting to his environment, in his heart he knew he didn't belong there. William didn't want Trevor to know about his mother just yet, and prayed that no one had told him. He was afraid of building false hope for the little boy who really didn't seem to have any hope at all.

After one week, Ann was slowly recovering. Her limbs were very weak and still she couldn't talk. According to Dr. Garfield a lot of therapy would be necessary and her speech and mobility would return.

After observation they were positive that she would recover one hundred percent.

The next morning both William and Mae were sitting in the waiting room when Paul, unaware of their presence, rushed past them.

"Paul!" William shouted. "Paul!" William yelled again as his voice echoed down the hall.

It was apparent that Paul couldn't hear him and William proceeded after him. Paul turned and noticed William approaching.

"Hello William," Paul said with a smile.

"Where are you rushing to in such a big hurry?"

"It's time William."

"Time for what?"

"I'm meeting with the DA's office to question Ann about the night of the incident."

William became speechless. His lips were completely immobile. This was the day he's been waiting for and now he had nothing to say. William looked at Paul and then down the hall towards Ann's room. Paul smacked William on his shoulder and smiled. A look of sheer delight said that William was thoroughly relishing the conversation. Even Mae, though getting a somewhat muffed version seems to like what she heard.

"I must go now. I'll talk to you after the questioning—and William keep your fingers crossed."

Paul crossed his fingers and held them in the air. William couldn't say a word. He stood there and watched as Paul rushed down the hall swinging his black briefcase back and forth. William walked slowly toward Mae, still staring down the hall.

"What was that all about?" Mae asked when he joined her.

"The DA's office is about to question Ann."

Mae lifted herself from the chair in an upright position. "Get out of here!" she cried, laughing helplessly.

"Paul asked me to cross my fingers in hopes that everything will turn out okay."

"Cross your fingers," Mae said as she shrugged her shoulders. "We don't need luck, we need a miracle."

At that moment, Mae struggled to her knees and began to pray. She smiled and kept on praying.

Meanwhile inside Ann's room was the staff from the DA's office. A large well-dressed clerk was sitting behind a desk and was preparing to take notes using a dictation machine. Paul turned to the secretary who was waiting patiently nearby and smiled down at her. In the corner where Janet had sat for the past several months was a video camera resting on a tripod. Dr. Garfield was standing by Ann's side and Nurse Kelly stood at her feet. First Paul spoke quietly to Dr. Garfield, and then he spoke to Ann. As he stood over Ann he admired her beauty for the first time, he took a good look at her. To him she was cute, better than cute and maybe even pretty. Her skin glowed and there was a flicker of brilliance in her eyes.

Within minutes the attorney representing the DA's office entered. He was a tall man wearing a dark blue suit. His face was clean shaved only showing a few freckles and his reddish hair was cut very short. Paul stared at the young attorney for a few minutes, studying him and then he looked back at Ann. The attorney strolled over to Paul and introduced himself.

"My name is Christopher Wine."

Paul returned the greeting and shook his hand. Dr. Garfield asked to speak to both attorneys alone. He led them into the hall and closed the door.

"My name is Dr. Garfield," he began quietly, "My patient is still very weak and she has not regained her speech yet. The only way she can respond to your questions is by the use of her right hand. So the questioning must be brief."

They agreed with a nod and followed him back into the room. When Paul came back into the room, he saw how rapidly Ann had changed. Even though Ann was wearing the white hospital gown, her shimmering silhouette was a perfect match. The technician was instructed to turn on the camera. When the green light flickered on, it indicated that the camera was ready. Dr. Garfield gave them permission to proceed. Christopher began slowly with his inquisition.

"Hello Ms. Sanford. Can you hear me? If you can hear me please raise your right index finger."

Ann's bright eyes were opened wide. All eyes were focused on her right hand. Within moments she gradually raised her index finger. Everyone in the room smiled. The attorney continued.

"Ms. Sanford is your first name Ann?"

Again she raised her index finger.

"Do you know why we're here?" he asked with complete gentleness.

They waited patiently and again she raised her finger in the air.

"Do you have a son?"

Paul held his breath when that question was asked. He waited intently and suddenly became afraid. Paul turned to Ann with terror in his eyes, while coughing on a lump caught in his throat. After several moments they waited in silence and Ann didn't raise her finger. Christopher moved to a spot on the other side of the bed where he could see her clearly.

"Do you have a son name Trevor?" without hesitation Ann raised her index finger.

"Can you remember what happened to you on October the twenty-second, nineteen ninety-nine?"

Everyone in the room was stunned into silence, but they all watched for the movement of her hand. Slowly she lifted her finger. In spite of the trauma she had gone through, she was doing a fine job at answering the questions.

"Did your son Trevor shoot you in the head—did he try to kill you?"

Paul knew the answer would tell it all. The direction of the finger would determine the fate of his little client. Christopher stared at Ann while eyeing her hand closely. Nurse Kelly looked as if she stopped breathing. Paul looked away, afraid of knowing what the answer could be. As Paul turned his head toward the window, he noticed that there was a dove nestled on the ledge looking in. When he turned his attention back in Ann's direction, her finger still had not moved. Paul let out a sigh and smiled at Christopher.

"Ms. Sanford I have one question left," Christopher stated seriously. "On October twenty second, did you try to kill yourself?"

Paul cleared the lump from his throat and crossed his fingers. There was dead silence in the room. All eyes were glued on Ann. Paul continued to look at Ann and back to the dove. After a brief moment they noticed a tear drop from her right eye. But yet she had not moved her finger. Christopher leaned in closer and asked.

"Ms. Sanford, do you understand the question?"

They were warned from the beginning, unfortunately there was no choice. They had to continue. Paul's face showed worrisome look for a moment. Then, Ann's finger slowly raised high in the air.

"Will you answer for me?" he asked, mildly repeating the question.

"Did you try to kill yourself?"

By now, Paul had begun to sweat. He looked at Christopher nervously, afraid of what the answer might be. His heart was pounding in fear for Trevor. After several moments, Ann frowned as she fought back tears. Everyone slowly watched her petite and much needed manicured finger rise. She aimed it high in the air with very little movement and it remained there. Large teardrops rolled down and dripped off her cheeks.

Needless to say, Paul was relieved that it was all over, and Ann had just confessed that she tried to kill herself and now his client was free of all charges. Paul smiled at Ann and within the same movement; he saw the dove fly away from the ledge. Having finished a difficult session, Christopher touched her small hand and thanked her. They packed up their things and everyone left the room within seconds after the last question was answered. Outside in the hallway, Christopher informed Paul that he would complete the paper work as soon as he returned to his office.

"Your client will be released within hours," Christopher said with a smile.

They exchanged handshakes and went their separate ways. Then Paul disappeared down the hall swinging his briefcase, heading in William and Mae's direction. William and Mae were elated about the report Paul had given them. The news was so overwhelming, Mae started to cry and praise God all at once. William danced a jig. Mae watched with concern as he danced and smiled at him with joy. She started another prayer. After her prayer she laid her head on William's shoulders and cried inconsolably for a long time.

"Mae it's all right to cry."

As William spoke those words, tears rolled down his own face as well. No matter what the two of them did to stop the flow of tears, the teardrops just wouldn't cease. Paul stared at them, wondering what it must feel like to be released from the pain they carried in their heart for so long. He was overjoyed for them as he left them weeping in the middle of the hallway. He simply smiled as he skipped down the hall whistling, never looking back.

William managed to hang around the house for the remainder of the day. Around 7:00 that evening, he received the telephone call he'd been waiting for. He picked up the phone after the first ring. When he hung up from the short conversation, a smile automatically stretched across his face. Trevor was now free. Although, he didn't have Janet in his life, he did have his mother again. She's not the same Ann as she was before. Being in the coma for so many months she was now a new creature. Her soul and heart had healed from her pain and grief and she was able to let it all go. God had given her another chance at life, and in her mind, this time she would not fail.

Chapter 36

After breakfast, William hurriedly dressed so he could get on the highway. The morning traffic was light for once as he sped through town. He was so excited about seeing Trevor and could hardly wait for his reaction once he realized that this mother had come out of her coma.

William's happiness had been temporarily stripped from him. Losing Janet was extremely difficult and he didn't think he could ever be jubilated again. But, now some resemblance of life was resurfacing. He was so overwhelmed with emotion that he couldn't hide his feelings any longer. When he arrived at the detention center, the tears had begun to fall. William quickly wiped them away when he saw Trevor step outside the barbed wire gate. He lit a cigarette and smiled. The moment Trevor recognized William's car, he ran to meet him as fast as he could.

"Hello Unc, I see you still have the big stinky Lincoln." Trevor said as he opened the door and hopped in the front seat.

William grinned. A tune by Al Greene was softly playing on the car stereo as they quietly rode to the hospital. Trevor didn't talk much at all, and at times when William glanced at him, it appeared as though he was ready to break down and cry.

William refrained from displaying any emotions. He hummed to the tunes of his oldies but goodies tape, knowing that Trevor would smile again before the day was over. He chuckled within as he thought about the big surprise that was in store for him as he drove the Lincoln down Main Street. William smoked one cigarette after another and was thankful that their nightmare was finally over.

On route to the hospital, William saw Jenkins's Pawn shop. He parked the car and asked Trevor to wait for him as he disappeared inside the building. Trevor waited in the car and watched the great world of freedom, with its cars and people. William returned and jumped into the driver's seat carrying a box and envelope in his hand. He handed the box to Trevor and placed the envelope in the glove compartment and drove away from the curb.

Out of curiosity, Trevor lifted the top off of the box and peered inside. There they were—the beautiful laced napkins with the initials 'AL' folded neatly inside. Trevor marveled over the napkins and smiled when he placed the top back on. Trevor swung himself around, he noticed the purple sweater that Janet had knitted for Ann was lying on the back seat of the car and a smile flashed across his face.

"Hey Unc, I see Aunt Janet finished the sweater."

Trevor passionately stroked the soft fabric and he felt his heart thump. For a tender moment, a hint of sadness flickered in his eyes. Not another word was spoken until they turned the corner to the hospital. William parked, turned off the engine, and yanked out the keys, smiling at Trevor while grabbing the sweater.

As they walked through the lobby past the receptionist desk, they were greeted with an admiring crowd. The news about Ann's confession had traveled throughout the hospital quickly and everyone that looked at the little boy smiled, feeling joyous for him.

"Welcome home Trevor," a nurse said as he strolled past her.

Trevor smiled and uttered, "Thank you."

Steps away from section B12, William stopped Trevor outside the door and started a father-like-son conversation with him. He spoke briefly to Trevor and then asked him to go in alone. Trevor stood beside William and respectfully waited for him to finish talking. By now, Trevor had become scared and nervous. He didn't ask any questions and did just as William had ordered.

Trevor slowly walked into the room and Ann was sitting up in bed, dressed in a lovely egg shell white nightgown. The long silky sleepwear fit impeccably on her body and her eyes were opened wide and she wore the biggest smile that her face would allow. The pearl necklace that Janet placed around Ann's neck was shining from the glare of the sun, and the gold cross that Bernita hung above her head twinkled. When Trevor spotted the necklace he smiled because he knew this was

Janet's doing. Trevor rushed over to Ann and reached out, and affectionately hugged his mother.

"Mom you're up!" The tears began to freely flow. "You came out of your coma." The smile that was on his face had not been there in a long time. "I'm sorry," he groaned guiltlessly, "I'm so sorry."

Both of them understood perfectly and if Ann could speak to him her words would have been.

This was my fault—no son I'm sorry. Please forgive me.

He cried even harder as he laid his head on Ann's chest.

"I love you so much, and I don't want you to die," he moaned as he clung to Ann.

His words by now were coming quite fast, very loud, and strong. Trevor kissed her on her eyes, nose, and mouth. He took Ann's hand and laid it upon his chest, and then he took his hand and laid it upon hers.

"Mom," he whimpered, "I can feel your heart beat." He glanced up at her and asked, "Can you feel mine?"

Ann didn't say a word. The sparkle in her eyes said it all. Her eyes that once filled with darkness were gleaming and full of life. Ann and Trevor wept until William entered the room.

The evil curse that had befallen on the family that he loved so much had been lifted, William thought.

It was a terrible ordeal for them, but through faith, their love had prevailed. He looked at Ann and saw the love that filled her eyes, and he knew than that everything was going to be okay.

For now, the dove was nestled on the ledge. And when Trevor looked up and noticed the bird, he cheerfully said, "Hey look," smiling and pointing at the bird. "Look at the beautiful bird, watching us."

Trevor giggled. William gradually turned his head in the direction of the bird and watched it fly off the ledge, high into the heavens. William stood in the doorway with the purple sweater draped across his arm and chuckled while he smiled at his family. He thanked God for answering their prayers and sparing Ann's life. As he clung to the sweater with tear stained eyes, a vision of Janet crossed his mind. In his heart he knew Janet would have been pleased. He closed his eyes and breathed a sigh of relief. William strolled over to the corner and neatly placed the sweater on the arm of the oversize chair that housed his sister for months. He turned and slowly walked away, glancing over his shoulder at Ann and Trevor's loving interactions.

The pearl necklace that Janet placed around Ann's neck was dashing as it complemented her gorgeous gown. And for a brief second, Trevor stared at the necklace and then secretly he slipped his hand into his pocket and touched the link that was given to him by Janet. All of a sudden, Trevor realized he felt Janet's love. Trevor glanced around his mother's room and it was still decorated the way he remembered. There were vases of flowers, cards, and balloons and then he remembered the card Bernita had given him months ago.

"Mom, I have something for you to read."

Ann blinked her eyes and Trevor located Benita's card and opened the sealed envelope. He held the card in the air and Ann read the words and her face became emotional as she tried to laugh. Trevor glanced at the words, read them and burst out in laughter.

"Aunt Be is funny, isn't she, Mom?"

Ann's right index finger swung high into the air.

The card read:

Ann I know Snook is going to forget to read this card to you in a week. If you are reading this card, welcome back girl. All I want to say to you prissy—you need a manicure, a pedicure, a good shampoo with a deep conditioning—finishing with an updated haircut. P.S. And don't forget a visit to the dentist. Phew! Love, Be.

After reading the card a strong surge of happiness overcame him, stronger than anything he had felt in a long time. Trevor laid his head on Ann's chest again, this time close to her heart. He silently lay there with teary eyes.

"Thank you, Lord," he finally said in a gravelly cry. "Thank you for answering my prayer."

The words were barely a whisper. Trevor knew how much he loved and needed his mom—more than he ever needed her before. Now for the first time, he was at peace. Trevor smiled as he continued to lay his head close to her heart. Once a lost sheep, today he knew he had found his way home. The secrets of the pearls were what Janet carried with her. Trevor knew the only people alive who truly knew the secret was him and his mother. In his heart he knew they also would carry it to their grave. A tear rolled down Ann's cheek. Although she once felt she had nothing to live for, today she realized she had everything to live for and her love for Trevor was more valuable than any gem. The joy and happiness shared by Ann and Trevor over Ann's recovery was tempered by the sense of awesome love which each experienced. Not knowing whether to pray or cry Trevor and Ann knew that their task of rebuilding would require patience, caring, and most importantly—unconditional love.

"I love you, Mom," Trevor whispered honestly.

His voice trailed off as he fell into a deep peaceful sleep. Ann smiled down at him passionately and within minutes she was asleep, too. The last thing she remembered was the words *I love you* that came from the lips of her precious gem—Trevor.

www.ingramcontent.com/pod-product-compliance
Lightning Source LLC
Chambersburg PA
CBHW051148030726
47504CB00004B/1102